THE SOCIETY OF RELUCTANT DREAMERS

Also by José Eduardo Agualusa
in English translation

Rainy Season
Creole
The Book of Chameleons
My Father's Wives
A General Theory of Oblivion

José Eduardo Agualusa

THE SOCIETY OF RELUCTANT DREAMERS

Translated from the Portuguese by
Daniel Hahn

Harvill *Secker*
LONDON

1 3 5 7 9 10 8 6 4 2

Harvill Secker, an imprint of Vintage,
20 Vauxhall Bridge Road,
London SW1V 2SA

Harvill Secker is part of the Penguin Random House group of companies
whose addresses can be found at global.penguinrandomhouse.com

First published by Harvill Secker in 2019
First published with the title *A Sociedade dos Sonhadores
Involuntários* in Portugal by Quetzal Editores in 2017

A CIP catalogue record for this book is available from the British Library

penguin.co.uk/vintage

ISBN 9781787300552

Co-funded by the
Creative Europe Programme
of the European Union

The European Commission support for the production of this publication
does not constitute an endorsement of the contents which reflects the views
only of the authors, and the Commission cannot be held responsible for
any use which may be made of the information contained therein.

Typeset in 10.25/16 pt Nexus Serif by Jouve (UK), Milton Keynes
Printed and bound in Great Britain by Clays Ltd, Elcograf S.p.A.

Grateful thanks for permission to reproduce Pablo Neruda's '*Si cada día cae*',
El mar y las campanas © Pablo Neruda, 1973, and Fundación Pablo Neruda.
Translated here by Daniel Hahn.

Penguin Random House is committed to a sustainable future
for our business, our readers and our planet. This book is made
from Forest Stewardship Council® certified paper.

For Yara, this and all my dreams.

For Patricia Reis and Sidarta Ribeiro.

*For Laurinda Gouveia, Rosa Conde, Luaty Beirão,
Domingos da Cruz, Nito Alves, Mbanza Hamza, José Cheick Hata,
Samussuko Tchikunde, Inocêncio Brito, Sedrick de Carvalho,
Albano Bingo, Nicola Radical, Nelson Dibango,
Arante Kivuvu Lopes, Nuno Álvaro Dala, Benedito Jeremias,
Osvaldo Caholo, and all Angola's young dreamers.*

'*The Real gives me asthma.*'
E. M. CIORAN

'*Let us always remember that to dream is to look for ourselves.*'
BERNARDO SOARES / FERNANDO PESSOA

1.

I woke very early. Through the narrow window, I saw long black birds fly past. I'd dreamed about them. It was as though they had leaped from my dream up into the sky, a damp piece of dark-blue tissue paper, with bitter mould growing in the corners.

I got up and went out to the beach, barefoot and in my underpants. There was nobody on the sands. I didn't notice the man who was watching me, sitting in a dark-green rocking chair, as the sun climbed the hillsides. Soon the air would be filled with light. Small waves, one and then another, embroidered their foam into fine bands of lace. The cliffs rose behind me. Atop the cliffs cacti grew like tall cathedrals of thorns and then, beyond them, the quick blaze of the sky.

I entered the water and swam, taking slow strokes. There are people who swim out of pure pleasure. There are those who swim to keep in shape. I swim to think better. I often remember a line from the Mozambican poet Glória de Sant'Anna: 'Inside the water I am exactly right.'

I had divorced the previous day. I'd been at the offices of

O Pensamento Angolano newspaper, transcribing an interview I had carried out with a pilot, when the telephone rang. The pilot, Domingos Perpétuo Nascimento, was a soldier. He'd trained in the Soviet Union. He'd fought in Mavinga, in the biggest battle on African soil since the Second World War, at the controls of a MiG-21. Years later he was captured by guerrilla forces, in an attack on a column of civilian vehicles travelling from Luanda to Benguela, and crossed over to the kidnappers' side. After the end of the war he joined the national airline. A few days ago he had found a bag containing a million dollars in one of the bathrooms on the plane and handed it over to the police. It was a good story. The kind of story I specialised in. I was so excited about it that I ignored the ringing. The phone fell silent for a brief moment, then started back up again. I answered, finally. I recognised the harsh, authoritarian voice of Lucrécia.

'Where are you?'

'At the paper . . .'

'Well, you're supposed to be at the courthouse – the divorce hearing is scheduled for fifteen minutes from now.'

I told her I had no idea. Nobody had informed me. Lucrécia's voice went up a notch:

'The court sent you a summons, but it ended up at the wrong address. I only just realised. I wrote your address down wrong. Whatever, you've got ten minutes.'

I first met Lucrécia at a party. No sooner had I seen her than I knew I was going to marry her. I remarked to a friend that I thought her practically perfect:

'Just a shame she straightens her hair.'

In all the years we were married, I never managed to convince her to wear her hair in its natural state, curling down over her shoulders.

'I look like a wild animal,' Lucrécia would complain.

We started dating in September 1992, during the first elections. Back then, euphoria walked the streets arm in arm with terror. My days passed between rallies, parties, trips to the provinces, unending conversations in bars, on verandas, in back yards. People would fall asleep with the certainty that the country was approaching its end, and then awake convinced they were living through the dawn of a long age of progress and peace. Soon afterwards the war started up again, more violent than ever, and we were married. At the time, I was running the culture section of the *Jornal de Angola*. I wrote about books. I interviewed writers, musicians and film-makers. I liked my job. Lucrécia was enrolled on an interior decorating course in London. Work didn't take up much of her time.

Her father, Homero Diaz da Cruz, had got rich mysteriously in the latter years of the one-party system and the centralised economy, when expressions such as 'proletarian internationalism' and 'revolutionary democratic dictatorship' were still popular, and nobody talked about 'primitive accumulation of capital' as a euphemism for corruption.

Homero had graduated in Law, from Coimbra, in 1973. Right after independence he was named director of an important state firm. He abandoned the public sector in 1990 – by which time he was very rich, and also a member of the central committee of the party – to set up a company supporting the mining industry. He's a brusque, cold man, often rude to his staff and his business associates. Yet he was always an attentive husband and an affectionate father. To this day, although his children are all over forty, he makes a point of organising their lives. We, for example, were offered an apartment. We lived in Maianga. We led a peaceful life. The war did not affect us.

Lucrécia got pregnant. Our daughter was born on a glorious sunny morning in March, in a private clinic in London. We named her Lúcia. She grew to be a happy, healthy child, who early on showed a burning passion for birds. Homero had a huge cage in his back yard, in which there lived, noisily and chaotically together, dozens of blue waxbills, long-tailed tyrants, lined seedeaters, finches and canaries. Lúcia would cling to the bars of the cage and spend hours trying to communicate with the birds. She learned to imitate each one's song well before she learned to speak. I assumed this was why my father started calling her Karinguiri, after the little bird from Benguela. The nickname stuck.

It was only after a Portuguese newspaper took me on as a correspondent, and I started covering politics and society, that the problems between me and Lucrécia began. Not that Lucrécia disapproved of what I wrote. She never took any interest in politics. It was Homero who didn't approve.

'We should always wash our dirty linen in private,' he pronounced on one occasion. 'I don't like you going around bad-mouthing our country in a foreign paper.'

I tried explaining to him that we mustn't confuse the government with the country. Criticising mistakes made by the government wasn't the same as insulting Angola and the Angolans. On the contrary, I criticised the government's errors because I dreamed of a better country. Homero waved away my arguments with irritation:

'You have no need to write for that newspaper. How much are they paying you?'

'A thousand dollars a month.'

'A thousand dollars? A thousand dollars?! All that work for a thousand dollars? Well then, I'll give you ten thousand a month not to write. You have a daughter now. You need to pay more attention to your family.'

I looked at him, astonished, and I refused his offer. A few days later I was called to the office of João Aquilino, director of the *Jornal de Angola*. Aquilino knew that everyone on the editorial staff despised him. Nobody ever referred to him except by his nickname, the Mole, which suited him perfectly. He was a haggard-looking guy, slightly hunched, with narrow little eyes and a sallow complexion, somewhat rustic in appearance, which none of his expensive suits managed to improve. He had been named director not for his qualifications as a journalist, of which he had none, but for his history as a committed party activist. He told me, in a reedy little voice, that I was contravening house rules by collaborating with a foreign publication. The paper insisted on exclusivity. Either I stopped collaborating with the Portuguese or he'd have to fire me. I pointed out that several other staff journalists, including the editor-in-chief, also worked for foreign publications. If the journal wanted exclusivity, they should pay better. The Mole stood up. He walked around the desk, arms behind his back, and positioned himself in front of me on his tiptoes:

'Do you know why I haven't fired you yet? Out of the great respect I have for the gentleman who is your father-in-law. I'm tired of your insolence. You, senhor, you think you're God's gift. You think you're better than all of us just because you studied abroad and you've read half a dozen books in English. But be warned – one more article in a settler paper and you're out on your ear.'

I took two steps back and turned to leave. I was already at the door when the spirit of Devil Benchimol – that's what I call him – descended on me. I closed the door again and advanced on the Mole, pointing my finger at him:

'And you, senhor, aren't you ashamed?'

The wretch hopped back away from me, terrified.

'What?!'

'You aren't even a journalist! You, senhor, are a policeman of thought, a political agent in the service of the dictatorship.'

'You're fired! Fired! Get your things and leave!'

I left to the applause of half the editorial staff. The other half pretended they couldn't see me. That night, when I told her what had happened, Lucrécia got angry with me. My father-in-law reacted even worse. He phoned in a rage to tell me that, with my behaviour, I had shamed the whole family. Two weeks later, during a Saturday lunch, he got up from the big chair he occupied at the head of the table and shouted at me:

'I'm sick of those articles of yours in that Portuguese news-paper, always bad-mouthing Angola and Angolans. Always talking our nation down. I'm going to buy the rag myself and you'll never write there again.'

One of Lucrécia's cousins, who had lived in Lisbon since

childhood and on completing his studies had decided to come back to Angola, tried to defend me:

'Take it easy, uncle. Daniel's allowed to write whatever he wants, and you have the right to disagree with him. We're in a democracy, and in a democracy it's healthy to have different opinions.'

'You shut up!' Homero commanded him. 'You've just set foot in the country and already you're talking about democracy? God made the lions and He made the gazelles, and He made the gazelles to be eaten by the lions. God is not democratic.'

An uncomfortable silence descended on the table. I got up, and left. Two weeks later, somebody – I never learned the name of the businessman or the corporate group – bought the Portuguese newspaper for which I worked. The director called, regretfully, to tell me he could no longer continue working with me.

'We belong to an Angolan firm now, I can't tell you the name. They promised not to mess with our editorial line, but they want your head. Try to understand, my friend, I've got a family – I can't afford to lose this job.'

Lucrécia took her father's side. I became the enemy.

'You don't like my family,' she said. 'You don't make any effort to fit in. Anyone who doesn't like my family doesn't like me.'

I called around a number of papers and magazines in Luanda, begging for a job, but got nowhere. I spent my days at home, reading, surfing the net, watching movies on TV, playing with my daughter. Lucrécia would come home from work and argue with me. They were terrible months. I would wake up crying. I would take long baths in dirty water, and it felt as if I was sinking into night itself. I was saved by a friend, Armando Carlos, who one evening came by our house for a visit and yanked me out of my torpor.

'Get dressed. Pack a bag and come with me.'

'Where?'

'My house. You can't stay here.'

Armando Carlos lived in an apartment across the street. He'd inherited it from an elderly aunt, a spinster without children, who had died three years earlier. It was on the fourth floor of a very dilapidated building. The wooden floorboards were loose, and some of the planks needed replacing. The paint was peeling on the walls. The outer coat, in lime green, matched harmoniously with the colour of the original coat, a faded yellow. The general impression wasn't of decadence so much as a weary luxury, perhaps because of the lushness of the magnificent light that came freely through the enormous curtainless windows and reflected on the walls. The apartment consisted of a huge living room, a kitchen and three bedrooms, two of them en suite. The lack of furnishing made it seem clearer. It had almost nothing inside, apart from three mattresses, one in each room, and half a dozen books.

'I gave away the furniture. I gave away the records and the books. I gave away almost all my clothes,' Armando explained while he showed me around the apartment. 'I've just got two shirts, two pairs of trousers, two pairs of socks, two pairs of underpants and a pair of shoes. I don't need any more than that. Having stuff eats up a lot of energy. Keeping an eye on everything you have eats up even more – it erodes, it corrupts the soul. The really good thing is enjoying what you have. I don't want the sailing boat, I want the journey. I don't want the record, I want the song. You understand?'

His enthusiasm made me laugh.

'Yeah, I think I understand.'

'Man, I suffer from such a longing for not having. My greatest ambition is to have less and less. If you have nothing, you have more time for everything that really matters.'

'Is that Buddhism?'

'Nah, it's pure lazyism.'

'You think that's lazy? Seems like a huge ambition to me, specially in a country where everybody wants to have more and more.'

Armando thought a moment.

'Maybe you're right. I am a lazy guy, but I'm a lazy guy with great ambitions. If the aim is to not have, I want to not have a lot. If the aim is to not do, I want to not do a lot.'

His thick dreadlocks were not yet the immaculate white they are now. Light strands mixed with the dark ones, giving an overall impression of silver, in handsome contrast with the dark sheen of his skin. We went to the kitchen, the only room that was furnished and well-equipped, and he made me some scrambled eggs with cheese and ham.

'I don't know what I was thinking when I fell in love with that woman,' I admitted, after I'd finished my third beer.

Armando laughed.

'Passion is a moment of madness. People who marry in a state of passion should be considered of unsound mind, and those marriages annulled.'

'Not such a bad idea,' I agreed.

'People should only be allowed to marry when lucid. I don't know why it is that you aren't allowed to drive when you're drunk, but you are allowed to get married when you're drunk, or when you're in love, which is the same thing. A marriage isn't so different from a car as all that. If driven badly, it can hurt a lot of people, starting with the kids. If people always got married when lucid, they'd only ever do it out of self-interest, like my parents.'

'Your parents married out of self-interest?'

'Of course. They're still married today.'

I lived in Armando's apartment for several years. During that time, I wrote stage plays and did technical translations for various companies. Armando is an actor. He directs a small but dynamic company, Mukishi, that receives funding from northern European institutions to work on questions relating to human rights and public health. I didn't have all that much money. And yet, having adopted my friend's philosophy, I discovered I was able to live on almost nothing and be happy. I don't think I've ever been as happy as I was back then. Three or four years ago, I was invited to join the editorial team on a new online newspaper, an independent project, which I thought exciting. So I rented an apartment in Talatona, I bought a cat, whom I named Baltazar, and I went back to having a more or less normal life. That was when I got the call from Lucrécia. She had started seeing a businessman, a guy who'd been at high school with me, and she wanted to marry him. She asked for a divorce. I agreed. And yet, for reasons I couldn't understand, she still went ahead with a lawsuit.

That was when I received her call summoning me to court. When I arrived, I found her with a famous lawyer, whom I knew from Saturday lunches at Homero's place.

'You haven't got a lawyer?' Lucrécia asked.

She knew perfectly well I didn't have a lawyer.

I left the courthouse divorced and defeated. I didn't go back to the paper. I got into my car and drove to Cabo Ledo. Halfway there a *candongueiro* driver crossed the central line at high speed, throwing himself at me. I veered out of the way, I'm not sure how, just pure instinct, while his minibus climbed the pavement and hit a huge cactus. I stopped, got out of the car, and ran over to see if they were all OK. Fortunately, nobody was hurt. The passengers were yelling at the driver. I continued on my way. About an hour later I slowed down, turning left onto a beaten-earth track, finally stopping in the shade of a mango tree. Seven bungalows, thatch-roofed, each painted in a different colour, red, orange, yellow, green, blue, indigo and violet, were lined up along the coast. One of them had a sign with the name Rainbow Hotel, and that's where the reception had been set up. I went in, greeted the owner of the establishment, a skinny guy with a drawn face, thinning dishevelled hair, and fierce crow eyes, and told him I was planning to stay one night. I'd been there several times before. I knew the man, I knew his name, Hossi Apolónio Kaley, but we'd never exchanged more than two or three words of small talk. Hossi scratched his rough beard with dirty nails:

'You haven't brought any luggage?'

I ignored his question. I snatched the key from his hand and headed for the blue bungalow. It was, just like all the others, cramped and ugly. Inside they had squeezed a metal bed, a chair, a TV set and a minibar. I opened the minibar. It was empty. I turned on the television. It didn't work. I took off my shirt, folded it, and put it on the chair. I took off my shoes and socks. I took off my trousers, stretched out on the bed and fell asleep.

'Every woman is a path.' The words came to me while I was swimming, as if I'd heard some other person saying them. That other person paused briefly, then went on. 'In every woman there's a beginning of the world.'

'A beginning of the world? Bullshit!' I retorted, addressing the person who was speaking within me. 'Every woman is a trap, that's the truth of it.'

Cursing, even in thought, even while swimming, is a balm to the spirit. I saw something floating to my right. It was a waterproof camera, in mango-yellow. My first reaction, in irritation, was to grab it and hurl it somewhere far away. The destruction of the oceans saddens and disgusts me. I once spent two months on board the *Rainbow Warrior* (I was twenty-four at the time), not long before the Greenpeace trawler was sunk by the French secret services in the port of Auckland, in New Zealand. This terrorist act killed a photographer friend of mine, Fernando Fernandes. It really shook me, and I gave up my eco-warrior role, though not its ideals.

Maybe the camera still worked. In any case, the least I could do was get it out of the water. I attached it to my right wrist, since the object came with a strap, and I carried on swimming, towards the beach now. That night, merely out of curiosity, I removed the camera's memory card, plugged it into the computer and downloaded the photos. What I found frightened me. It couldn't be, and yet, there it was. Until four in the morning I looked at each of those pictures over and over, dazzled by the sudden revelation that had come to me in such an extraordinary fashion, and thought about what it meant and about the mysterious movements of the tides and destiny.

2.

Let us picture an amphitheatre. A hall sloping down towards a stage of dark waxed wood, framed by a heavy scarlet curtain. A woman, totally naked, is playing a piano, while parakeets flutter all around her.

I'm seated, also naked, in the back rows, right up near the top, and I'm watching the concert through tear-filled eyes. I don't know the pianist personally, but I know everything about her. An old man, seated to my left, wearing a brilliant admiral's uniform, whispers in my ear:

'That woman's a fraud!'

I restrain myself so as not to hit him. I've never heard such beautiful music in my whole life. Besides, I feel a deep admiration for that woman. I know she's been arrested, and tortured, she's survived a tumour and a cruel, violent husband, who forbade her from pursuing a musical career. After she was widowed, she went back to the piano. She established a neo-pagan church, the Cult of the Goddess, which accepts only women. In her concerts, she usually has herself accompanied by animals, the parakeets I saw there but also dogs and even wolves. Sometimes she fires a pistol up into the air, using real bullets, to the annoyance of the owners of the halls.

A dream. I woke up with it on the morning of the day I got divorced. I recalled some fragments the following morning, while I was swimming back to land with the camera attached to my right wrist. The dark stage, the naked woman with her shrivelled breasts hanging down over her belly. I often dream about people I've never met. Sometimes I dream the whole of these people's lives, from their births all the way to their deaths. At the end of the concert I walked down to the stage to congratulate the woman. She hugged me, tenderly. She said:

'Everything passes, my friend. Time covers the world in rust. Everything that shines, everything that is light, will soon be ash and nothingness.'

'Almost everything is ash already,' I answered. 'They've incinerated my past.'

At the moment when I awoke, the conversation made no sense. By the end of the day, when I had come back from the courthouse, it did. These kinds of conversations often happen in my dreams – implausible, mysterious, affected, even ridiculous. Later, though, they attain an unexpected coherence. Sometimes, I dream loose lines of verse. I also dream interviews. I've interviewed Jonas Savimbi four times: twice awake and twice in dreams. Muammar Gaddafi I've only interviewed in dreams. He told me his last days had been terrible. He'd slept in abandoned houses, fleeing his pursuers, trying to reach the village where he'd been born. Planes dropped bombs on the column he was travelling in and he found himself forced to get out of the car and take shelter in a drain.

When I interviewed him, Gaddafi was in the drain, bent double, pressed against the cement, wearing a khaki shirt and with a black cap on his head. The following morning, I woke up, turned on the television and saw him with his head uncovered, hair in disarray, his face covered in blood and a look of dazed surprise, astonishment, his delicate hands trying to brush away the hard blows he was receiving.

'God is great! God is great!' his killers were shouting. I felt sorry for him. I felt even sorrier for God.

In the interviews I've done in my dreams, the interviewees have often proved more authentic, and especially more lucid, than when I've been alert. Others, however, make use of mysterious languages of which I'm able only to guess at fragments. Julio Cortázar, for example, a writer with whom I'm not even particularly well acquainted, appeared to me in the form of an ancient giant cedar, with a twisted trunk and crinkled leaves. He answered my questions by moving clouds in the sky. The clouds were a kind of alphabet, the sky a blank page. I remember that dream because seated in a straw chair, in the shade of Cortázar, ramrod straight and very remote, was the Cotton-Candy-Hair-Woman. The Cotton-Candy-Hair-Woman appeared in my dreams often. She was tall and elegant, and almost always wearing the colourful cloths of our local *bessangana* women. A long, angular face, interesting without being beautiful, and a *quindumba* hairstyle that was very tall and soft, and copper-coloured. The Cotton-Candy-Hair-Woman waited for Cortázar to leave the clouds at peace and then said:

'I once met a man who was dreamed by the sea.'

3.

I like sitting on the veranda of my bungalow in the early hours, waiting for the sun to rise. I was there today, sitting quite still, when I spotted Daniel Benchimol on the beach, wearing white underpants. I thought it was strange for the mulatto to be wandering about in underpants like that in a public place, even if there was nobody else around.

He got into the water and swam away, breaststroke. He was swimming straight ahead, determined, as though he had no intention of coming back. I calculated that if he managed to maintain that same speed and the same course he'd arrive in Recife, in Brazil, in less than a hundred days.

The guy had been here, in the hotel, on seven occasions, always alone. I was a bit surprised to see him arriving today, a Tuesday, and also that he was carrying only a small briefcase. During the week, apart from in the holidays, not many customers showed up here. Daniel snatched the keys from my hand without a word, without the slightest gesture of thanks. On previous occasions, he'd always been polite. A bit distant, but polite. Something must have happened to upset him.

All my customers interest me. I like Tolentino, the old boy from Portugal, grey hair, white beard, still tough, in good shape, and an extremely nice guy, who has a different girlfriend every month. He sambas past me, giving me a wink. 'The love of my life,' he whispers, and the girl, her arms around him, smiles shyly. They're all very young, very tall and thin and supple.

I also get frequent visits from a former minister and his wife, both of them fat, both of them arrogant. They complain because there isn't enough toilet paper, because the air con has broken down, because the room's full of mosquitoes, because the steak is very tough. The cook makes a point of spitting in their soup. I pretend not to see and say nothing; I'm inclined to do the same myself. I have done, if I'm honest.

There's a young couple I like, him almost black, her not far off being white, who look like they're straight out of a fifties movie. The man's always very well dressed, sometimes in suit and tie; the woman in long skirts and cheerful blouses.

I investigate everybody's pasts. It's a bad habit I've kept since the old days. Tolentino de Castro is a lawyer. He arrived in Luanda in the sixties. He lived first in Benguela and then in Luanda, where he befriended the composer Liceu Vieira Dias and other important figures in the city's cultural life and the nationalist movement. After independence, he spent many years working as an advisor at the Ministry of Justice, before opening his own firm. Today he defends the interests of some of the largest fortunes in the country. He has become rich, but his habits remain modest. He spends a good part of what he earns on funding an organisation that supports street children. His *philanthropy extends to trees, too. About ten years ago he got the idea of buying baobab trees that are under threat. He doesn't buy the actual trees, obviously; he buys the lands where they grow, and on which the former owners are intending to build homes. Today Tolentino owns two dozen small plots of land, maybe more, wedged between horrendous apartment blocks, and surrounded by high walls. And inside: baobabs. One afternoon he took me to see one of those trees, a huge specimen, whose trunk had already begun to be cut when he saved it. First, he paid the workers to turn off their machines. Only then did he go and find the owner of the land. The cut is big enough for a man to lie down in. Tolentino stretched himself out in it to show me.*

'Sometimes I come here in the evenings,' he said. 'I lie down and sleep.'

I wanted to know why he did it.

'Why I sleep inside the baobab?'

'No, why you spend so much money to save baobabs. They're only trees.'

Tolentino climbed out of the trunk. He shook himself down. He looked tenderly at the baobab:

'Take a good look. It's so beautiful, isn't it?'

Tolentino also squanders a lot of money on his young girlfriends. But that does seem like a good thing to squander it on, if you ask me.

The ex-minister is called Nzuzi Sincero da Maia; he was born in Pointe-Noire, in the Congo, and he was a nurse in the colonial times. President Agostinho Neto enjoyed his company. He named him minister of fisheries for a brief period, then ambassador to Ethiopia. He is diabetic, impotent, and not likely to live long. I know because I've talked to his doctor.

The elegant young couple have a rather more curious story. Melquesideque was born in Luanda, but left Angola when still a baby in the arms of his maternal grandmother. His parents were shot, back in 1977, having been accused of involvement in an alleged attempted coup. The kid grew up in Lisbon. He later moved to London, to study medicine, and there he met his wife, Tukaiana, who was completing a photography course. They quickly fell in love. They went everywhere together. One evening, when he arrived at his girlfriend's apartment, he found her hugging a pillow and weeping buckets.

'Go away!' shouted Tukaiana.

The guy came over to console her. 'What is it?'

'I can't tell you. You'll never want to look at me again.'

But she did tell him: she had learned that afternoon that her father, a friendly, happy man liked by everyone, the owner of a small chain of hotels scattered around Angola, had tortured and killed Melquesideque's mother in front of her husband. Then he had shot the husband. One of her cousins had reported this tragedy to her. She had sat down opposite her, at the kitchen table, a very serious expression on her face:

'There are some things you need to know about your father, girl.'

And she started talking. João da Gruta, that's what Tukaiana's father was called, was one of the founders of the Political Police, shortly after independence. He was a young man at the time, tall and thin, with a long face, Arabic features and a thick, coarse, black beard, that earned him the nickname the Ingombota Christ.

I remember him, that Ingombota Christ. I mean, I don't remember him physically – I only ever saw him in photos – but I remember the terror his name inspired. 'So-and-so is in Christ's hands now,' people would say, and we all gave him a wide berth whenever So-and-so walked past, our eyes down, because he was someone who had been to hell and back, and of course he was no longer even a man, not really; he was a kind of amazed shadow who sometimes still smiled, still laughed, as though he was one of us.

Melquesideque listened to his girlfriend in silence. Finally, he looked up and walked out of the apartment without closing the door. Tukaiana didn't hear from him for two weeks. One morning, when she came out of the apartment, she found him sitting on the steps. The lad looked fragile now, and at the same time more mature. He got to his feet, held out a bunch of roses, and asked her to marry him.

Daniel awoke my curiosity the first time he showed up at the hotel, because of the profession written on the registration card: journalist. Only then did I connect the name to the face. I remembered one of his reports, the astonishing story of the hijacking of an aeroplane, a Boeing 727, from Luanda airport. The guy specialised in disappearances. Cases where people, sometimes very well-known people, simply evaporated during the war. Public funds that vanished in a puff of smoke. Kidnappings of foreign businessmen. Those kinds of news stories. The government didn't like him much.

He was born in Huambo in 1960. His father, Ernesto Benchimol, an employee on the Benguela railroad, came to be quite famous, in Angola and even in Portugal, as a footballer. He played for Benfica. After giving up football, he devoted himself to hunting, fishing, to recreational shooting and swimming. For many years, he taught swimming at the Railroad Club, after hours. Daniel is the youngest of three brothers. All three studied at the same school as me, Monte Olimpo, but I don't remember any of them. Samuel and Júlio were swimming champions, fulfilling their old man's dream. The youngest, however, never showed the least talent for any sport. Let alone for hunting. I talked to a Portuguese man, Vasco Go-with-God, who worked as a janitor at the Railroad Club for more than three decades. He must be nearly ninety. He's half-blind and only moves a few metres at a time, with the help of a frame. Poor thing, they've done a total laryngectomy on him. He has a hole in his neck. He communicates through a device, a kind of amplifier, that he holds up to the hole when he talks. The voice that comes out, a sort of Robocop voice, entertains children and scares adults. Although his body is no longer much use, after seventy years abusing alcohol and cigarettes, his head does seem very healthy. He smiled when I mentioned Daniel:

'Kid didn't swim at all,' he said, in that metallic voice. 'I remember him in the late afternoons, always huddled in one corner of the pool, skinny and shivering with cold. He was the shame of the family.'

I told him I'd seen him swimming – and that he swims very well.

The old man smiled. An almost happy smile. 'Really? Perhaps. The sea teaches you.'

I tracked him down on one of my visits to Huambo, where I was seeing some distant cousins. At a certain point, Go-with-God put the fragile bones of his left hand down on my leg, while at the same time bringing the amplifier to his throat:

'You know the story about the lion? The story of that boy, your customer, with a lion cub?' he asked.

I didn't know. Then he asked me for a cigarette. I tried to resist:

'You really shouldn't smoke. Your wife warned me you'd ask for cigarettes. She made me promise not to listen to you.'

'Oh, for fuck's sake, man! Just give me a cigarette.'

I glanced over my shoulder to check his wife wasn't watching us. She was still a young woman, thirty-five at the most, who had received me at the front door straightening a dressing gown. She prodded a hard finger in my chest, while warning me about her husband's health:

'The old goat mustn't smoke!'

I took a cigarette from the pack I had in my pocket, lit it, then with an incredibly quick movement the old man snatched it from my fingers and stuck it into the hole in his neck. I watched him inhale the smoke while the dusk flung itself against the eucalyptus trees with the rage of a storm. We were sitting in the yard of the small house where he lived. There had once been a wall a few metres over; it was still possible to make out the ruins, a heap of bricks in the middle of the very green grass, but now the yard stretched out into the bush, all the way to a little eucalyptus grove.

'What I'm going to tell you happened a few weeks before independence, or a few weeks after.' Vasco Go-with-God coughed, a prolonged rattle. Then he calmed down, stubbed out the cigarette on the beaten-earth ground and went on. 'My brother Hermínio worked at the zoo. That boy's family, what was his dad's name . . . ?'

'Ernesto. Ernesto Benchimol.'

'Right. Ernesto. So the Benchimols lived very near here, a couple of steps from the zoo.'

The following day I went to visit the zoo. Or rather, what was left of it. I walked alone through the undergrowth. I found the old lion cage almost intact, though with its walls pierced by bullet holes and the cement floor all cracked. Inside, behind the bars, was a boy wearing orange shorts. He was sitting on a wooden crate, with his eyes closed, whistling. I was surprised to recognise the tune: 'My World Is Today' by Paulinho da Viola. I don't like Brazilian music. I don't like

23

anything that comes from Brazil. I hate Brazil. Except Paulinho da Viola and Pelé. Oh, and Mangueira, I'm a Mangueira supporter, I don't even know why.

As I was wandering the ruins, I returned to November 1975, a few days before independence, or a few days after, either way. It must have been hot, even there, in the zoo, surrounded by a eucalyptus grove. One afternoon, Vasco Go-with-God received a call from his brother:

'We're going to have to kill them.'

Hermínio said this, and he started to cry. Vasco waited for his brother to calm down. 'I know a hunter, Ernesto Benchimol – you know who that is? The mulatto who looks like a movie star who teaches swimming at the Railroad? Guy's a hunter. He's hunted lions, he's hunted elephants, he must know how to do it.'

The next morning, Ernesto showed up at the zoo suitably equipped. He had brought his three sons to help him. He wasn't happy:

'A hunter is not a killer,' he explained to his sons. 'Hunting is a game between hunter and prey. It must be played freely. What we're going to do in the zoo is something different, a humanitarian act – we're going to kill those animals because they're suffering.'

'Couldn't we take them some food first?' asked Daniel.

His older brothers laughed at him. His father got annoyed:

'And what do you suggest we feed them, tell me that?'

Daniel fell silent. He was fifteen and already as tall as his brothers. Taller than Ernesto. He put the shotgun on his back and followed his family. Vasco and Hermínio were waiting for them. They went to see the elephant. The animal, who was called Jamba, lived on a kind of little island surrounded by a moat. In the good old days, people would offer him peanuts and Jamba would thank them for their kindness by ringing a little bell. Jamba was lying on his side, thin and dry like a coat-hanger, his trunk covered in flies. He waved it slightly when he saw them coming, and the flies flew off. A dark swarm like an ill omen. The hunter put a plank of wood down over the moat and walked across. He stroked Jamba's ear, put the barrel of the shotgun against his head, just above the eye – a liquid globe, round and bright like a marble – and fired. Daniel gave a cry, his eyes filled with tears. His middle brother, Júlio, said something to him with a cynical smile, but Samuel, the oldest, silenced him. Then they killed the crocodile, the hyenas, the ostriches and the giraffes.

'The monkeys?' asked Ernesto. 'Where are the monkeys?'

'Somebody let the monkeys loose,' said Hermínio. 'They're round about here somewhere, in the eucalyptuses, screaming, absolutely famished. We fed the forest buffalo to the lions. The forest buffalo, the antelopes and the warthogs.'

Daniel stepped forward:

'So now you can give them the meat from the elephant, the giraffes and the ostriches. So we don't need to kill them.'

Hermínio felt sorry for him. 'It's got to happen, kid. Worst bit for me is the little lion cub.'

Two months earlier, the lioness had given birth to two cubs, but one of them had died hours later. The survivor was born blind in his left eye, which was how they'd come to call him Moshe Dayan.

'I'm going to count to three,' said Ernesto. 'At three we fire. All of you deal with the female, I'll take the male. Point at her head.'

He counted to three and they fired. The lion fell. The boys, perhaps because they were nervous, were less lucky. The lioness gave a leap, crashing her head against the bars with a terrible roaring. Ernesto turned his gun on her, an instinctive gesture, fired, and killed her.

Hermínio went to fetch Moshe Dayan. They had put him in a different cage so he would not witness the killing of his parents.

Daniel hugged the little creature:

'Kill me!' he shouted. 'You're going to have to kill me first!'

'We shouldn't have brought him,' said Ernesto, making no effort to hide his displeasure. 'The kid only brings trouble.'

Samuel, who was very patient, tried to convince his brother to let go of Moshe Dayan. Ernesto, however, thought the whole thing no better than a little girl's tantrum.

'Leave him!' he told Samuel. 'Now he's going to be the one to have to kill the animal.'

Daniel started to cry. 'I'd rather kill myself.'

'And I'd rather have a dead son than a faggot son. Kill the animal!'

Then Daniel got up. He took the shotgun and placed the barrel under his chin. 'Nobody move or I fire!'

His father just laughed. 'You're going to fire, kid? How? Sure, I know you've got long arms, but in that position there's no way even you can reach the trigger. I've never understood how the hell Hemingway managed to kill himself with a damn shotgun.'

He was right. Daniel was holding the barrel with both hands. There was no way to keep the gun firmly under his chin while at the same time reaching the trigger and firing.

'Drop the gun,' ordered Ernesto, very calmly. 'Take the cub home and look after it. He'll end up starving to death, poor thing, and he'll suffer a lot more than if we just killed him now, but you've made your choice.'

That was how Daniel came to take a lion cub home. He sold his bicycle and with the money bought the last tins of powdered milk in the city. For the first few weeks he fed Moshe Dayan milk, first from a baby's bottle, and then from a saucepan. He started hunting the neighbourhood cats, which pained him terribly, because unlike his brothers he had a great love for all living things. Júlio and Samuel used to catch frogs in the river at night-time, dazing them with a flash-light. They would bring them home, keep them in a big bucket and the following morning they'd line them up against a wall and shoot them with their air rifles. Daniel would often go out after dark, hidden from everybody else, and return the frogs to the river. When he ran out of cats, the lad remembered all those frogs that, over the years, he'd saved from such a cruel death, and went to find them in the mud. The little lion cub, though, refused to eat that elusive meat, even after it had been cooked and well seasoned, with salt, hot capsicum and lemon.

Most of the Portuguese settlers had fled. Thousands of handsome old houses were shut up, with thick iron chains and padlocks on the gates. Daniel persuaded his best friend, 'Gato', a very fat boy, the son of a nurse, to break into the houses. Getting over the walls was easy, at least for Daniel; Gato didn't always make it. Then they would break a window with a rock and go inside. Some of the houses were perfectly tidy, beds made and floors waxed, as though the owners had just gone on a short holiday. Others were in complete disarray. In one they found shards of glass scattered all over the bedrooms and hall-ways. In the next they found a crude trap with a grenade attached to a wire, which only didn't go off because Gato, who had earned his nickname from his cat-like eyesight and strange night-time predator's instinct, had noticed a strange glint in the middle of the hallway and froze just in time. On the opposite wall, the owner of the house had left a message in red paint: Die, commies!

'Fucking whites!' Gato complained. 'They steal from us for five hundred years, and even after they've fucked off, driven out by gun and blow, they're still trying to kill us.'

I know all this because, besides talking at length to Vasco Go-with-God, I also talked to Gato, aka Estêvão Chindandala, an absolutely vast man, who if he were a motorised vehicle would have been a lorry, as he said himself, laughing so loudly and so vividly that it was like he had waterfalls and torrents of light leaping from his mouth. He didn't say it because of being fat, though, but because he likes lorries. He's the happy owner of a road haulage company. He never left Huambo. We talked in the company office, a cramped, low place; or at least it seemed cramped to me because the huge Estêvão occupied it completely with his gigantic body and powerful voice.

Daniel, said the huge Estêvão, brought all kinds of objects back from their night-time incursions, from watches to cameras, which he then tried to exchange for meat to feed the insatiable stomach of Moshe Dayan. He entered into an agreement with a butcher, a man called Robert Williams, the name copied from the English millionaire who'd built the Benguela railroad. The Portuguese had given the millionaire's name to Caála. After independence, the town had its African name restored. This guy, the butcher, continued to be called Robert Williams and nowadays nobody connects his name to the town. Robert dealt in stolen goods, and though I say stolen it doesn't seem like the right word; people in those days used the euphemism 'recovered'. In truth, they were neither stolen nor recovered, but abandoned. And so Robert would exchange these products for two or three kilos of meat that Moshe Dayan would swallow down greedily.

One night the inevitable happened. On returning home, Daniel found his father with his belt in his hand. He didn't have time to say a word. Ernesto started beating him with the belt, furious blows, while he shouted that there was no place for thieves in this family. The brothers tried to intervene, with no success, until Dona Angelina put her arms around her son, crying – and fainted. They had to take her to hospital, where she spent the night.

The next morning, Daniel could not find Moshe Dayan.

'Father took your lion,' murmured Júlio.

Daniel never saw another trace of the little cub. Years later, when Ernesto was dying, his son took his hand and asked him what he'd done with Moshe Dayan. The old man turned his surprised eyes towards him:

'I don't remember!' he said in a whisper. He closed his eyes. 'All I remember now is the sea.'

4.

The Rainbow Hotel has a restaurant overlooking the beach. There are seven wooden tables, arranged across a kind of stage, each protected by a broad sunshade. Each of the shades is a different colour: red, orange, yellow, green, blue, indigo and violet. The restaurant was empty, so I chose the table closest to the sea, under the blue parasol. I called over one of the staff and ordered a Cuca and a grilled chicken. The man walked away. He returned moments later with the beer. The chicken will take a while, he apologised, with a lovely smile. I thanked him for his frankness. Frankness is a rare quality in restaurant staff nowadays. These people seem more and more to resemble politicians. The customer asks, say, whether the fish is fresh, and instead of telling us right away that, no, it's frozen, the waiter launches into praise of the butter sauce. Anyway, I poured myself some beer, looked out towards the beach and settled in for a wait. Hossi Apolónio Kaley came over, smoking a cigar.

'OK if I join you?'

I agreed, though a little surprised. The owner of the Rainbow

Hotel sat down opposite me. He looked at me alertly, as though I were an ancient artefact displayed in a museum:

'I've read your articles. What's a journalist doing in Cabo Leda on a Tuesday?'

'Journalists need to rest, too. And often on weekdays.'

'Tomorrow we celebrate independence – it's a national holiday. You could have come tomorrow.'

'I hadn't even remembered. It was today I needed a rest. But I'll stay an extra day. Make the most of the holiday.'

'You won't be celebrating independence?'

'There's not a lot to celebrate . . .'

'You don't think so? I didn't fight for independence – I was too young – but if I'd been old enough I'd have fought for it. I did fight later on . . .'

'You were a soldier?'

'I was. On the guerrilla side . . .'

'You were a guerrilla fighter with UNITA?!'

'Yes. I went through hell.'

'I'm sorry to hear that . . .'

'Don't be sorry – a dog who knows how to kill also needs to know how to carry what it's killed.'

'Look, I don't believe violence can be liberating. And that means I don't believe in wars of liberation. All wars imprison us. That thing you call a war of liberation was the origin of the civil war.'

'How so?'

'How so?! We'd had three independence movements before independence, right? And people were already fighting one another. Killing one another.'

'You believe the Portuguese ever would have left without force?'

'Yes. I believe we could have achieved independence by peaceful means. What you get through violence remains poisoned by violence. Just look at what happened next.'

'The Portuguese left, they went back to their country – that's what happened next. Now we're independent.'

'Sure, Portuguese colonialism came to an end, but we aren't any freer or any more at peace.'

'Maybe not. But in any case, I'd rather be ordered about by a black man than by a white or a mulatto – no offence, my friend.'

A waiter approached with a tray. He served my chicken and chips. I turned to Hossi:

'Will you join me?'

'No, thanks very much. I don't eat meat.'

'You don't eat meat?!'

'No, I'm a vegetarian.'

'A vegetarian? Seriously?! My daughter's a vegetarian, too.'

'You look amazed. You think that's so strange?'

'A bit. There aren't all that many vegetarians in Angola.'

'Hitler was a vegetarian. Gandhi was a vegetarian, too. I'm not Hitler, or Gandhi, and yet just like them I don't eat meat.'

'Why don't you eat meat?'

'Why doesn't your daughter eat meat?'

'Ethical reasons, I guess. Probably health reasons, too.'

'And Hitler?'

'I don't know. Health reasons?'

'Also health reasons. But not just that. He liked animals. The Nazi regime set up all kinds of laws to protect animals.

Hitler wanted to put an end to slaughterhouses and the consumption of meat.'

'I didn't know that.'

'No, of course you didn't. People prefer not to know. It's hard to accept that a man who did such harm to humanity was sensitive to the suffering of animals. It's easy to accept that Gandhi was a vegetarian who liked animals. But we find it hard that Hitler wasn't completely evil. Tell me, what do you know about death?'

'About death? "Dying is only disappearing from view," that's what Fernando Pessoa said.'

'Only disappearing from view? The "only" in that line's redundant. Dying is disappearing from view, and that seems to me to be a dreadful thing.'

'Yes, you're right.'

'You don't know anything, do you? You don't know anything about death, or about evil!'

'Right again. My ignorance is limitless. The older I get, the more it seems to grow. And about death I know less still. I've never killed anybody.'

Hossi looked at me with contempt.

'You think a man only learns what fire is by lighting a bonfire? Killing isn't the same as dying.'

I smiled.

'You mean you haven't only killed, you mean you've also died?'

The hotel owner shook his head, with an expression of genuine bewilderment. His voice, which was naturally harsh, turned almost soft.

'Yes. I've died twice, but I only want to tell you about the second time.'

5.

On the afternoon when Hossi Apolónio Kaley died for the second time, two years before the end of the war, I was in a Huambo yard looking for memories of myself. In front of the house where I was born and lived my whole childhood and adolescence, there opened up, just like in the old days, a vast horizon. The sun still lay on the grasslands, a huge, round, red ball, and then, straight afterwards, night fell. The boy I used to be enjoyed lying on his back on one of the upper branches of the avocado tree, while the firmament spread out, up there, revealing the millions of stars in motion, like glow worms flashing in a well.

The avocado tree was still there. They had pulled down the medlar trees and the guava trees, they'd cut down all the Surinam cherry trees. Only the avocado tree was still in the same spot, just a little bit taller and with its trunk very badly damaged. The yard had been transformed into a car park. The house, somewhat dilapidated, covered in the sediment of decades, rust-coloured, housed a Military Recruitment Centre. My father's study had become the finance office. The shelves fixed to the walls were the same, but they were full of files now. Ernesto Benchimol had had a fine library. I remember the encyclopaedias. There were several collections, some of them comprising dozens of volumes, like the *Luso-Brazilian Encyclopaedia*. My father particularly liked the *Lello Universal*, in two volumes. It had all disappeared. But no, not all. In one corner, very badly kept, I discovered a rare copy of the second volume of the *Great Encyclopaedia of the Worlds*. I grabbed hold of the book, quite emotional, and wiped it clean with the end of my shirt. A clerk, who had been dozing at the desk, head in hands, was surprised at my behaviour.

'What are you doing with that book?'

'It's mine!' I growled. 'I'm taking it.'

The man got to his feet, threatening.

'No, you aren't!'

It was lunchtime. We were alone. Our shouts ended up attracting more people. I put my hand in my trouser pocket and pulled out a high-denomination note.

'Here. I'm taking the book.'

The man accepted the note. He shrugged.

'Were you really born in this house?'

'Yes, I was born here. Me and my two brothers.'

We weren't. We were born in the Benguela Railroad clinic. We grew up in this house.

'Take the book, then,' said the official. 'It's yours, really.'

I remembered this episode after my conversation with Hossi. Back in the blue bungalow, still stunned by the story I'd just heard, I turned on my computer and consulted my journal. I'd started it more than twenty years earlier, because I was tormented by the idea that I'd end up like my father. Old Ernesto started losing his memory straight after leaving Huambo. The process happened fast. The past was erased from front to back. First he couldn't remember what he'd done the previous week. Next, what had happened five or six years ago. Finally, all he had left was the odd image from his happy boyhood, in Benguela, in the distant thirties of the last century. I was with him when he died.

'The sea,' he murmured. 'I only remember the sea.'

I consulted my journal to try and work out what was going on in the world on the day Hossi died for the second time.

I went to see the house. There was a boy, in the bit of open ground right in front, flying a paper kite. I didn't find the Surinam cherry trees or the guava tree, but the avocado tree is still there. I met, at dinner – we were having dinner in the same restaurant, at adjacent tables – the correspondent from the Lusa agency. He told me Blondin Beye died today in a plane crash, in the Ivory Coast. It's a strange and unfortunate coincidence, the disappearance of the mediator of the peace process happening at the exact moment when everybody is preparing for war. To me it's just one more sign, of so many, that this country is on the verge of a terrible convulsion. The guy from Lusa also told me he'd been in Andulo; the white man responsible for maintaining the airstrip told him that there had been a UFO four hundred metres in diameter floating around there for some time, in the evening, not long before the storm.

Hossi saw something inexplicable floating over Andulo. That's the last thing he remembers. He can't recall what happened in the days following the accident. To this day, he doesn't know for sure how many memories he lost. Nor does he know how much of him was lost along with those memories.

'Losing memories isn't like losing an arm,' he said. 'When we lose an arm, we know we've lost an arm. People look at us and know we've lost an arm. It's not like that with memories. We don't know we've lost them, nobody notices, but as we lose them, something in our spirit stops working. You know, sometimes these creatures show up here who know me. I don't remember them. I pretend I do, as a matter of courtesy, or so I don't have to give them big explanations, but I haven't the faintest idea. They're people from those days I lost – or maybe weeks, maybe months, maybe years – from those huge holes in my memory.'

Hossi saw something floating over the little town. He was squatting down, in the rain, on the roof of the house, trying to fix an aerial, when a strange bluish blaze lit up the night. He got up, shaking with terror, while something resembling the belly of an enormous blue whale pierced the clouds and slipped noiselessly above his head. The blue whale disappeared, the night closed in again, and there he was still, standing, his arm pointed towards the mystery. It was then that it started to thunder. The first lightning bolt hit him full on, and Hossi dropped down dead.

'I woke in a place where the rivers don't flow – they remain totally still,' he tried to explain. His voice trembled. I moved my chair closer so as better to hear him. 'Butterflies were floating, motionless, over the waters of the rivers. There, in that place, nobody grows old. My grandmother was with me and she was laughing. I don't know how long I was dead. Then I was hit by a second lightning bolt and I woke up. I came back to life.'

I laughed.

'Seriously? Come on, old man – don't tell me that! The first bolt of lightning, fine. I can even believe that. That place without time, I can believe that, too. But a second bolt of lightning? And this second one brought you back to life . . . ?!'

Hossi threw me a furious look. He stood up and took off his shirt. A scar, like a black lightning flash, came down from his neck to his belly, unfolding and blossoming into a thousand delicate, precise bolts of light.

It was horrible. It was so beautiful.

Then he turned around, and on his back I saw a similar scar, even leafier and more detailed than the first, like a tattoo drawn by a brilliant artist.

'It was like those two lightning bolts had always been waiting for me. As if every moment they'd been bursting onto my skin.'

I put down my cutlery, appalled. Astonished.

'I'm sorry. I don't know what to say.'

The next evening, on my way home, I hunted out the second volume of the *Great Encyclopaedia of the Worlds*. I kept the book on the shelf of curiosities along with the four precious photograph albums of Angola, from Cunha de Moraes, in 1885 and 1886. I opened it at random, the way I always do when I want to take my spirit for a wander. I read the story of a Cuban dwarf, El Negro Juan, who for a few years had accompanied the famous automaton maker Wolfgang von Kempelen on his travels.

Juan would hide inside a chess-playing machine, known as the Turk, to face astonished opponents.

I opened the book at random again:

NEIPPBERG, Sara, Brazilian pianist and mystic, b. Porto Alegre 1866, d. Rome 1963. At the age of six, she went to live in Paris, with her parents. She taught herself to play the piano and by the age of twelve was already performing in public concerts. At sixteen, she married a rich Armenian businessman, who forbade her from pursuing her career as a pianist. After her husband's death, in 1904, she went back to giving concerts, performing her own works and those by avant-garde composers, such as Erik Satie, whom she had befriended. In her concerts she would use tame animals, including wolves, incorporating the animals' barks and howls with the sounds of the orchestra. At one point, she brought a flock of sheep onto the stage. She was arrested and tortured by Nazi troops, at the time of the occupation of France, on suspicion of having maintained links to the Resistance. After the end of the war, she established a clandestine neo-pantheist society, for women only, called the Secret.

I closed the book. I must have read that before, as a child. The information had been kept in some abandoned drawer in my brain, for years on end, only to reappear in the fantastical form of a dream. That's what I thought. It seemed the most reasonable explanation.

6.

The fig tree twisted in the evening as though the wind were tickling it. I liked it at once. The tree, as it laughed, was leaning over the wall. A crow – or maybe it wasn't a crow, in any case it was a bird that was solid and dark as a crow – watched the curious figure of a man. Then it snarled. Other identical birds appeared. They surrounded me, snarling. The fig tree was no longer laughing. Now it was closing itself up, threateningly, like an octopus ready to attack.

I understood that I was dreaming. The wind sweeping across the patio was not real. The patio was not real, nor the fig tree threatening me, still less the noisy pack of crows. I made an effort to wake up. 'Wake up!' I commanded myself. 'Open your eyes! Move an arm!' I couldn't do it. A terrible distress weighed down on my chest. I heard a voice behind the fig tree:

'Yes, you are sleeping. Let it take you. Fighting a dream is not like fighting the current of a river. Let it take you.'

The Cotton-Candy-Hair-Woman came out from behind the fig tree. She was walking with her beautiful feet bare, sinking into the soaking earth.

'Let it take you. A dream is only a dream, and you will wake up someplace.'

I noticed her hand, I noticed her long fingers, with blue-painted nails, weaving slow figures in the air as she talked, and I thought about the flutes played by snake charmers. At that moment, one of the crows was transformed into Hossi Apolónio Kaley, though still retaining the physical form of a crow. It was Hossi in the form of a crow. He fixed his harsh eyes on me:

'Dreams are delicate artefacts,' he murmured. 'Most of them crumble in the light like the skin of a vampire, and then not even ashes remain. Not many people know how to dream. You have a calling, but you lack practice.'

'Practice?'

'Train yourself to dream. Believe in your dreams. Now, wake, man!'

'No, not yet! Tell me about death.'

'What ... ?!'

'You said you'd died twice. The second time you died you woke up in a place without time ...'

'Yes. Time is a lie, but a necessary one. Death, too. Wake up, wake up, wake up! If you don't wake up, you'll lose this dream, and you won't have another tonight.'

I woke up. I struggled to my feet and went over to the window. Outside, it was raining. Water was beating heavily against the cold glass. The darkness crossed the street and swirled between the tents of the poor wretches who had been turfed out by the development of new luxury condos. There was an old man sitting on a stone, looking towards me. I often saw him there. I thought about speaking to him. Instead I sat down at the desk, turned on my laptop and made a note of the dream. Then I opened the folder where I kept the photos from the camera I had saved from the waters. There she was, the woman from my dreams, the Cotton-Candy-Hair-Woman, looking at me. They were strange pictures, which produced an effect on the soul kind of similar to the effect a grain of sand in a shoe has on a sensitive foot. To an inattentive gaze, they might seem like innocent landscapes. Looking at them again, more attentively, you'd notice that the grassland, behind the river, couldn't possibly be real. The woman (the woman from my dreams) was standing there, naked, in the bottom left-hand corner, and casting no shadow on the sand. Birds were flying across the sky with their eyes closed, as though dead or asleep.

I dreamed about crows one Thursday. The following Saturday I returned to Cabo Ledo. Hossi didn't seem surprised to see me.

'Staying in blue?'

'What?'

'The blue bungalow?'

'Yes, yes, in blue. You know, I dreamed about you.'

The hotel owner didn't hide his shock.

'Seriously, you dreamed about me?'

'I'm sorry. But it's not what you're thinking . . .'

At that moment, a Portuguese couple came in. The woman was tall, with long blonde hair, a lifeless pallor to match her voice:

'Have you got any rooms?'

Hossi handed me the key.

'I'll talk to you at lunchtime.'

I moved away, disappointed. In the two hours leading up to that moment, at the wheel of my car, I'd imagined many possible ways of approaching the hotel owner. None of them resembled this. I tried to read a book, but I couldn't focus on the pages. I took a shower, got dressed and headed to the restaurant. The hotel was full. I managed to get a table under the yellow awning, in a corner, without a view of the beach. I ordered a grilled grouper.

'It'll take a while,' the waiter warned me.

'Fine. Bring me the beer.'

I was on my third bottle when Hossi appeared. He sat down opposite me, sweating, his beard dishevelled.

'Sorry about that. We're very busy today. You were saying you dreamed about me . . .'

I was getting embarrassed:

'Yeah, I know it must seem a bit weird.'

'Was I wearing a purple coat?'

'A purple coat?!'

'So I wasn't?'

'No!'

'Just as well. That's a bit of a relief. It's been a while since people dreamed about me. But it used only to happen when I was nearby. I used to appear in their dreams wearing a purple coat.'

'I don't understand . . .'

Hossi leaned back in his chair.

'People used to dream about me when I was nearby. Those dreams – ah, those dreams! A friend once told me she thought dreaming was the same as living, but without the great lie that life is. Maybe that's how it is. Maybe it's the opposite. I don't know. It sometimes happens – I believe in a given idea and in its opposite with identical passion, or with no passion at all. In recent years, actually, I've been losing my hair and my passion. I've been losing ideas and ideals, too. Maybe it's old age, maybe it's nirvana. What do you think?'

7.

I'm finally writing in this journal again. I was struck by lightning twice, the first time killing me and the second bringing me back to life, and I was left paralysed. I was blinking, talking, but unable to move a muscle from my neck down. I'm now in a clinic in Havana, Cuba.

A few days ago, I saw a news report on TV about a family who were struck down by a bolt of lightning. A witness to this event, a fisherman, described seeing a huge lightning flash unleashed on two parasols. The people who had taken shelter beneath them fell to the ground, like the petals of a flower opening, one in each direction, that's what the fishermen said. And that's how I imagine it happening to me. I fell to the ground like a flower petal.

The leadership of the movement decided to send me to South Africa. I travelled in a military column, towards Andulo. I was due to board a small plane to a tiny secret airstrip in Zambia, and from there head on to Lusaka and then, finally, to Johannesburg. We were ambushed just a few kilometres from our destination.

What I remember of the attack:

The hot air. An eagle, up there, motionless, pinned onto blue card. The jeep that was travelling ahead of us rose up, as if it was made of cardboard and had just been struck by a sudden gust of wind. There was a kind of vacuum, which pulled it forwards, and the next moment the explosion. Gunshots. Shouting. Death shouting and dancing all around me and there I was, screwed down into my seat, unable to move.

I don't remember everything that happened. At nightfall, in Huambo, a kid from military intelligence recognised me. The following day they sent me to Luanda. I was treated like a prince. They made me promises, offered me positions and money. They didn't even realise I would have given them what they were asking for free of charge. I hate Savimbi. I hope he dies a cruel death. I've never talked about this to anyone. I've never even written anything like it in this journal. I'm scared that the agents from the movement are going to read it. I have nothing else. I've lost two children. I've lost my wife. It's been a long time since I believed in war. And so I came to an agreement – I told them everything I remembered. My memory was, and still is, full of holes, like the Canjala road. They were suspicious of me at first, they thought I was faking forgetfulness to try and deceive them. I spent three months in the military hospital. I recovered from my paralysis, my wounds scarred over, but my memory didn't come back. Finally, they sent me here, to a clinic specialising in war trauma. I'm OK. Everything here is very clean, very calm.

Sunday, 21 June 1998

The poet David Mestre died last week. I learned the news from an Angolan general called Amável Guerreiro, a mulatto from Calulo,

who's being treated for an attack of schizophrenia (he hears voices).
David Mestre died in Portugal angry with the regime. I had lunch
with him in Luanda, in 1992, shortly before the elections. He gave me
a signed book: For a UNITA supporter who is (almost) sorry. *I*
don't know how he was able to tell I had doubts. I'm kind of scared of
poets. The good ones are like fortune-tellers.

Monday, 22 June 1998

Yesterday a psychologist came to talk to me, a pretty woman, still
young, very pale, who everybody calls Snowflake. I don't know her
real name. 'Tell me about your life,' she said.

She's so beautiful, she has such a glow in her eyes, that I started
to talk. I told her what I remembered. I enlisted at seventeen in the
Galo Negro troops, right at the start of everything, in the country's
terrible infancy. In the first months, I told her, in the first months it
was wild – everybody wanted to fight. We were killing one another in
those days, we were killing ourselves in those days, but we knew why.
We believed in all that. The communists on one side; us on the other,
fighting for democracy and against the Russians and the Cubans.

Snowflake corrected me:

'No, comrade, you on one side, the puppets of imperialism, sup-
ported by the South African racists; and the socialist comrades on the
other, along with the proletarian internationalists.'

I couldn't tell if she was winding me up or if she really believed
what she was saying. I agreed. It's all the same to me. The war lasted
too long. From a certain point, we stopped knowing why we were kill-
ing. People were killing out of habit. Some out of addiction. Yes, a lot

47

of people really got a taste for firing guns. They dived laughing into the middle of the bullets, like somebody jumping off a cliff into a turbulent sea, like somebody going all in during a poker game, like somebody declaring himself to the most beautiful woman in the world. I was put in military intelligence. One of my functions was to interrogate prisoners. On one occasion they brought me a man who was very frightened, his whole face beaten up. It took me a while to recognise him. Play-in-the-Sand, that was what we'd called him, but I think his name was Abel. We'd grown up together. We were both sons of engine drivers. The engine drivers' neighbourhood was behind the station. Low houses. Yards growing fruit trees. Dogs barking. Chickens pecking away among the collard stems. That's what I remember.

Play-in-the-Sand must have been a bit older than me. He asked after my sisters, my cousins, my father. We laughed about old stories. The way we used to serenade the girls from the Youth Home. The hot bread rolls we'd go to eat, in the early hours, at the Confiança Bakery. That time Júnior fell asleep drunk, after a night partying at the Athletic Club, and Alvarito shat in his hand. Then Play-in-the-Sand put a filterless cigarette in Júnior's mouth until the flame burned him and the poor guy brought his smeared hand to his mouth and woke up. We laughed about it together. As we laughed, we went back to being friends. Then I fell silent and he started to cry.

Snowflake doesn't believe that my memory problems, all those holes tormenting me, are anything to do with the lightning. She thinks my amnesia is only to do with the violence of war. Traumas, she says, a hell of a lot of traumas. She takes an interest in me the way an entomologist does a rare insect. I'm a rare insect. I'm much rarer than I seem. And much more of an insect. But I didn't tell her that.

Sunday, 16 August 1998

Slightly strange morning. I woke up with bad pain in my back and chest. I walked past the TV in the rec room, and it turned itself off. This has happened a few times before. The crazy people try and start a fight with me. They think I mess with the electric devices. Maybe I do. I'm a lightning bolt in slow motion.

. . .

Snowflake showed up at the hospital looking really excited, wearing a broad smile.

'I dreamed about you,' she said. 'You were wearing a silk coat, in purple.' I looked at her, suspicious. I've never had a coat that colour, I've never seen one.

Tuesday, 18 August 1998

Snowflake sought me out again today:

'There you were, comrade, in that coat in an impossible colour, speaking Portuguese, but I was also speaking Portuguese, and what you were saying to me was sensible, a kind of common sense that doesn't exist in dreams.'

I listened to her in silence.

She added: 'If your dreams still make any sense after you've woken up, maybe that's because you haven't woken up yet.'

Wednesday, 19 August 1998

Today it was General Amável Guerreiro. Then two nurses showed up. Right after that, one of the guys who works as a cleaner. All of them had dreamed about me. It's like an epidemic. I think it's funny. I've laughed about it quite a lot. I've never been a specially popular guy – on the contrary, I don't even know how to make friends, and now, all of a sudden, I've become famous.

Saturday, 22 August 1998

I must be the only person in this place who doesn't suffer mental disorders. It reminds me of a story my grandmother used to tell. In some little hamlet or other it started raining a strange kind of water. Anybody touched by that water went crazy. The whole population went nuts, except one old man who had been sleeping in his hut when the rain fell. So the old man went out and a kid came over to him and spat in his eye, then a lady came over and showed him her ass, then another started following him screaming insults, and so on for the rest of the day. As night fell, the old man, desperate now, threw himself down a well. I feel afflicted in just the same way. Everybody is dreaming about me. Me, wearing a silk coat, in purple, doing something or other. At first I thought it was kind of fun. Now it's started to seem frightening. The same individuals who used to greet me, playfully, have started looking at me with distrust.

Today a madman came over and stood in front of me, blocking my way to the canteen. He started shouting at me. I couldn't understand everything he said, but I understood enough. He thinks I'm a quimbandeiro, *a witch doctor. Another man stood next to him, and then a third, a fourth and a fifth. It was a whole wall of rage. I took a step back, then returned to my room. I locked the door. I could hear their roars outside, a growing unrest. They started thumping on the door. I thought they were going to lynch me. Finally, Snowflake came to my rescue, protected by three soldiers. We got into a car and left.*

'You're not safe in the hospital,' she said. I was afraid she was going to start crying. 'There are a lot of backward people. First the collective hysteria, which – I'm so sorry – I started myself. Then the accusations of witchcraft – because you know that's what they're accusing you of, your people, my people, everybody – you do know that, right?'

I didn't answer.

During the war, I saw things that cannot be explained. Lights passing through walls; rains of spiders and dead birds. I can still remember a lake out of which fat frogs were leaping, as yellow as lemons. Anybody who ate those frogs started speaking some unknown language. People wanted to speak Portuguese or Umbundu, but they only managed to speak this language. They could understand one another. We, the ones who didn't want to eat the frogs, couldn't under-stand a thing. I also remember an old man who vomited up little snakes as though they were strands of spaghetti. I remember trees laden down with tiny glowing crabs. At night, they looked like Christ-mas trees. There was a baobab tree that as darkness fell would sing the saddest songs in the world. I saw women being shot, stoned, burned alive, because the soldiers had accused them of flying in the night, with the bats, or of seducing them with sweet songs only then to transform them into birds. I saw soldiers who believed they had been transformed already, chirping, squatting on the branches of tall trees. One time they brought a man to me, a famous wizard, who was accused of having tried to poison Savimbi. While we talked – though the word 'talk' doesn't really do it justice – the guy was ageing. He never got to confess to anything because he died of old age in my arms.

Tuesday, 25 August 1998

I often remember a South African captain, in Mavinga, Captain Petrus Viljoen. I remember him after he'd stepped on a mine and lost both legs, I remember him holding my hand, like a bride, and whispering in my ear:

'Oh, mate, mate, my dear friend,' in a Portuguese that was full of rolled r's and errors, 'your country is so green, your country is so green, I wish I was as green as your country'.

He asked for whisky, he liked whisky, but we didn't have any whisky so I gave him a bit of Marufo wine, and he died smiling in my arms. That night I dreamed he was a green man, as green as the grasses after the rains, a hippopotamus head in place of his own, but I still recognised him, I recognised him by his smile, and he said to me in a voice that was as sad as the singing baobab:

'Oh, mate, mate, we're killing with no reason at all, the people now sending us to our deaths are already preparing to switch sides.'

From then on, I started to dream about Captain Petrus often,

I started to dream about other dead people, even some of those I'd sent across myself, and all the dead talked to me of unrelated tomorrows, and of the stupidity of war, and then I started to slacken in my duties, in my hygiene, and above all in my own safety. My superiors called me in:

'What's up with you, brigadier? You've always been such a model of discipline, of organisation, of military flair, and now you go around talking to yourself, and you look such a wreck, unshaven, flip-flops on your feet – you look more and more like a tramp, like a madman . . .'

And I had no answer, I just looked at them, with a silence that made them angrier still. So one morning I climbed up onto a roof to fix an aerial – it was raining, and I received two bolts of lightning to my body, I died and was resuscitated, and in the process lost a part of my memory, or rather lots of parts of my memories.

. . .

I'm now in a small apartment, in a building very much like some of the buildings we have in Luanda. People grilling pork chops on the verandas (with almost no meat, just fat and bone). The things they eat here we wouldn't give to our dogs. These people are going hungry. Snowflake has forbidden me from going out. I mustn't talk to the neighbours.

Friday, 28 August 1998

I've spent these past days a prisoner. I do practically nothing. I listen to the voices of the building. A maid comes in the morning to tidy the house. She brings me food and drink. She's called Concepción and she seems very old. She's kind of deaf. Maybe she works for the cops and

53

she's just pretending to be deaf all the better to hear me. What's for sure is that I can't keep up a conversation with her.

Saturday, 29 August 1998

This afternoon, Snowflake appeared here at the house accompanied by a soldier. The guy was wearing yellow shorts and a flowery shirt, like my older cousins used to wear in the sixties. He even had round glasses, with a very thin frame, the John Lennon kind. He could have been a hippy lost in time, but the moment his eyes accidentally met mine I could guess what his profession was. Fellow professionals recognise each other at first sight. The man sat down opposite me, gave me a gentle pat on the knee and said quietly:

'Well then, moreno, seems you've been infiltrating other people's dreams. How do you do that?'

I didn't like the racial undertones when he called me moreno. But he smiled and I did the same. He started to laugh. We both laughed, uproariously. Then finally the soldier sat up. He straightened his shirt. He turned very serious:

'Man, it's such a crazy story, what a fucking story. One of these days they're going to send me to interrogate the invisible man.' He said this in a deep voice, and I sat up, too. 'Amigo, the man you see sitting before you is a rare breed of Cuban, a genuine Marxist-Leninist. I don't believe in voodoo crap, or in Jesus Christ, or His holy mother, who ascended to the heavens on the fifteenth of August on board a silver cloud. It would be easiest if you could just tell me what poison it was you gave those lunatics to get them all to dream about you. I want some of it, some of your blessed poison, as I'd like to be dreamed about by a certain woman by the name of Isabel – I'd like to spend Sundays strolling through her dreams, as if I was back on the Malecón.'

He left a long pause. I felt his breath, the slight smell of rotten fruit. Maybe he suffered from diabetes. Maybe he hadn't eaten in a while. The bags under his eyes were as deep as wells. Most likely he'd been working for twenty-four hours without a rest. Any man is dangerous when he is tired and hungry, and all the more so if he is an operative of Cuban military intelligence. It wasn't in my interest to fall out with a guy like that.

'I'm sorry, amigo,' I murmured, eyes lowered, with the same tone of voice I would have used to address God, if He had appeared there in that moment, and He was a hungry lion. 'Just tell me what's expected of me. I'm ready to help in any way you need.'

The man relaxed a bit. He wanted to know what I thought about it all. I told him I thought the whole thing total nonsense. The Cuban seemed to like my answer:

'That's just as well, brigadier,' he answered. 'You are a brigadier, aren't you? I know you fought on the side of those stooges. I'm grateful for your candour. My name's Pablo, Pablo Pinto, and I'm a captain. It might sound impossible, but the men up there don't think the same way we do. They want us to investigate. They'd like to have an agent capable of travelling through other people's dreams. Between you and me, word is that the CIA takes projects seriously that are even more ludicrous than this. So we're going to investigate it.'

I couldn't hide my amazement. The captain smiled.

'Take it easy, comrade, take it easy, it'll be night-time, you'll go to bed and sleep, the good people of Cuba will sleep, the next morning we'll talk to some of your neighbours. We're starting from the

55

principle that you're only able to invade the dreams of those sleeping nearby.'

I shook my head, wearily. 'No offence, captain, sir, but you've gone crazy!'

'Yes, yes, it's crazy, you're right. We'll get everything sorted within a week, then you'll go back to Angola. I remember the women of your country. Beautiful women. I also remember the food, roast baby goat, chicken with palm oil and that manioc paste – funge, that's what it's called, right? – all of it really nice. Excellent food, pretty women, music almost as good as ours. Your problem is a lack of discipline, and arrogance. If it weren't for our intervention, in '75, and later in Mavinga, you'd be a province of South Africa today. What do you say, brigadier, would you like Angola to be a province of South Africa?'

'No, that was never a possibility. South Africa never had any intention of annexing Angola.'

'It didn't?! So you're still talking like a stooge, then . . .'

I couldn't tell if the guy was kidding or being serious, so I just kept my mouth shut, and my eyes down. 'If you want to live,' my father used to say, 'play dead.' It's something all poor people learn from a very early age. To play dumb, deaf and blind; to make themselves tiny, buried away, like the dead.

Friday, 4 September 1998

I awoke to the lovely smell of coffee filtering in from the apartment on the right. There is a refrigerator in the kitchen. On top of the fridge, next to a window, somebody has positioned a wire cage with two canaries. The window looks out onto a narrow, deserted street. The birds sing all day long. They fall silent when evening comes, and the silence makes the house turn sad. I change their water. I give them birdseed and pieces of banana, which they peck at with pleasure. I've named the larger of the two Hardy. Laurel is the smaller. I talk to them a lot. Maybe these guys dream about me, too.

. . .

I'm always in bed very early. I listen out for sounds, stretched out in bed, until sleep comes. I'm already able to identify most voices. There's a couple living in the upstairs apartment. She must be very young. He's not. They argue every night, and then they go to bed.

'Give it to me, daddy, give it all to me!' screams the girl. The man wheezes and goes into battle. 'Hit me, daddy, hit your woman. Do it, slap my face. Hit me harder!' screams the girl, and I hear the man's palm cracking against her flesh. Their exertions make the chandelier on the living-room ceiling tremble.

On the right-hand side, there lives a family with four children and a sick grandfather. The old man coughs, coughs, coughs all night long. I wake up, now and then, to pee, and I hear him on the other side of the wall, struggling against the catarrh, cursing Jesus Christ and the Virgin Mary in an exuberant Spanish, cursing Fidel Castro, cursing his children, all his children, who take no care of him and leave him there, rotting away, instead of sending him to Miami.

The other apartment is home to a jazz pianist and two cabaret dancers. The pianist has a piano. He plays old-time boleros I know very well: 'Porque Tú Me Acostumbraste', 'Solamente una Vez', 'Bésame Mucho', 'Angelitos Negros' or 'Las Simples Cosas'. I do like the last of these. Out in the bush, when I was with the guerrillas, we used to listen to Afro-Latin music. Once we captured a Cuban captain, a funny guy, really good fun, called Ramirez. This Cuban guy

57

sang. He sang well, really well. One time I got to hear him sing accompanied by a band of kids in Jamba called the Black Jaguars. Unfortunately, the Old Man decided to have the Cuban shot. The pianist, my neighbour, plays those songs with an emotion that's genuine, reinventing them as he plays, in such a way that I feel like I'm becoming less familiar with them the more I recognise them. It's always the best part of my day.

Saturday, 5 September 1998

Pablo doesn't want me to get too close to the windows that overlook the shared courtyard. The neighbours mustn't know I'm here. So I hide behind the curtains and spy on the neighbourhood. I've seen the pianist a few times getting ready to go off to work. I've also seen him in the company of the dancers, exchanging impressions of the people who frequent the cabaret where all three of them work. On another day, I saw him chatting to a girl with long legs. I think she's the upstairs neighbour. Yesterday I got up really early and surprised him with his arms around a thin young man, with red hair and a strong American accent.

Sunday, 6 September 1998

Pablo has come back. I could see, no sooner had he closed the door, that he was not bringing good news.

'Oh, brigadier, my dear brigadier,' he said first. 'Your story is getting more and more demented. We've talked to some of your neighbours.

We talked to them separately. The last thing they were expecting was for us to take an interest in what they've been dreaming. One old man swore at me.' Pablo gave an appreciative laugh, shaking his head. He imitated the old man's voice. He was a good mimic. ' "You son of a syphilitic goat, so dreaming's a crime now?" I had to summon all my patience. I made up this whole story. No, I'm not a policeman. I'm a psychologist. We've been doing this study of the dreams of the Cuban population. Anyway, the whole thing wasn't easy, not at all. It's been the weirdest mission of my life.'

I looked at him, livid. He looked straight back, as if we were two boxers before the first punch was thrown. He was waiting for me to say something. I kept quiet. An agent, and I was a good agent, learns how to manage his silences. So then the guy pulled up a chair and sat down opposite me.

'The thing is, they've all fucking dreamed of the same person. A man in a purple coat. I showed them a photo of you and they were astonished. Astonished and perhaps a little frightened.'

'They recognised me?'

'Yes, yes, almost all of them. Not the old guy. Or he did recognise you but didn't want to give me the satisfaction. In any case, he knows I'm no psychologist.'

I shook my head, increasingly troubled: 'And what the hell was I doing in his dreams?'

Pablo took off his glasses. He wiped the lenses clean with the hem of his shirt. 'You seriously don't know?'

'How the fuck would I know?'

Pablo poked me in the chest with the index finger of his right hand:

'Hey, careful with the language, asshole, have a bit of respect. You seriously wander around these people's dreams and you don't remember any of it?'

'No. No. I remember nothing.'

'Right – well, no point us getting angry. This is what we're going to do – I'll stay and sleep here, with you, the next few nights. You OK with that?' He reminded me of a cat toying with a sparrow. He put his glasses back on. His eyes looked smaller and harder now. 'Don't worry, amigo. I'll sleep here in the living room, on the sofa. You'll keep sleeping in the bedroom. To be honest, I'm kind of curious. You must be, too. I get these weird nightmares. Seriously, really weird. I don't even recognise them as mine. And you're going to have the privilege of wandering through them.'

. . .

Pablo is in the kitchen frying green bananas.

. . .

We ate together, in the living room, in our underpants, with the intimacy of a husband and wife. Round about midnight, the old guy upstairs started shouting at the woman with the long legs.

'Are they always like that?' the captain asked.

'Yes, it's been like that every night. They'll go to bed soon enough.'

A few minutes later the lamp started to dance about. Pablo's shadow grew over mine, as if about to devour it, and then flew away to hide in a corner. The captain shook his head, impressed.

'That old bastard was a journalist. Name's Nicolás Santa-María and he's seventy-four, would you believe it?'

'Seems to be in excellent shape.'

'He is. As tough and lucid as Commander Fidel. Nobody would think him a day over fifty-five. You'd be even more surprised if you knew the guy had been imprisoned for twenty years. But I'm not going to tell you why he was in prison for so long, it's a state secret.'

Pablo waited till the couple were done with their furious night-time gymnastics, then he got up and wished me sweet dreams, and I went back to the bedroom. He lay down. I can hear him now in the living room, snoring.

. . .

I'm writing. I can't sleep. I was terrified at the thought of closing my eyes and waking up, with a start, inside one of Pablo's nightmares.

. . .

Monday, 7 September 1998

It's two in the afternoon. I've just finished lunch. When early this morning, around six-thirty, the captain got up and came into my room without knocking, I must have looked really glum. He looked at me with displeasure:

'Christ, moreno! You look like someone who's spent the whole night travelling around other people's dreams. That must be exhausting.'

I said I was sorry to disappoint him: I hadn't slept a wink. I'd spent the whole night tossing and turning in my sheets. Pablo sat down at the foot of the bed, facing the window, with a mixture of anger and disappointment.

'That's why I didn't dream about you. I had one of those outlandish nightmares, but you didn't show up. I waited all night, and you never showed up, asshole.'

I got annoyed. I told him I couldn't care less about his nightmares. I couldn't care less about the dreams and nightmares of the Cubans. I wanted to go back to Luanda. Pablo ignored me. He got up. He began a nervous dance around the room. Four steps that way, four steps this way. Four steps that way, four steps this way. He looked for something in his coat pocket, then gave up.

'I never should have quit smoking. Not smoking is ruining my health. But as for you, moreno, you got to sleep! We've a simple agreement – we give you a bed, food and clean clothes, and you sleep. If you refuse to sleep I won't take it well, I'll get angry with you. I could arrest you for . . . for . . . Oh, who knows what the hell pretext I could arrest you on . . .'

'So get on with it! Any pretext would be fine. In Cuba, just like Angola, any reason's good enough for arresting somebody – the books people read, their haircut, the length of their trousers, the visas in their passports, their religion, their tastes in sex or food. You can even have me arrested for refusing to sleep!'

'You're right, I'll have you arrested for no reason whatsoever. You know, I could be home at this moment, in my own modest palace, standing at the window and eating my bread soaked in milky coffee and looking outside, watching the girls going by. I live next door to a school. That's right, a school. All those young girls with their short skirts and tight little blouses. Just thinking about them is enough to make me feel more of a man. But instead I wake up on a sofa left over from Batista's time and I see this sad dog's expression on your face. Tonight I'm going to take drastic measures.'

. . .

Pablo arrived at ten at night with those drastic measures: two sleeping pills. He showed them to me:

'Swallow these.'

I swallowed the pills without an argument. Let's see if I sleep.

I slept like a mountain range. I woke up a new man, my skin glowing and my soul lighter. Pablo was waiting for me in the kitchen, frying eggs. 'You look extremely well this morning, amigo. I can see you've slept.'

I answered yes, I'd slept, I'd slept very well.

'You slept eight hours and twenty-two minutes. And I dreamed, amigo, but I didn't dream about you. Two possibilities, then – either we're looking at a fine collective hoax, or you're avoiding coming into my dreams.'

I ate the eggs, irritated, frowning, eyes glued to my plate. In the afternoon, Pablo came by the apartment to notify me, somewhat perplexed, that for the last two nights, nobody in the building had dreamed about me. 'We're going to try again tonight. This time without the pills.'

He returned some hours later, with grilled chicken for dinner, and two bottles of a Chilean wine called Gato Negro. I don't really like wine, I'm more a beer kind of guy, but I did like this one. We ate well, we finished the Gato Negro. Pablo told me a bit about his life. At eighteen he'd volunteered to fight in Angola, not out of any ideological conviction, since in those days he didn't believe in anything at all, but to escape a tyrannical father who wanted to see him graduating in medicine, just like he, his grandfather and great-grandfather had done before him. He returned to Havana transformed into a real

communist; and into a soldier, too, he added. He spoke the word 'sol-
dier' very seriously, 'sol-di-er', looking me in the eye.

I held his gaze. At this point in my life all I want is to get free from
the army. I'm sick of soldiers. Nevertheless, I do understand the dedi-
cation. A military institution is much more than just one large family.
The army is like a symphony, a perfect symphony, amid the disjointed
roar of a giant city. By enlisting, a man becomes a part of this sym-
phony. We are a note in the score. Being there, standing to attention
in that score, gives you a feeling of harmony and comfort.

Wednesday, 9 September 1998

When I woke up this morning I found Pablo sitting on my bed. I
must have awoken when he sat down. He didn't try to hide his
excitement:

'How do you do it? It was just like Snowflake said. Like the others
said. There you actually were, in a really strange coat. If it hadn't
been for the coat you'd have looked as real as you do now. Something
to do with the contrast, perhaps. Because of how unreal everything else
was. You came in suddenly, you wandered right across the madness of
my nightmare with a smile, and you started talking.'

'What did I say?'

'What did you say?! If you don't remember, I'm not going to be the
one to tell you. Otherwise, what use are you to us, even if it's true you
can go into other people's dreams, if you don't remember anything?'

'Yes, yes, that's exactly it, I'm no use to you! I'd never be able to act
as an undercover agent, as I wouldn't remember a thing. What use is
an agent with amnesia?!'

'Who knows? We could always use you to pass on certain messages to the dreamers.'

'And how would you do that? I can't control dreams.'

Pablo frowned. He took a small notebook and a tiny pencil out of his shorts pocket and jotted something down. The two of us knocked back a little pick-me-up, and then he left. He returned at two in the afternoon, accompanied by Snowflake. When I saw her, I just fell apart. I threw my arms around her:

'Get me out of here! Tell them this is all a terrible mistake. I'm not what they think. They're all crazy. I want to go back to my country.'

Snowflake was as nervous as I was. She wiped away my tears with the back of her hand as she tried to calm me down. She agreed with me. She just wanted to clarify this one 'small mystery'. That's what she called it: a 'small mystery'. Then I'd be able to go back home. Pablo sat down at the table, pretending to write in his notebook. I turned to him. I demanded to speak to someone from the Angolan Embassy. He gave me a conciliatory smile:

'The Angolan authorities have been notified, you needn't worry. We're going to continue with this programme just a few more days. Come on, you went through worse things in Mavinga. Yes, I know you were in Mavinga. Even in Luanda, in the barracks, when you go back to Luanda, I'm sure the food won't be this good. Your mission, moreno, is very simple. All you have to do is sleep and dream.'

'Don't call me moreno!'

'Easy now,' Snowflake intervened. 'Calm down now, Hossi. We're going to talk. The captain has nothing else to do here. You and I are going to talk.'

Pablo got up. He held out his hand: 'Right, for now I'll leave you with the doctor. I have more serious things to deal with. A maid will come every day, like she's been doing up to now, to bring you food and tidy the house. Don't go near the windows. Don't let anybody see you.'

'I shouldn't let anybody see me?! And for how long am I supposed to do that? How much longer do I have to be kept prisoner here?'

'You aren't a prisoner. You're carrying out a mission. You're an Angolan combatant and you're on a mission. If it were up to me, I'd send you home now. I'm sick and tired of you. But I can't. I'll give an order for you to be brought some more bottles of wine, that one you like. Get some rest and sleep.'

He said goodbye to Snowflake with a nod, and left. The psychologist sat on one of the chairs. She looked at me for a while, shaking her head:

'This must seem strange to you.'

I sat down, and wiped my face with my shirt. It was very hot. All I wanted was for Snowflake to go and leave me alone to have a cold bath. I watched her furtively, like a chameleon looking at a cat, unable to hide my nerves. I'd been sent to Havana because I was suffering memory problems. I had come here for treatment. And instead I'd leaped from the frying pan into the fire. The psychologist tried to offer me some consolation:

'You were a little disturbed when you arrived here. And I think it's completely natural – who wouldn't be disturbed by the horrors you experienced? Dreams, let's talk about dreams. Have you ever thought about what dreams are for?'

'I have no idea! My grandmother used dreams as a way of know-ing things. She predicted the future with her dreams. It might be sunny in the morning, but she'd know it was going to be raining later in the day.'

'Yes, dreams and fortune-telling are connected. Dreams have always been a discipline of magic. But you don't believe in magic, do you? I'm a psychologist. I do believe, a bit.'

I told her that throughout my life, especially in the forest, I'd seen many strange phenomena, I'd heard many stories, but nothing as ludicrous as the things the Cuban intelligence officers were making up. Snowflake told me dreams help us to face the real world. Ex-fighters tend to suffer from nightmares. These nightmares tend to be recurring. I shook my head firmly:

'I don't have nightmares! Pablo does. Pablo is a raving lunatic.'

'Pablo also fought in Angola. What I'm trying to say is that maybe nightmares help people to deal with traumatic memories. Besides, it does seem as though dreams help to make memories stick. Finally, they can help us find solutions to problems that are troubling us when we're awake. Mendeleev created the periodic table of elements after a dream. August Kekulé dreamed about a snake biting its own tail and when he woke up he realised he'd discovered the structure of the benzene molecule. They also say that in their dreams, Beethoven and Wagner heard fragments of compositions they were working on. Sometimes they dreamed entire pieces of music. Paul McCartney dreamed 'Yesterday'. He woke up with the tune in his head, sat down at the piano and played it from one end to the other. He was convinced he must have heard it somewhere before, and so he didn't dare record it. He thought it wasn't his. For months he went around whistling the tune to his friends, to try and find out who had come up with it, until he was finally convinced he really had found it in his dreams. You know that on average a person spends six years of their life dreaming? It's got to mean something . . .'

I listened with interest, but feigning uninterest. I told her again that I almost never had dreams. She became annoyed. She implied, raising her voice, that maybe I didn't want to tell her my dreams. Then I got up, went over to the door and opened it:

'Please leave!'

Snowflake left. I took a cold shower, and made dinner. I ate in the living room, distracted, while reading, or trying to read, old literary magazines. I finished eating, did the washing-up, and stretched out on the sofa with a book in my hands: The Autumn of the Patriarch by Gabriel García Márquez, which I had found yesterday hidden under the bed, in a cardboard box. Night fell, but the heat got no less intense. Finally, I put down the book. I had another cold shower then took up a position at the window, in my underpants, watching the courtyard. I couldn't see anybody. I felt like I was suffocating. A breeze pushed aside the curtains and coolly stroked my skin. I was suddenly overwhelmed by a need to leave, to run away, to lose myself in the city streets. I put on some jeans, pulled aside the curtains and jumped out of the window. The little courtyard led to a kind of inner patio, in which five or six husks of 1950s' American cars were rotting. I sat there on the wall, my back to the yard, looking out at the chaos. I heard a woman's voice:

'Hello! So you must be our neighbour from number thirty-three.'

I turned to look. She was leaning on the door frame and smiling. She was wearing a short dress, very light and loose, with a peacock print. Where I was sitting, partially plunged into the night, the girl couldn't see my face. But as she came closer, the teasing smile with which she'd greeted me transformed into an expression of amazement:

'Sweet Mother of God! It's the man from the dreams!'

She took three steps back, towards the staircase.

I raised my hands, trying to pacify her.

'You dreamed about me?!'

The young woman hesitated.

'Me and lots of others. The police have been questioning all of us. Who are you?'

I tried to calm her down, but I was nervous myself, and stumbled over my words. I told her I wasn't Cuban, but African, that I was being kept hidden here against my will. I had effectively been kidnapped by Cuban security.

'Please, don't tell anyone you saw me.'

The girl seemed to grow calmer. She took a couple of steps forward. She held out her hand:

'Ava. My name's Ava, like Ava Gardner.'

'I'm Hossi. Hossi means lion in my language. I had a twin brother. He died in the war. In my culture, when two boy twins are born, one gets called Hossi, and the other Jamba, elephant.'

We talked for two hours. I've only just left her. She promised to wait for me tomorrow at the same time.

Thursday, 10 September 1998

Since waking up I haven't stopped thinking about Ava. I tried to read, but I can't. Concepción found me in the kitchen talking to the canaries. She said nothing. She didn't seem surprised. The old lady made a soup, cleaned the house, and left.

. . .

Ava appeared at the agreed time. I jumped out of the window and

went over to meet her on the terrace. She was wearing a blue dress,
something very simple, and she was barefoot. She seemed even younger
than yesterday. I was scared to ask her age. We talked till two in the
morning. I told her I'm a soldier. I told her I've been struck by light-
ning twice. Unlike most people, she didn't question my story. She
wanted to see the scars:

'They're beautiful!' she said.

She brought two fingers to her mouth then ran them down my
skin. Now I'm sitting at the kitchen table, talking to the canaries –
again. Hardy seems interested. Laurel is asleep with his head under
his wing. I ought to go to bed but I'm not sleepy.

Friday, 11 September 1998

I close my eyes and I see Ava's eyes, big and honey-coloured and full
of light. Tonight I heard her, upstairs, while the old man forced him-
self on her. I waited for her, sitting at the window, but she never
showed.

Saturday, 12 September 1998

Pablo had lunch with me. He brought me a tape recorder:

'In case you happen to remember a dream, record it.'

I told him, yet again, that I don't dream. It's been years since I've
had a dream. Or maybe I do dream, but I don't remember.

. . .

Ava didn't come tonight either.

I spent the whole day thinking about Ava. I've thought about her so much my stomach hurts. My eyes hurt from squeezing them so tight thinking about her. I spend hours imagining what life would be like if we ended up together. Maybe I could stay in Havana doing translations from Spanish to Portuguese or fixing electrical devices. There's nothing stopping me. There's no one waiting for me in Angola.

. . .

Ava came round. I'd been lying for hours on the living-room floor, looking up at the ceiling, imagining that the ceiling was a shadow theatre, when I heard light taps on the glass of the window that looked onto the hallway. It was her. She smiled when she saw me. She gave me a hug. She kissed me on the cheek.

'Can I come in?'

She didn't wait for my answer. She moved her right leg, then her left, then she was in. She hugged me again. A long hug. She put her lips to my neck.

'You smell nice,' she murmured.

I pushed her away, scared. I was honest with her.

'It's been years since I've been with a woman.'

Ava took three steps back. She pulled up the hem of her dress – the same one I'd seen her in before, with a peacock print – to reveal her legs.

'Do you think I'm beautiful?'

'Yes! Yes!'

'Kiss me!'

And I did. And I forgot all my fears.

Monday, 14 September 1998

I look back, to what I've retained of my life, and I can't think of any time when I've been as happy as I am now.

I can't remember having been happy.

Tuesday, 15 September 1998

Ava showed up in the middle of the afternoon. I opened the door for her, nervous that somebody might have seen her. She came in, unhooked the straps of her dress and let it slide to the floor. She was naked.

'I like that look in your eyes when I undress,' she said. 'When I'm wearing that look, I'm invincible.'

I'm the one who's felt invincible since she appeared in my life. Invincible, and also fragile, both at the same time. Invincible whenever she's with me, when she is mounted on top of me, moaning and screaming, and fragile each time she goes, not knowing if she'll be back.

Friday, 18 September 1998

Last night I heard her moaning in the old guy's arms once again. I don't mention it to her. I haven't got the right. I make out that I don't know she lives with another man. Ava talks a lot about her father, about her difficult childhood, but rarely says anything about her day-to-day life. I know she studied nursing, but she gave it up. She studied

IT but gave that up, too. Once I asked her how she sees herself in the future.

'With you,' she said, and bit my ear.

. . .

Pablo showed up. He wanted to know if I'd recorded any dreams. I said no. He asked me to return the tape recorder. He told me about five Cubans who'd been arrested a few days ago in Miami, who were being charged with spying. He spoke warmly about one of them, as though I also knew him, as though we'd all been childhood friends. He gave me a hug when he said goodbye.

Sunday, 20 September 1998

Tonight I pressed Ava against the wall, her back to me. I had to make a great effort not to cry out. It was good.

Tuesday, 22 September 1998

I close my eyes and I see Ava again, raising her smooth, round, firm ass, revealing herself completely. I feel her shuddering in my mouth. She's biting her lips, silent.

. . .

I wake in the middle of the night. Ava's scent. The certainty that something bad is about to happen.

Concepción didn't come this morning. I thought that strange. Just after three, Pablo showed up, accompanied by two soldiers. He told me to get my things together and pack my bag.

'You're going back home, brigadier!'

I looked at him, dazed:

'Now?!'

'Now. There's a plane waiting for you at José Martí airport.'

'That's impossible.'

'Why? You were so keen to go home. And anyway, you were right all along. It was completely crazy. Let's forget the whole thing. Forget about these days.'

I sorted out my few belongings, helped (or watched over) by one of the soldiers. I was trying to think of some way of getting word to Ava. Nothing occurred to me.

'I had a dream,' I said. 'I've had some amazing dreams.'

Pablo turned his back on me.

'I'm not interested in your dreams. Never have been, to tell the truth. I'm a soldier, I follow orders. Let's go!'

He drove me to the airport. We got out and he escorted me to the steps of the plane. He hugged me. He put his mouth to my ear.

'I'm sorry, moreno, I'm really very sorry. Want me to tell your girlfriend something?'

I struggled to hold back my tears:

'Tell her I'll be back for her.'

I went up the steps. I sat by the window, next to a fat, sweaty man who fell asleep the moment the plane had taken off. He snored the whole trip. Now we're coming in to land in Luanda. I don't know what I'm going to find. I don't really care.

8.

I'm used to hearing weird stories. Not a lot surprises me any more. What seems strange to some people might be trivial to others. When Hossi finished talking I asked him a few questions:

'What happened to Ava?'

The hotel owner was expecting the question.

'I never spoke to her again . . .'

'You didn't try?'

'No. I don't even have the address of the building where they kept me. And anyway, Ava was married, remember? Her husband, Nicolás, was her father's best friend. When they arrested her father, Nicolás invented some kind of conspiracy so that he'd be imprisoned, too. He let himself get put in prison just so he could help his friend there. He helped him. He protected him. The old man died in his arms. Ava's mother died a few months later. When he came out of prison, Nicolás found an orphan waiting for him. Gratitude is a more solid emotion than love. She never would have left her husband to be with me.'

There was silence. Hossi was thinking about Ava. I was thinking about the Cotton-Candy-Hair-Woman.

'To tell you the truth, I wanted to talk to you about my dreams,' I admitted. 'I dream about people I don't know, but who really do exist, or did exist.'

'It would be strange if you dreamed about people who didn't. Apparently in our dreams we aren't able to invent faces. We only dream about real people. I read that somewhere. Tell me more about your dreams.'

'I have very detailed dreams. I dream the whole lives of these people and sometimes I talk to them. I have conversations which don't often happen in dreams. My friends don't believe me.'

'Of course not. You think I do?'

'You don't?'

'Why should I be any more gullible than your friends?'

'You told me an implausible story and I believed it.'

'Then you're stupider than most people. As a journalist, you should make a habit of being sceptical. You'd do very well out of it if you were.'

I felt Devil Benchimol descending on me:

'So that stuff you told me, the dreams, the killer lightning, your passion for Ava, actually all those stories – you were lying to me?'

'I was lying, yes, I invented the whole thing. Or – no, no, I wasn't lying. What difference does it make?'

'It does, it does make a difference!' I shouted.

'It doesn't, seriously. It doesn't matter in the least. What matters is that you believed it. While I was telling you my story, you believed it. While I was telling you my story, the whole thing was true.' He sighed, a long sigh like the whistle of a train bidding farewell. 'No, I'm not going to help you. And how could I, anyway? Go get help from a psychologist.'

9.

I'd become obsessed with the photos. I had them printed. I used to look at them before going to sleep. I would look again as soon as I woke up. There would be moments when I would lose myself looking at that naked woman, so distant, so beautiful. I would run my fingers over her small breasts, down her long legs. I would fall asleep and find her once again in my dreams, and now she was parading past in the distance, not like a person, more like a landscape. Only the somnambulant birds talked to me.

One evening I discovered Google had a tool that could search for pictures. I uploaded one of the photos to the search engine. I was surprised to see sixty-eight results. *Most relevant result for this image: Moira Fernandes.*

I searched for 'Moira Fernandes'.

I recognised the Cotton-Candy-Hair-Woman at once: *Artist, born in Maputo, Mozambique, 7 August 1983, a family originally from the Island of Mozambique. She studied at the Byam Shaw School of Art, in London, thanks to a scholarship from a British institution. At twenty-five she moved to Cape Town, South Africa, where she still lives. She has received a number of national and international prizes. She works with photography but also with oil paints and watercolour. She became well known after exhibiting a series of photographs in which she stages her own dreams.*

I phoned a South African journalist, Peter van der Merwe, whom I'd known many years ago during the war. We'd become friends. Peter works at the *Mail & Guardian*, one of South Africa's most respected newspapers. I asked him if he knew Moira Fernandes.

'Moira, the artist?' Peter laughed. 'Has she disappeared?'

'I hope not. But she's lost something, and I've found what she lost. I want to return it to her.'

'Aha, so you are still working at lost and found after all. Though in the old days you never used to find anything . . .'

'I did . . .'

'What did you find? That damn plane? Did you find the plane . . . ?!'

We chatted for a few more minutes, laughing and teasing. I promised to visit him in Johannesburg, with no expectation that I'd do it – I hate Johannesburg. I said goodbye and hung up. Half an hour later I received Moira's email address. I sat down to write: *Hi Moira!*

I hesitated a moment. I'm never sure how to address somebody I don't know. And it was even worse in this case, because I really did know her but I couldn't tell her that. I corrected myself: *Dear Moira, My name is Daniel Benchimol, I'm a journalist and I live in Luanda. Recently while swimming on a nearby beach I found a camera that turned out to contain photos you took. I imagine the camera belongs to you. I'd like to return it to you. Yours truly, Daniel Benchimol.*

I sent the message and went to make some tea. While I filled the kettle I started thinking about Lucrécia again. I felt a twinge of bitterness. I had handed my future to that woman and she had tossed it in the trash, and my past with it.

10.

Dear Daniel,

Thank you very much for your message. I was pleased and incredibly surprised to receive it. Yes, the camera's mine. In your message, you said you're a journalist. Journalists are trained to ask questions. After a certain point, they become compulsive question-askers. I thought it extraordinary that you didn't ask me a single question. Not even whether the camera belonged to me. I've been thinking about that. I guess you must have made a special effort, a huge effort, not to do it. I'm grateful for your tact.

And so I'm going to try and answer the questions which, I'm sure, you at least considered asking me.

Daniel Benchimol – How did you lose the camera?

Moira Fernandes – I lost it in Cape Town more than a year ago. I went on a boat ride with a good friend of mine, Hugo, who organises excursions for tourists. The tourists go underwater in cages to see sharks. I took the camera intending to photograph the sharks. I had a few photos already on the memory card, which I'd already worked on, to show my friend. You must have seen those pictures and also some others of sharks. I hope you weren't too frightened by the former. Just a little, since, according to Hugo, art is different from a tourist postcard in that while a postcard soothes, art unsettles.

– So tell me, were you frightened?

At a given moment, one of the sharks rushed against the cage, hitting the bars head on, and I nearly died of shock – I've never been that frightened in an art gallery. So I let go of the camera.

– Your photos remind me of dreams. Are they inspired by dreams?

– They are. I dream, wake up, make a note of what I've dreamed and then I stage those dreams and include myself in them.

– Why do you include yourself in all the photographs?

– They're my dreams. If I staged your dreams I'd include a picture of you in those photographs.

– And why are you naked?

– I'm always naked in my dreams.

– But isn't there some vanity in that, too? Do you like looking at yourself?

– You're right, I am vain. I do like looking at myself. I was a troubled teenager. I was taller than all my friends and much, much thinner. Besides that, I never had a pretty face. I still think my face a bit strange, my nose too big, my cheekbones exaggerated, but now I know how to use that strangeness to my advantage. In those days, I used to cry. I hated my face. I hated my hair. Until I was twenty I used to straighten it. One day I got tired of doing it and started letting it grow naturally. Today people notice me because I'm tall, but mainly because of this head of hair, my haughty nose, my cheekbones. I like wearing turbans in bold colours. I wear turbans to match my clothes. I design the clothes I wear myself, taking inspiration from Ndebele patterns. I paint my nails blue, green, bold colours, so that people don't only notice the hair. People do, however, notice the hair more than the hands. I hear praise for my hair every day. I also hear insults – there are stupid people everywhere.

– Let's get back to the photographs. They look like landscapes . . .

– I hear that a lot. It's not an observation I like. Landscapes are for crossing, for passing through, not for experiencing. When landscapes wound us, or move us, or anger us, they stop being landscapes and start being occurrences. I'd like my photos, my oils, to be occurrences. I want my work to wound, to move, to annoy whoever sees it. Only yesterday I asked Hugo, my best friend, whether what I do is necessary:

'Do you think my work is unnecessary?'

Hugo looked at me, afraid. He's a big man, really very big, a giant with broad shoulders, a solid back, powerful arms. A big man, when afraid, looks more afraid than a tiny man.

'No! Your work is vital!' he assured me.

'Why?'

'Because it confronts us with our most intimate terrors.'

Hugo, as I mentioned, has a sailing boat. He takes tourists to dive among the sharks. The tourists are lowered into the sea, shut inside cages. They pay to experience fear, though they're in no danger at all. In ten years, there's only been one problem, one occasion when a young American got out of the cage, wanting to prove he wasn't scared of the sharks. Hugo waited for the guy to come back on deck. Then, without shouting, without saying a word, he slapped him twice.

'Terrors? What terrors?' I asked him.

'Dreams,' Hugo stammered, nervously. Whenever he's nervous he starts stammering: 'All your work is about dreams, isn't it?'

'Yes, dreams, they're my dreams. My dreams are frightening?'

'All dreams are frightening, because they're intimate. They're the most intimate thing we have. Intimacy is frightening.'

Hugo is right when he says such things. And what about you, what do you think of my work?

You'll have to tell me some day. In the meantime, thank you for your kindness. There's no need to return the camera. Send me the photos of the sharks by email, just as a memento of that afternoon with the great shocks.

If you visit Cape Town, it would be a real pleasure to receive you in my studio.

All best,

        Moira

11.

When I was a child, just a few weeks after turning twelve, I killed a cat. To this day I don't know why I did it. I saw the cat stretched out on top of the wall in the shade of the avocado tree. It was a beautiful animal, with luxuriant black fur. I remember that the light was streaming vertically down, dazing the afternoon. For years, I blamed what I did on the excess of light. As if the sunshine, the vast, resplendent sky, had authorised me to kill. My intention was to climb up the avocado tree and sit up there watching the world go by, as I often did, but then I spotted the cat. One of my brothers had left an air rifle leaning on the laundry sink. I grabbed the gun, aimed at the animal's head and fired. The cat fell. I had a moment of panic. I'd imagined it giving a leap, mewing loudly. I never would have thought a tiny pellet would kill it. I hadn't wanted to kill it. I looked around me. Nobody nearby. Grandma was sick, in hospital. My dad was having his siesta, in the study. My brothers must have been indoors, playing. My mum was doing the washing-up. I prodded the body with the barrel of the gun. There was no reaction. I grabbed hold of it, horrified, and hurled it over to the other side of the wall. The side where there was nothing, except a huge patch of open ground covered in grass.

No one ever discovered my little crime. On the afternoons that followed, after lunch, I used to climb the wall and look at the cat. The ants came. There were so many of them, working away inside the corpse, dismantling it, that the cat seemed to be wheezing, as if it was alive. This lasted about three days. When the ants went away, there was no more cat. What remained of it was to a cat what a glove is to a hand. The sun did the rest.

I think about that cat a lot.

'Have you noticed that the sun that gives pomegranates their colour, or leaves a glow on the skin after an afternoon on the beach, is the same sun that yellows and erases the photos of our youth?' I asked Hossi. 'The light strengthens the colours of everything alive, and fades whatever is inanimate. The sun lights up the living and wipes out the dead.'

'And so you carry a corpse around!' concluded the hotel owner, scorning all my arduous philosophy. 'It's not only me. You have your dead bodies, too.'

I look at him, annoyed:

'For God's sake, Hossi! It was just a cat!'

'A cat, a soldier, a child, every death has whatever weight our conscience gives it. That dead cat weighs more to you than a whole village devastated with gunshots and katanas does to a lot of generals I know.'

I had decided to come back to Cabo Ledo to show him Moira's message. I found the hotel owner on the beach, fishing. I sat down beside him. I told him about the camera I'd found in that very spot, in that beautiful sea, about the strange photos and the South African artist who had made them.

'She also has uncommon dreams. She works with dreams. You don't think that's an amazing coincidence?'

'First of all, I don't dream. I'm the one other people dream about. And second, most people have incredibly weird dreams. Dreams are weird. If they weren't weird, maybe they wouldn't be dreams.'

'Don't screw me around. You're always saying you don't dream, but when you told me your Cuba story you said that in the forest you used to dream about the people you'd killed and who you'd seen die. You said you dreamed about that Captain Petrus . . .'

'Oh, Captain Petrus! I told you about Petrus?'

'You did.'

'Yes, I used to dream – before taking those two lightning strikes, I used to dream quite a lot. After that I never dreamed again. Or I dream very little. Or I do dream, but I don't remember my dreams.'

'Either way. You knew exactly what I meant. Know what I've been thinking?'

'No, and I don't want to, either.'

'Do you know the origin of the word "shaman"?'

'No.'

'Shamans, like our *quimbandeiros*, practise their dreaming. They use their dreams to understand the world. The word "shaman" comes from a language in eastern Siberia, meaning he who sees in the darkness.'

'Shaman – he-who-sees-in-the-darkness?! That's what I call

the power of synthesis.' Hossi pulled in his line. He put the rod down on the sand and turned towards me, anger blazing in his eyes. 'So is that it, comrade? Now you're going to say we're basically *quimbandeiros*, me and you and this woman?!'

His reaction scared me. I didn't know what to say. Hossi went on, a crooked smile on his lips:

'Aberrations, that's what we are. Me and you. Your friend, well, she's slightly less than us. At least she's found some way of earning a bit of money from what she dreams.'

He jumped to his feet, before quickly winding back the line and dismantling the rod.

'Come with me. I want to show you something.'

I got up. I shook the sand off my trousers.

'Can I ask you a question?'

'You can ask. I'll decide if I want to answer.'

'You said you were vegetarian. I thought it was strange to find you fishing.'

'If you paid attention to everything around you, like a journalist should, you'd have noticed I don't use a hook.'

It was true. At the end of the line there was a weight, but no hook. I laughed.

'Why do you do that?'

'I like to be out fishing. What I don't like is to fish. I could like to fish and still be a vegetarian. One thing has nothing to do with the other. But I don't. I buy fish from the fishermen. Right next to us here, as you must have noticed, there's a fishing village. The fish you eat has been fished by them. Now come with me. I'm going to show you something.'

He walked up to the yellow bungalow, and invited me inside.

All the walls of the small space were covered in bookshelves, floor to ceiling, made to measure in good-quality wood. The shelves held dozens of boxes and files. I spotted a small wooden statuette. I picked it up, curious:

'I've never seen anything like this . . .'

Hossi snatched the statuette out of my hands.

'It's my twin brother, Jamba. He was a soldier, like me, but he fought on the government side. He died years ago. In our tradition, I'm sure you know, since you're a mulatto and you're also one of our people, you're an Ovimbundu bastard – when one twin dies, the surviving one keeps a figure of the deceased.'

He put the statuette back on the shelf from where I'd taken it. He offered me one of the chairs (there were two), he selected a file and only then did he too sit down.

'You had a twin brother?' I asked, amazed.

'Yes, I told you that already.'

'Hang on a moment – did you study at Monte Olimpo?'

'Yes, me and my brother.'

'Sweet Jesus – we were at school together! I remember you, the twins!'

'Because we were twins, or because we were the only black kids?!'

At the time, I didn't really know what a mulatto was. I didn't know what a white was. I didn't know what a black was. I remembered Hossi and Jamba because they were twins and because they spent their time playing tricks on their schoolmates and their teachers. One of them, I don't know if it was Hossi or Jamba, had a higher pain threshold than his brother, or he was more selfless, and he offered himself up to take a beating in the other's place. Hossi was surprised I remembered this.

'It's true. I messed around, and Jamba got beaten for me. That teacher, what was her name . . . ?'

'Tarsila . . .'

'Right, Tarsila Zarvos. A really fierce woman. Serious nationalist. Did you know my brother and I never had to pay? And that's got to have been an expensive school. We didn't pay anything because my uncle had been arrested, for links to the nationalists. He was imprisoned with a brother of hers. They became friends. She used to beat us a lot, or rather, she used to beat Jamba. Poor thing got thirty strokes in a row one time. His hands swelled up.'

'I got beaten, too. I still get nightmares about that ruler today.'

'I remember the ruler. I don't remember you, though.'

'I was a nondescript kid. No one remembers me.'

We spent a good while recalling our school. One memory drawing out the next. Finally, Hossi opened the file:

'Look at this. I've got a bunch of newspaper cuttings that might interest you. Read this one. Read the bit I've underlined.'

I read:

Thathánka Íyotake (Sitting Bull), chief of the Lakota Sioux Indians, was a member of the Buffalo Dream Society, a secret order of mystic dreamers devoted to premonition. Thathánka Íyotake explained his victories by saying he discussed his combat strategies, in his dreams, with a huge white bison. That white bison was God.

I couldn't help laughing.

'Personally I find it easier to imagine God as a white bison than as a huge gaseous invertebrate, as Aldous Huxley put it. Dreaming that you're talking to a white bison is preferable to a gaseous invertebrate, too.'

Hossi took the folder from my hands. He leafed through quickly.

'Now read this one.'

I read:

Evaldson Bispo dos Santos lives in São Francisco, a small city in the state of Minas Gerais, five hundred and thirty kilometres from Belo Horizonte. He was born and raised in abject poverty. Because he liked milling aimlessly round the city, people started calling him Dizzy Chicken. The name stuck. One day – he was seven at the time – he knocked on the door of a house to ask for food. The maid let him in. She gave him a plate of soup. On finding him in the yard, just moments later, the owner descended on him, screaming; she kicked away the bowl he was eating from, and chucked him out.

Dizzy Chicken returned to the shack where he lived with his parents in tears. That night, he dreamed about three children: a Japanese boy, Toshio; a German, Hans; and an English boy, Paul. The three boys introduced themselves and explained that they were going to teach him to speak and write in their respective languages. Months went by. Every night, the boys would show up for their lessons. One day his mother heard him speaking strange languages. Believing that the Devil had taken over her child, she took him to the church. The priest, who himself had German origins, was frightened when he heard him. Dizzy Chicken was able to communicate in German and even write a few words. Yet he couldn't write in Portuguese.

Toshio, Hans and Paul continued to frequent Dizzy Chicken's dreams, over the next fifteen years, growing up with him, helping him to perfect the three languages. Today, Dizzy Chicken teaches these same languages to people who don't have the money to attend private schools. In 2004 he agreed to tell his story in a widely seen TV programme. The programme took him to language schools in São Paulo, where Dizzy Chicken showed off what he knew to German and Japanese teachers. According to the Japanese teacher, a normal student would have to study at least two and a half hours a week for five or six years to reach Dizzy Chicken's level.

I closed the file, amazed. Hossi brought his face close to mine.

'Well? What do you say?'

'What do I say?! For someone who isn't interested in dreams, you've done a good job.'

Hossi thanked me with a slight nod.

'This is what I know how to do. Gather information. That doesn't mean I believe everything I read. It means I'm a curious person. When are you going to Cape Town?'

'When am I going?'

'You are going, aren't you?'

'I wasn't planning to.'

'Of course you were. Go on, go talk to the woman. This is starting to get interesting.'

12.

Moira Fernandes lived in a spacious house, painted a dull green, with a broad veranda wrapped all the way around it and a small garden at the back. The floor of the veranda, in ceramic tiles, formed geometric patterns in shades of blue, which brought back memories of my childhood. In the kitchen, in our house in Huambo, the floor was identical. Or maybe it wasn't, but it's how I imagine it. My brothers and I spent a lot of time sitting at the kitchen table. Our grandmother would prepare our tea when we got home from school: lemonade, with lemons collected from our own back yard, cake and toast. I remember the light that used to slip through the open door and stretch out, dazzling, onto the sky-blue.

Moira had put out two yellow sunloungers on the front part of the veranda. That was where I found her. She had fallen asleep with a book open in her lap. She was smiling. I spent a long moment just looking at her. It was as though I'd experienced that exact same moment before. The last light of the afternoon was dying on her hair. Her skin gave off a honey glow. I coughed. I was about to say something. Then she opened her eyes and looked right at me.

'I'm sorry,' I said, a bit anxious. 'My name's Daniel Benchimol. I'm looking for Moira Fernandes.'

Moira put the book down on a little table beside her, and got up. She was even taller than in my dreams.

'Daniel? The gate's open. Come through, and come on up . . .'

While I climbed the five steps that separated us, while I held out my hand to greet her, I once again experienced the sensation that I'd been through all this once before. Moira was and was not the Cotton-Candy-Hair-Woman I'd dreamed of so many times. She seemed fake, all of a sudden, a rather crude copy of the woman from my dreams. I fought to control the chaos inside me. She frowned in an involuntary display of surprise.

'Are you OK?'

I tried to see myself through her eyes. A man slightly taller than average, dark-skinned, with a vigorous mop of hair, almost as rebellious as hers, though black, very black, and a grey goatee lengthening his chin. That afternoon, in the hotel, I had selected one of my favourite shirts, in petrol blue, and black jeans. Maybe my hands were shaking, maybe it was my voice; what I do know is that Moira noticed my nerves. I walked into the living room, pretending to pay attention to the enormous framed photographs, some of them hanging on the walls, others on the floor, leaning up against the bookcases.

'You like my photos?'

I turned to face her.

'I do. I like your work and I like you. You're a very beautiful, very brave woman.'

'Thank you. I don't know what to say. That makes me happy.'

'I like the photographs, but I'm not sure I understand what they mean.'

'What they mean? I'm not after anything that has meaning! On the contrary, I want something that undoes the common meaning of things.'

I fell silent. I sat down in a leather armchair, which looked like it had been there for longer than the house itself, and at once a black cat jumped into my lap. Moira laughed.

'Don't be scared. Of me, or of the cat. His name's Morpheus, by the way.'

'Morpheus?!'

'Yeah, I know, it's not very original. You're thinking I don't have much imagination?'

'No, no! I didn't mean that. If anything, you could be accused of having too much imagination, never too little. I live with a cat, too. Mine's called Baltazar.'

Moira sat on a kitchen stool, which was painted red and yellow, opposite me. She looked at me, serious.

'So, you're from Angola?'

'Yes.'

'An Angolan Jew?'

'I'm not Jewish. I'm an Angolan with Jewish heritage, but it's been several generations since anyone in my family has known what that means. Besides, I inherited the name from my father. My mother's name is Vagamundo, a very rare surname. But I don't think it's a Jewish one.'

'I understand. You look Jewish. Or at least more Jewish or Arab than Angolan.'

'What?!'

'Sorry. I was kidding. I know you Angolans have quite the tradition of mixing the races. I was born in Maputo, but I'm from the Island of Mozambique. There, on the Island, we also have a lot of mixing. I myself am part black, part Arab, part Indian. I even have a great-grandfather who was Portuguese.'

I opened my backpack and took out the yellow camera, which I had found floating, weeks earlier, in Cabo Ledo. I held it out to Moira.

'I've come to return your camera.'

Moira put the camera down on the floor, beside her stool, distractedly.

'No. That's not why you came. Why did you come?'

I couldn't take my eyes off her fingers. Moira had painted her nails an intense, twitchy blue. Each time she moved her hands, her nails scratched the air.

'Dreams!' I admitted. 'I've come to talk to you about dreams.'

Moira straightened up. She placed her hands on her lap, hiding her nails, and only then was I able to lift my eyes.

'Do you dream? I think I attract dreamers.'

'Everybody dreams. I dream about people's lives. Sometimes I see them being born. I see them moving through the years. I see them die.'

'That sounds interesting.'

'It's not just that.'

'It's not just that? Let me guess – you dream about people who really exist?'

'Yes, people who exist, or existed.'

'Without actually knowing these people?'

'Some of them I meet. For example, I've dreamed about you. I've dreamed of you saying the exact thing you said a moment ago.'

'What did I say?'

'That you're looking for something that undoes the meaning of things. In my dream, you were in a garden. You were talking to me in a garden, and telling me that, you were saying that through your photographs, through your canvases, you were not trying to achieve meaning, that you wanted to see things from behind, or back to front, that you wanted to undo the usual meaning of things.'

'What was there in this garden?'

'Orchids. I remember there were orchids.'

'Yes, orchids always go well in dreams. You always know you're really dreaming when an orchid appears in your dream. When orchids occupy reality, reality becomes a little less real. A little more scented, perhaps. Though there are some orchids that smell of rotten flesh. There are nice orchids and nasty orchids, but what they all have in common is a certain degree of madness. That's why I like them so much. It's important to drive reality mad.'

'And platypuses?'

'You're right, platypuses are like something that's escaped from Salvador Dalí's dreams. I don't understand how there can be people who don't believe in God but do believe in platypuses. Do you?'

'Believe in platypuses?'

'Yes.'

'No. I don't believe in God, or in platypuses.'

We both laughed. Anything is possible after a man and a woman have laughed together for the first time. Moira looked at me, curious:

'Tell me, have you talked about your dreams to anyone else?'

'I've got a friend, back in Angola, an ex-guerrilla. He told me a story that's hard to believe. A story involving dreams. We've talked a lot.'

'What's the story?'

'My friend doesn't dream. He says he doesn't dream. Other people dream about him. People who've never seen him, who don't know him. Hossi – his name's Hossi – appears in these people's dreams. He travels through them, but when he wakes up he doesn't remember a thing. He travels through other people's dreams like a sleepwalker.'

Moira stood up. She was wearing a blue bodice, in satin, very tight, and a knitted skirt with red, yellow and black checks, that showed off the shape of her broad hips. Her intense, honey-coloured eyes intimidated me.

'I'm going to make some tea. Do you drink tea?'

'Yes, of course.'

'Come with me.'

We walked down a long, well-lit hallway, with a series of photographs of dreams running along the walls. It was like a gallery of stuffed animals. A gallery of dead animals, carefully prepared to look alive. The corridor opened into a modern kitchen, with large windows overlooking a small garden. The first thing I noticed was the orchids. There were at least a dozen orchids, attached to the walls or clinging to the wrinkled trunk of a huge orange tree.

'The orchids . . .'

'Yes, you were right about the orchids. Perhaps you saw them in one of my photographs. I have several photos where these orchids appear. These ones, or others, either way.'

The way she said this bothered me.

'You're right, that must have been it.'

Moira was a collector of tea. She had dozens of jars filled with all kinds of leaves. She chose one, spooned out a small amount and put it into an infuser. She put water to boil in a kettle. Once the tea was ready she invited me to come out to the garden. In the scented shade of the orange tree, there was a square iron table, Moroccan style, inlaid with blue and white ceramic. The tree was in full flower. I'd never seen such a tall, lush orange tree before.

'I'm going to tell you something.' Moira lowered her voice as she poured my tea. 'You're the first journalist I've told. It goes without saying that I'm not talking to the journalist now, I'm talking to the dreamer.'

I scratched my beard.

'You needn't worry. I'm not here as a journalist.'

'I've received messages from people who've been to exhibitions of mine and who have recognised some of my dreams, or recognised themselves in them. Hossi, your friend, is dreamed about by other people, but he doesn't remember these incursions. In my case, it's like I go around dreaming other people's dreams, even if they aren't aware of me being there. If your friend is a sleepwalking intruder, like you said, I'm an invisible witness, like a birdwatcher.'

'Like a birdwatcher?'

'Yes, I remain hidden, to observe those dreams that come to rest near me.'

I looked down at the tea. I added a spoon of honey, and the liquid, a bold red, took on a duskier colour. I tasted it, trying to guess what it might be made of. Rooibos. Tangerine. It was a good mix.

'Your case is easier to explain than Hossi's,' I said. 'Maybe there are just a lot of people who've had dreams like yours. That's all.'

'Yes, it's possible. But you've seen my photographs, you've seen my canvases, haven't you?'

'You're right, your dreams are very original. Besides that, they have a style, a lineage, as if they were born from each other.'

'That's what I think. I'm an aberration.'

I laugh.

'Hossi said he and I were aberrations. But that you weren't. You make money selling your dreams. You're a successful artist. A successful artist, meaning a crazy person who manages to make money out of their own craziness. In other words, not a crazy person at all.'

Moira laughed.

'Your friend must be a very interesting guy.'

'There's another possibility I can think of.'

'What's that?'

'Listen, I'm just thinking out loud, it's an insane idea . . .'

'Great! I like insane ideas.'

'Maybe what's happening is the opposite. Maybe you're spreading your dreams.'

'Like a virus?'

'Like a virus. Or like the antennae of a radio broadcaster. You broadcast your dreams, and some people, who are tuned in to you, receive those dreams. They dream those dreams.'

Moira laughed again, even more delighted now.

'I like it! Synchronised dreaming. Like the hearts of singers in choral groups that come to beat in unison, slowing and accelerating their pace according to the structure of the music. Or like those women who live under the same roof, nuns in convents, prostitutes in brothels, young students in university residences, women like that who end up synchronising their menstrual cycles. It's believed that some women with particularly strong personalities, alpha females, cause the others, through chemical commands, to follow their cycles. So you think I'm an alpha dreamer?'

She made another pot of tea. She brought toast and scones. Night-time was slipping across the slope of Table Mountain, silencing the birds, awaking the cicadas, but neither she nor I noticed that the air was being emptied of light. It was only when Moira got up to fetch a catalogue for her latest show from the living room that she stumbled, suddenly, on the astonished blindness of dusk.

'God, it's almost night!'

I got up quickly, knocking over my chair. The orange tree shook and a tiny shower of white flowers filled the air with a sweet scent.

'I'm sorry, Moira, I didn't mean to take up so much of your time.'

She held out her hand.

'You aren't one of those people who takes time, you're one of those who adds to it. Give me your hand – I'll take you inside.'

I took hold of the blue gleam of her fingers, and went.

13.

I dreamed that Moira was stretched out on her side, laced around my legs like an orchid around the trunk of a tree, moving her head, slowly, up and down. Her tall hairdo shone in the gloom. Behind her there rose the head of a dragon breathing fire. I woke up with my heart pounding. I got up and went to wash my face. Dawn was breaking. At that moment the phone rang. It was her.

'Did I wake you?'

'Yes, kind of . . .'

'Kind of?'

'No, you didn't wake me.'

'Have you eaten?'

'No.'

'In that case, let me introduce you to the best toasted sandwiches in the city. I'll be outside your hotel in half an hour. We can walk.'

She took me to Malecón, on Long Street, a place with tall, wide windows, magnificent wooden floorboards, photos of Havana everywhere. One of the walls held a huge portrait of

Che Guevara smoking a cigar. It felt like I'd been transported to the Caribbean island, not because of the pictures, but because of the light, which as it came through the window-panes took on a lively golden colour. I remembered a similar light, many years ago, one December evening, after I'd run away from a press conference to meet a young activist on the actual Malecón. I close my eyes and I can see it again, in front of us, the blue ocean, and behind us the handsome ruined mansions. I had travelled to Cuba with a group of former fighters and I ended up publishing a report in a Portuguese newspaper on child prostitution in Havana.

The toasted sandwiches arrived, with eggs over easy, bacon and cheese.

'They're good,' I said. 'Almost as good as my grandmother's.'

I finished one and ordered another. I had already bitten into my third when an idea came to me. I called the waiter over.

'Say, is the owner of this place Cuban?'

The waiter, a tall young man with a long, solid horse-face, thick hair close cropped, confirmed this with a slight nod.

'His name's Juan Miguel.'

'Could we talk to him?'

Juan Miguel came out just moments later, wiping his big solid hands on his apron. He looked partly drowsy, partly out of place, in the false dusk of that beautiful Sunday morning. I congratulated him on running such a charming establishment and on the quality of the food. I told him I'd been in Cuba several times, that I'd left many good friends on the island. I asked him if by any chance he knew a psychologist everyone called Snowflake.

'Elena!' The Cuban smiled. 'Elena Ribas. Such a generous woman. She never should have died the way she did.'

'She died?! How did she die?'

'I'm sorry, you didn't know?' Juan Miguel looked down at his hands, astonished, frightened, as if he were watching them sprouting out of his thick wrists at that very moment.

'Elena was attacked one night, very late, almost morning, on her way out of the hospital. Tramps, drunks, maybe the same lunatics she'd been treating, I don't know. No one ever found out. To tell the truth, I don't even really want to know who it was. They raped her. They slit her throat.'

I was speechless. Moira sat back in her chair and closed her eyes. Juan Miguel said goodbye and went back to the kitchen. That afternoon, as Moira and I were walking in Sea Point, I told her Hossi's story, from the moment when he was struck by two bolts of lightning to the strange saga in Havana where he'd met Snowflake. If the psychologist really did exist, maybe all the rest was true, too. Moira teased me.

'You think one single truth can make an entire fiction true? Oh, you really are so naive! A fifty-year-old man really shouldn't be that naive.'

'Fifty-five.'

'Even worse.'

'So you don't believe Hossi's story?'

'Does he believe in platypuses?'

'Hossi? Doubt it . . .'

'A man with such an imagination and he doesn't believe in platypuses?'

'I don't know if Hossi has as much imagination as all that . . .'

'You don't?!'

'No.'

Silence. Light coming through the windowpanes.

14.

I dreamed about God and God was an old dog, barking in the darkness. God was the birds wandering aimlessly in a distant sky. God was the orchids in the small back yard at Moira's house. God was everything, and indifferent to everything, like Table Mountain. God said to me:

'Resign yourself to it. There won't be bright lights, there won't be a garden to receive you. Nobody will give you their hand after the end.'

Moira didn't seem very impressed.

'Echoes,' she said. 'Dreams are always echoes of something.'

It was very sunny. We were both sweating as we made our way up the mountain. I'd been the one who suggested it. Moira had tried to talk me out of it.

'I've been living here for years and I've only been up there once. I've never been on foot. Why do you want to go on foot?'

'For the feeling of triumph.'

'Triumph?! You think if we get up to the top, on foot, we'll have triumphed over the mountain?'

'No, no. We'll have triumphed over our own indolence.'

Moira smiled.

'I'm at peace with my indolence. Laziness is the mother of all art.'

I finally managed to convince her. Despite the sharp, violent sun, there were plenty of people scaling the rocky, dusty paths. The one we took ran alongside an almost vertical wall. After an hour and a half, we stopped in a broad concave opening in the rock, just centimetres from the precipice. From there we could see a good part of the city, the houses, the ugly apartment blocks, like pieces of Lego strewn in disorder across the valley, and right down to the bay, way over there, and then the calm blue of the sea.

That was when I remembered the dream.

'I watched my father die. I gave him my hand as he was dying. Just before he died he said something about the sea, about the shining of the sea. I like to think my hand was there to meet him on the other side.'

'And at the same time, you're afraid there's nothing. There is no other side.'

'Of course. Aren't we all?'

'I find it consoling that there's nothing there.'

'Consoling?'

'Calming. No one to judge us. No duties to fulfil. We close our eyes and it's the great silence, the infinite nothing. The end.'

We remained seated there, sweating. Moira took my hand, lacing her fingers through mine:

'Silence is good.'

'Silence is good for a few moments. When it stretches out for too long it stops being silence and starts being deafness.'

I brought my face close to hers. I was going to kiss her. But then Moira drew her hand back and got up.

'Let's go!'

A man burst past us, at a run. He was wearing short shorts and a T-shirt with marijuana leaves against a black background. South Africans are proud of the ethnic diversity of their country, the Rainbow Nation, etc., etc., and there's a reason for that. I like sitting in the late afternoon in some café on Long Street, looking out to the road, because it's like watching a procession of the human race. However, it only took the briefest glance at this stranger to know he had not been born on African soil. There was something in him that made him foreign, even if the dark skin and tightly curled hair revealed a considerable likelihood that he had African ancestry. He stopped, surprised, when he saw Moira.

'I'm sorry, are you Moira Fernandes?' Moira, rather taken aback, confirmed that she was. 'Amazing coincidence. I've been looking for you. I've come to Cape Town for a medical congress. Somebody showed me a documentary about your work.'

The man was slightly shorter than her. He had a soft, deep voice. I recognised the accent: Minas Gerais. He gave me a firm handshake.

'Hélio de Castro.'

'You're from Minas?' I asked.

'You, too?'

'Oh, no, I'm from Angola.'

'Amazing. First Angolan I've met.' He turned to Moira. 'I went to see an exhibition, at the Cape Gallery. They've got a lot of your photos. I loved them. I'm a neuroscientist. I work with dreams.'

'We should set up a Republic of Dreamers,' said Moira.

Hélio received the suggestion with a laugh.

'An empire! We'll be imperialists! I'm in.'

He accompanied us for the rest of the climb. The man climbed the paths without any apparent effort. He remained light and cool, indifferent to the heat and the dust, as though he were sliding through the air-conditioned corridors of a shopping mall. The three of us came back down by cable car.

'Come have tea at my place,' said Moira.

'Hélio must be tired,' I heard myself say.

'No, no – I'm very well. Walking doesn't tire me – on the contrary, I find it invigorating. Tea would be wonderful. And we can talk some more.'

That's how we found ourselves, the three of us, a few minutes later, beneath the flowery crown of a huge orange tree. Hélio poured himself some tea. He praised the beauty of the orchids. Finally, he put the teapot down on the table and smiled at Moira.

'Like I was saying, I work with dreams. I started getting interested in the role dreams play when I was doing my doctorate in the US. My doctorate was on the representation of birdsong in the brain. Nothing to do with dreams. It just happened that in those first months I was sleeping fifteen hours at a stretch. I was always tired. I had a lot of dreams about things connected to my thesis. I thought my body was betraying me. However, after that time, my thesis started to flow and I understood that, on the contrary, the dreams had helped me.'

'You're saying dreams help us organise our thoughts?' asked Moira.

'It's more than that. Dreaming is rehearsing reality from the comfort of our own beds. There was an interesting study on the dreams of women who get divorced. First, they dreamed that everything was OK in their marriage. Then they started to dream about their husbands dying. Some of them saw themselves killing their husbands. Then they got divorced.'

'I hope none of them really did kill their husbands,' I said.

Hélio ignored my question.

'Unfortunately, people have stopped seeing the value of dreams. We need to restore dreams to their practical vocation.'

'What do my dreams mean?' asked Moira.

'I don't know. Only you can know that. Dreams relate to our own personal emotional experience.'

'What is it that interests you about my work?'

'What you're doing with your photographs is trying to translate dreams into images. In the Dream Lab, where I work, we're trying to do something similar. We've developed a technology that allows us to look at other people's dreams.'

I started to laugh.

'Why are you laughing?' asked Moira, annoyed.

'I'm sorry. It's not possible. He's saying they've invented a machine to take photos of dreams.'

'Yes, but we weren't the ones who invented it. We're just trying to perfect something that already exists. We want it to be an instrument capable not of photographing but of filming dreams. That's the aim.'

'How can I help?' asked Moira.

'I'd like to compare your images, the images of your dreams, with our own movie, as our Angolan friend would put it.'

'Daniel. My name's Daniel.'

'But in reality I'd like more than that. I'd like you to draw for us, to illustrate dreams.'

Moira got excited.

'Yes, yes! I'd love to do that!'

Hélio returned to Brazil the next morning. Moira called me mid-afternoon. She wanted me to go with her to a Moroccan massage parlour. I told her I don't go to massage parlours. The intimacy bothers me. I'm appalled at the thought of strangers running their oily hands down my back, stroking my legs, sinking their fingers into my thighs. No, it's really not the kind of thing I like. She insisted. I would like it, she assured me, a massage and a Turkish bath. Finally, I agreed.

We drove to the Malay neighbourhood. A woman in an earth-coloured djellaba met us at the entrance to a small house painted a very bright yellow.

The woman barely spoke English. She gestured towards a room where I could change clothes. Moira was led to the room next door. I took off my shoes. I took off my shirt, my trousers and underpants and sat down to wait on a stool. After a few minutes the woman came to fetch me. She took me into a little cell, lined with cobalt-blue tiles, stood me up against one of the walls and gave me a hot bath with a bucket and sponge. She wiped my back, then my chest, with a scented paste, which felt slightly rough, and then washed me again. She asked me to lie down on a table, then she gave me a long massage. I didn't like the massage. Finally, she led me to the Turkish bath. It was a very beautiful space, low and vaulted, with the same cobalt-blue tiles as the previous room. I lay down and fell asleep, or almost fell asleep. After a breath or after an eternity (I'd been asleep, or thought I had) the door opened. Moira advanced through the soaking air, which smelled of mint and burned my eyes, her breasts bare, illuminated by an amber light, which seemed to descend like a balm from some hidden place in the vaulting. She didn't speak. She sat down opposite me, eyes closed, in the lotus position.

'By the time my father died, all he could remember was the sea,' I said. 'I'm really scared of losing my memory. But if they told me I was going to forget everything, apart from one single moment, and they let me choose that moment, I'd choose this one.'

Moira smiled, a slightly teasing smile.

'Why?'

'Because if I can remember this moment, even if I've forgotten everything else, I won't have lost my whole life.'

'Seriously? Sad life you've got.'

Later, when I was getting dressed, I couldn't find my cellphone in my trouser pocket. I was sure I'd left it there. I asked the masseuse, but the woman didn't seem to understand. Moira didn't pay me much attention either.

'You must have left it at the hotel.'

'I'm sure I put it away in my pocket.'

'Is there anybody else here? Do you see anybody else? There's no one here. Only us and the woman. You aren't going to tell me she stole it from you . . .'

I agreed. I'd agree with anything Moira said. I paid the masseuse and we left. I didn't find the phone in my hotel room, or anywhere else. On another occasion, I would have got annoyed. That night I was on cloud nine.

I had dinner with Moira in a Thai restaurant. She took me back to my hotel and said goodbye with a kiss on the lips. The next morning, I set off back to Luanda. I sat in my allocated seat, wedged between the window and an unpleasant, enormously fat woman, who spent the entire journey looking at me with a mysterious unspoken hatred. It didn't bother me. I closed my eyes and the picture I saw was Moira.

15.

A lot of people are scared of plane travel. Lucrécia, for example, used to grip onto my wrist from the moment we sat down. Her hand would be hard and icy. One time, in Rio de Janeiro, she burst into sobs no sooner than we had taken off.

'I want to get out!' she screamed at the flight attendant.

The head of the cabin crew came over to talk to me:

'If your wife doesn't calm down, we're going to have to turn back, and there'll be legal proceedings. She's scaring the other passengers.' Finally, we managed to get her to swallow a Xanax. She slept the rest of the trip.

I'm not afraid of flying. I never have been. I have a less common, but related ailment: airports make me anxious. Or now I think about it, it's not really airports. It's airport police. The police generally. You know you were born in a third-world country when you're more scared of the police than of the thieves.

We arrived in Luanda on time. As I walked down the steps towards the tarmac a growing disquiet came over me. The anxiety grew as I headed towards the line for the Border Police.

A large, sweaty agent took my passport from my hand, opened it, tutted, and called a colleague over:

'Look at this guy, boss, must be the terrorist girl's dad.'

The other officer looked me up and down, with a mixture of pity and revulsion, whispered something to the first and then left.

'What is it?' I asked. 'What's happened?'

The first police officer shrugged, stamped my passport and handed it back to me.

'Go ahead, man, go! This country is your home. You can go ahead.'

I waited for my suitcase. An old man I'd never seen before, lean-fleshed, with big dreamy lemur eyes, put his hand on my right shoulder.

'Stay strong, kid. Things are going to get better.'

Armando Carlos was waiting for me at the exit. He hugged me.

'Have you heard the bad news?'

'What bad news?'

'You haven't had a call from your ex?'

'I lost my phone. What's happened?'

'They arrested Karinguiri,' said Armando.

'What?! What the hell did that girl do?'

'That girl did exactly what we all should have done, but never did out of cowardice and conformism . . .'

He didn't get a chance to say any more. His phone started ringing. Armando answered:

'Yes, I'm with Daniel . . . In the airport, yeah. How did you know? . . . Well, people do keep an eye on each other in this city . . . He's not avoiding your calls, my dear senhora, he lost his phone ... Look, you know what else, I'm not your husband, I'm not even your friend – the truth is I don't much like you, I never have, and so I don't have to put up with you. I'm passing the phone to Daniel.'

He handed me the phone. It was Lucrécia.

'It's your fault!'

'OK, you can calm down now ...'

'Calm down?! This is all your fault. You're the one who gets her going, with that armchair revolutionary talk of yours. She's going to end up a loser like you.'

'Calm down, I'm just arriving from South Africa. First of all, I need to know ...'

'Don't ask me to calm down! You're the one they should have arrested, loser!'

She shouted this at me and hung up. I turned to Armando, waving the phone in front of his face.

'What the hell is going on?!'

My friend said the same thing I'd told Lucrécia – 'Calm down!' – and just like Lucrécia, it only served to rile me even further. Armando took my suitcase and carried it to the car, a rusty but tenacious old carcass of a thing, which a neighbour lent him whenever he needed it. He waited for me to sit down, he settled himself next to me, and while he drove towards Talatona, he told me everything. Karinguiri, who was studying history in Lisbon but who came to Luanda whenever she could, had got involved with a group of young people who defined themselves as revolutionaries, or 'revos', and who filled social media networks with videos of protests against the dictatorship.

She used to criticize me for what she called my bourgeois complacency:

'The difference between you and Mamã is that she at least has a clear position – she supports the dictatorship. You pretend to be a democrat, but in practice you play along with the regime. The dictatorship is growing in the shade of your silent complicity.'

I got annoyed, because it was true, and we argued:

'You kids all want everything today,' I said. 'You don't know how to wait. This country has been through a terrible war. We can't create the conditions for another war.'

'The only party in a position to unleash another war,' replied Karinguiri, incensed, 'the only party that's threatening another war, is the ruling party.'

I fell silent, trying to make up an argument I could believe in myself. I pretended to be annoyed, but deep down, I liked losing arguments to her. I was surprised to see how quickly she'd grown up. At eighteen, Karinguiri looked like she had been designed by Niemeyer, with a single triumphant stroke. She was taller than her mother, prouder, more beautiful. Despite having inherited my hooked nose, it didn't make her uglier; rather the opposite, it emphasised her rebellious attitude. The day she turned eighteen she told me she wanted to get a tattoo. I promised to take her to a tattoo artist, Kenjy, a guy from São Paulo of Japanese origins, who was visiting Luanda, and who was, Armando Carlos assured me, one of the best artists in Brazil. Karinguiri appeared at my apartment with her head shaved on the right side, almost up to the middle of her skull. Little braids on the other side. I was shocked:

'Has your mother seen what you've done to your hair?'

'Not yet.'

'Have you told her you want to get a tattoo?'

'No.'

'I think you'd better call her.'

'I don't need Mamã's permission any more. I'm free! And anyway, you're coming with me, aren't you?'

So off we went. Karinguiri asked Kenjy to do her a tattoo from her neck up to her scalp. She showed him a design. It was a porcelain rose on whose petals you could read the word 'Freedom'. The tattooist got excited. Me not so much. By the time we left it was dark. I dropped her at home. She gave me a long hug:

'Thanks, Papá. I'm really happy.' She stroked my hair, and gave a mischievous smile. 'You don't want to come in and say hi to Mamã?'

I remembered all this while Armando told me what had happened.

The previous night the President had travelled to the newly inaugurated Congressional Palace, in Talatona, to give the opening address for the 1st International Anti-Corruption Congress. At the exact moment the man was getting ready to speak, a young woman jumped onto the table – 'like a lioness,' said Armando, unable to hide his enthusiasm – throwing blood-stained Monopoly money around her and shouting: 'Down with the dictator.'

Later I saw the pictures that had appeared on the television. Millions of people, inside and outside Angola, saw them, too. A tall girl, leaping onto a table at which the President was seated. The President's hands raised, palms open, as if in a kind of supplication, or adoration. The President's face, however, showed nothing but panic. The girl standing on the table, her hair arranged in long braids on one side, and on the other the scalp exposed to reveal the word 'Freedom'. Her eyes gave off a kind of glorious light, as if she were not there but at a rock concert or a Candomblé shrine.

Six other young people came onto the stage, shouting slogans against the regime, and hurling pamphlets over the stunned spectators. The President was hurried away by four security men. Taking advantage of the confusion, one of the young men grabbed the microphone and yelled: 'General popular resurrection!'

At least that's how it looked to me. In the days that followed, newspapers in Portugal, England, France and Brazil published a photo of my daughter being dragged out of the hall by a group of police officers. She was laughing. The blaze of her smile was exploding, like an untameable sunny morning, between the sweaty fat arms of the policemen. I still remember the headline, in the form of a question, from the *Guardian*: *Angola: Will laughter triumph over darkness?*

I spent those first few days on the phone. I only stopped to smoke. I took two melatonin pills before going to bed. I closed my eyes, counted to a hundred, got up again, picked up some book or other, opened it at random and read. I lay back down. I called Armando. On the third night, he stopped answering my calls. Finally, I fell asleep. I woke very early, more tired than when I'd gone to bed, my eyes swollen and hair dishevelled.

A well-known lawyer, Américo Kiala, prepared to defend

the prisoners. Américo defends both high-profile opposition figures and young revolutionaries without a penny to their name. The regime's critics call him 'the human rights lawyer'. The governing party call him 'the terrorists' lawyer'. I found him submerged in cigarette smoke and old pieces of paper, in Maianga, in a tiny, tumbledown apartment where years ago he set up his office. On one of the walls is a map of Angola with some three dozen red-topped pins in it. The pins mark those places where in recent years the government forces have committed some kind of violence.

'What do you think's going to happen to them?' I asked.

Américo smiled sadly.

'Your dear father-in-law, old Homero, is moving heaven and earth to try and get Karinguiri out of prison. He's hired a colleague of mine, a guy from the party, who knows everyone and all their secrets. Trouble is, those kids' action had really big repercussions, inside and out of the country. It put the Old Man in an unpleasant position – he felt offended, he felt humiliated. He's angry. Very angry. Do you know what the charge is going to be?'

'What?'

'Attempt on the life of the President, and attempted coup d'état.'

'What?!'

'Yeah, I know, it's nonsense, but they're scared. They'd like to let your daughter go, right away, not least because a lot of them, and I'm talking about generals, ministers, party leaders, are personal friends of Homero's. They see Karinguiri as a kind of niece. They know her.'

'But if they let her go, they have to let the others go.'

'Exactly. And they can't do that. It would look weak.'

'So?'

'They'll bring them to trial and I don't think they'll let them go in the meantime. You'd best get ready, it's going to be a long fight.'

I went with Américo to visit Karinguiri. Despite what I'd feared, it wasn't hard for us to get into the prison. Everyone was kind to me. Karinguiri looked thinner. I found her fiercely determined, however. One of the police officers, a very large young woman who barely fitted into her uniform, didn't bother to hide her smile each time my daughter raised her voice against the President.

'That kid, man, she's braver than Chuck Norris! Shame it won't do her any good. The President will stay in the Palace, he'll keep on sleeping well, and she's stuck in here.'

I got up, almost in tears, when I saw her come in, dressed in the prison uniform. It was only then, I think, that I was really convinced that she'd been imprisoned and that it wouldn't be easy to get her free.

'Why didn't you talk to me?'

'What would you have done?'

'I don't know. In any case, you wouldn't be here.'

'I'm where I need to be. We knew this would happen, we're not crazy.'

'You wanted to get arrested?'

'I knew I'd get arrested. Wake up, Dad, we're living in a dictatorship.'

I changed the subject.

'They're treating you well?'

'Kind of. There are only two women being held here for political reasons. Some of the other women prisoners respect us. Others are angry with us.'

I left the prison disheartened. I stopped at home, threw some clothes into a travel bag, fed Baltazar the cat, and got into the car. I needed to swim. Before I even knew what I was doing, I was pulling in to the Rainbow Hotel. Hossi came out from behind the counter as soon as he saw me arrive. He put his hand on my shoulder:

'Come, let's have a drink.'

He turned to one of his employees and told him to take my bag to the blue bungalow. He led me to the restaurant and offered me one of the tables overlooking the sea. Night had just fallen. A cicada was singing itself hoarse between the thick branches of the mango tree. Hossi ordered a bottle of whisky. I don't like whisky but I let him pour me some.

'I'm really sorry,' he said, and for the first time I sensed genuine warmth in his voice. 'I know what happened to your daughter. We're in this together now. Remember the boy who called for popular insurrection?'

'He called for resurrection . . .'

'What the hell? Seriously, man – resurrection? Insurrection!'

'Resurrection!'

'Insurrection, you misheard him. But anyway, he's my oldest nephew.'

'Your nephew?'

'Yes, my nephew. My sister's son, so it's like he's my own son. You didn't notice his name?'

'No!'

'Of course you didn't. If he'd been white or mulatto you'd have noticed.'

'Bullshit. What's he called, your kid?'

'Sabino Noé Kaley.'

I downed the whisky in one go and poured myself some more.

'Christ. Does he already have a lawyer?'

'Yes, Américo Kiala. Isn't he a friend of yours?'

'An old acquaintance. I like the guy.'

'I nearly wore myself out telling Sabino not to get mixed up in politics. My sister lived in Zambia during the war. All five of her kids were born there. When peace broke out, they moved to Luanda. As soon as Sabino turned eighteen, I decided to send him to Lusaka to study. He came back an electrician. A good electrician can earn a lot of money.'

I agreed, with a nod that was filled with silence and a sad darkness. My pain was growing, adding to the hotel owner's. A rage came to me. It arrived from some red smouldering place in my chest and opened up a path to the surface without my being able to control it. Damned Devil Benchimol.

'Those fucking crooks!'

Hossi got nervous. Several people turned to look at us with an expression that mingled curiosity and reproach. The hotel owner drove his dirty nails into my arm.

'Take it easy, Daniel.'

'They're all fucking crooks!' I insisted, not bothering to lower my voice. 'Starting with the tyrant himself, then his family and all the generals who've been getting fat over the years sucking the people's blood.'

'Relax! You see that skinny guy, over there, looks like a hairdresser? Well, appearances can be deceptive. His name's Rui Mestre, but he's better known by his *nom de guerre*, 20Kill. He was a member of the presidential guard and now he does odd jobs for the security services. He showed up here two days after your daughter and my nephew were put in prison . . .'

It was only then I realised he'd started using the familiar mode of Portuguese when addressing me, instead of the formal one, and I'm not sure why but for some reason that made me happy. I smiled.

'Man, your hotel's attracting quite the clientele.'

Hossi tutted:

'As long as he pays his bills, I can't kick him out. On the other hand, I don't think I'll go to hell if I just complicate things for him a little.'

'What do you mean?'

'The guy likes his whisky. He has it on ice. And, well, you know what the ice is like in this country. Sometimes people don't pay attention and they forget to boil the water, and it can cause intestinal trouble – nothing serious, of course. I might forget to put toilet paper in his bungalow, too. And water. As you know, there's often a water problem here.'

I started to laugh. The rage I'd been feeling was transformed into a kind of furious jubilation. I laughed until my stomach hurt. Hossi laughed with me. I noticed that 20Kill was looking at us, bemused, shaking his delicate little hairdresser's head gravely.

That night I went swimming. I swam for more than an hour, beneath the single eye of an enormous moon. I swam until the lights, back on the beach, mingled with the confused torrent of stars. Then I stretched out on my back, floating, pulled upward by the strength of the moon. If it had been just a little closer, it might have pulled me clean out of the water. I'd be levitating, a body freed, between the sea and the stars.

Hossi was waiting for me, sitting on the sand.

'I never know if you'll come back.'

'I never know if I'll come back either. But whenever I do, pal, I come back a little freer.'

16.

I wake up and say my name out loud:

'My name is Hossi Apolónio Kaley. I am the son of Pedro Kaley and Maria João Epalanga.'

Then I recall the names of my poor children and of my wife. I try to remember all my cousins' names. There are twenty-two of them. I can't always do it. Only then do I get up. I live in terror of one day waking up and not knowing who I am. Imagine some guy, any old guy, imagine he's had his eyes ripped out. We're going to give him a name and an occupation, to make things easier. For example: Sebastião Eusébio, farmer. Some people have ripped his eyes out, could be with a knife, could be with a teaspoon, the guy's still Sebastião Eusébio, farmer, though he's now blind. Now we're going to cut off his hand, then an arm, an ear, his nose; anyway, we're basically stripping Sebastião down, blow by blow, as though chopping the branches off a tree. Even mutilated in this way, he's still Sebastião Eusébio. Now let's try ripping out not parts of his body, which is easy enough – you just need a firm hand, some practice and a certain alienation of the spirit. We're going to be tearing out his memories. First we're going to rip out the image of his mother pounding corn with the other women, while they sing; then the happy memory of playing with his siblings and cousins among the sugar cane in the field beside the river; next, the coolness of the water out of a clay pot. We'll also take from out of Sebastião's head the stories his grandmother used to tell him, the smell of pipe smoke and her little laughter.

So answer me this question: this man who has never been a boy, is this man still Sebastião?

I wake up with the first rays of sunlight. I leap out of bed, clean my teeth, drink some lemon juice, savour a banana, and then I sit down to write in old notebooks, turned completely inward towards myself, covered in spikes on the outside, like a hedgehog. I remain like this for a long while, delving into my memory, in search of my pictures of childhood. I try to remember the faces of the people I loved. There are days when their images come to me with almost perfect clarity, like the scent of Surinam cherries releasing a red taste in my mouth. That is unusual. I know my late wife had a small scar on her chin. Her eyes were like mirrors. Her lips moist, well drawn. Despite this, I can't see her.

The same night they arrested my nephew, an ugly man showed up at the Rainbow, even uglier than me, limping on his right leg. The man looked at me shiftily, with a mixture of fear, hatred and curiosity. I haven't got the right word to describe that mixture. He looked at me in this multiple way, full of eyes, like a spider. His head tilted slightly to one side:

'Is it really you, Brigadier Kaley?'

'No, it's not me. Maybe I was that man, but I'm not any more.'

'And you think that's possible?'

His voice was hoarse, nasal. All those different stares were unsettling me. 'Sorry, I can't seem to recognise . . .'

'I once knew a Brigadier Kaley . . .'

'Are you here for a room, senhor?'

'Yes, I'd like a room.'

He showed me his passport, in the name Jamal Adónis Purofilim, and I immediately handed him the keys to the green bungalow, the one furthest from the beach. The next day he came over while I was playing chess with old Tolentino de Castro. He sat down next to Tolentino, pretending to watch the game, but in truth much more interested in me.

'I heard you had an accident.'

I didn't answer.

'They say you lost your memory.'

Tolentino laughed:

'He lost some of it. For example, he never remembers to protect his queen.'

I smiled – just very slightly. I let him take my queen. I managed a checkmate three moves later. It was four in the afternoon and the heat was oppressive. I was wearing some old Bermuda shorts, a Benfica T-shirt, with flip-flops on my feet that were two sizes too big. Tolentino was in swimming trunks, shirtless and barefoot. He's got to be in his seventies, but he has a body that's leaner, tauter and better defined than most kids of thirty. He does weight training every day, for three hours, with a personal trainer from Brazil. Jamal was stifling in a blue suit, which was too tight. His tie was like a garrotte. He got up slowly. Sweat was running down his face:

'I need to make a decision.'

Tolentino shook his head:

'Man, have a coffee! Have a coffee first. I've always replaced any big decision with a pot of coffee and it's always served me well.' He waited for the man to move away and then he turned to me.

'You only beat me because I was distracted by that ill-omened bird.'

'Distracted, how?'

'Don't know. He's got bad energy. Don't you think he's strange?'

'Why strange?'

'Nobody comes here on a Saturday wearing a suit and tie. This is a beach hotel, not a lawyer's office. And besides, he's armed.'

'How do you know?'

'Because I saw the gun attached to his belt, on his back, when he got up.'

I told him not to worry. I went to the office. I turned on the computer and googled Jamal Adónis Purofilim. It's an unusual name. If there were any references to someone with that name, it would have to be him, but I found nothing. If somebody isn't in Google, it can only be because they don't exist. I opened the safe and took out a Glock, a 9-mil, a gift from an Israeli friend. I loaded the gun, put it in my shorts pocket and went to find so-called Jamal. The door to the green bungalow was open. There was no one inside. No clothes. In the bathroom, I didn't find a toothbrush, a razor, nothing to suggest the presence of a guest. My phone rang. It was my sister, telling me her son had been arrested. I shut the door of the bungalow and that very moment forgot all about Jamal Adónis Purofilim.

17.

Swimming did me good. It did me even more good to be talking to Hossi. I had already been in Cabo Ledo for three nights when the hotel owner asked about my visit to Cape Town.

'And what about the artist, that Moira?'

I hadn't forgotten Moira. Her image continued to float, a sailboat among the tall waves, on the stormy sea that my life had become. Now and then I would let my heart rest on this image. But the noise would quickly bring me back to reality. I was glad Hossi had asked the question. I was honest:

'I fell in love.'

My friend laughed with a gentle manner I'd not seen in him before.

'Some good news at last. I'd like to fall in love again, but I fear it might be too late. It's not going to happen.'

'Why not?'

'I'm too old for that now.'

'Come on! We're the same age.'

'No, my friend. I've died twice already. I'm very much older than you.'

'But you did fall in love again, even after the second time you'd died.'

'You're right. I've died three times. Losing Ava was my third death.'

'You never told me what happened the first time.'

'I can't. I can't do it.'

Hossi fell silent, very serious, and I didn't insist. The hotel owner had had an awning set up on top of the cliff. Beneath it he'd arranged a table and a few chairs. He challenged me to the climb. From up there we could see the whole of the beach. The hotel staff had brought cold beer, grilled chicken, fries and even a banana cake. I told him I'd climbed Table Mountain with Moira and that halfway up we'd run into a Brazilian neuroscientist, a dream expert. The man was building a machine for seeing dreams. Hossi got interested.

'A machine for seeing dreams?'

'A machine that can translate the cerebral activity while we're dreaming into animated pictures, yes. I don't think they're films exactly, but almost.'

'Whoa, pal! Sounds interesting. He'd be able to confirm the thing of whether people really dream about me . . .'

'Dreamed. It hasn't happened again since, has it?'

'Except you! It's never happened since, because I take sleeping pills now.'

'Ah, right. I didn't know that.'

Hossi put his hand on my forearm, stopping me from saying any more. He picked up a pair of binoculars from the table and pointed them towards the hotel. He laughed.

'I've caught the crook!'

'What?!'

He passed over the binoculars. He told me to locate the green bungalow. I saw two of the hotel staff accompanying a small limping man in suit and tie. One of the staff was carrying a little suitcase. The three of them went into the bungalow.

'Look, look!' Hossi encouraged me, pleased with himself.

The three of them came out again, moments later. The small man was handcuffed and one of the staff was sticking a pistol in his back. I sat up with a start.

'What's going on?!'

Hossi took the binoculars from me.

'The guy came here to kill me.'

'Seriously? How do you know?'

'He appeared out of nowhere, in a suit and tie. Then he scarpered without a word.'

'He ran away without paying?'

'What do you mean, ran away without paying? No one leaves the Rainbow without paying – you know I make everyone pay up front!'

'So what happened? What's the problem?'

'The problem is that he was armed and he gave a fake ID. I thought his behaviour was strange so I went to investigate. I asked around.'

'And?'

'Nothing. I didn't learn a thing. Or not till yesterday when I got a message from the same guy booking a bungalow.'

'What are they going to do?'

'My men are going to bring him here. I want to have a quiet talk with him.'

'Why don't you talk at the hotel?'

'It's calmer up here. No one to bother us.'

Worried, I watched the three men's progress. The prisoner was finding the climb hard going, his steps uneven, tripping on the rocks, struggling not to get caught on the cacti and the brambles. The other two seemed to be mocking the poor man's difficulties, shaking their heads, laughing, shoving him instead of supporting him.

'Have another beer,' said Hossi, holding out a bottle. 'Drink it, and calm down. I'm not planning to kill the cripple. I'm just going to extract a little information from him.'

'Extract some information! What year do you think you're living in?! The war is over . . .'

A billow of wind whipped us with burning dust, blood-coloured. Hossi rubbed his eyes, which were very red; he shook out his hair, which was even more dishevelled than usual. He gave a bitter laugh.

'The war isn't over, my friend. It's only sleeping.'

The three men finally reached the summit of the cliff and started towards us. One of the hotel employees, called Adriano, who always wore shades, even at night, and whose voice I'd never heard, handed the gun to Hossi. The prisoner's suit was dirty. He reminded me of one of those tiny flies that bananas secrete after they've rotted. He was limping badly. The handcuffs were cutting into his wrists. He was crying.

'Why?! Why?!'

'For the love of God,' I shouted. 'Hossi, let the man go!'

Hossi ignored me. He got up. He walked around the unfortunate man, shaking the gun, a hyena sizing up its prey. It was like some unknown being, something cruel and cold, had taken control of his body. His voice had changed. A harsh voice, the voice of someone used to giving orders and being obeyed.

'So tell me there, cripple . . .'

'Yes, sir.'

'What's your name?'

'Jamal Adónis Purofilim.'

'No. Your name isn't Jamal! You're going to start by telling me your real name.'

The prisoner looked at me, entreatingly. I was as scared as he was. My throat was dry. I could feel my legs shaking. All the same, I got up and took two hesitant steps.

'Please, Hossi. Take off his cuffs. The man's bleeding.'

Hossi turned his red eyes towards me, and his amused smile. Then he addressed Adriano:

'Adriano, take off his handcuffs. And you, Jamal, have a seat with us. Wet your whistle, then talk.'

Adriano took the cuffs off Jamal. The little man sat down, fearfully, on one of the chairs. He looked like a bird on a perch. He was looking at the sea as though at any moment he might take flight and vanish into the undisturbed blue.

'Take a deep breath,' Hossi said to him. He put the pistol down on the table. He gave Jamal's injured leg a friendly pat. 'You're in luck – my friend Daniel here doesn't like violence. Daniel's a pacifist. You are a pacifist, aren't you, Daniel?'

'Yes, I'm a pacifist.'

'Hear that? Daniel's a pacifist. He's a protector of human rights. He even protects animal rights. When he was a kid he saved a little lion cub, he took care of a lion cub. He hunted cats to feed the little lion. Nowadays he feels guilty that he killed all those cats.'

I looked at him, shocked:

'What?!'

'Yes, I know all about it,' said Hossi, very pleased with himself. 'I know that when you were a kid you took care of a one-eyed lion, called Moshe Dayan.'

I couldn't help laughing.

'A lion? Moshe Dayan was a hyena. A hyena cub.'

'Are you sure? The story I heard said it was a lion.'

'A lion? You think I'd get a hyena and a lion mixed up? You think I'd keep a lion in the house? It was a hyena and it didn't eat cats, it ate scraps, it ate rubbish, like pigs. I've only killed one cat in my life and it wasn't to feed to some lion.'

Jamal was looking at me, he was looking at Hossi, with a confused half-smile. The brigadier gave me a wink.

'Well, it's like my grandmother used to say – in this country, whoever tells the tale, makes the tale a little taller. Fine, a lion or a hyena, it actually doesn't make any difference. You're a humane kind of guy who doesn't like violence, which is why, in consideration of you, we're going to have a civilised conversation. So tell me, what's your name . . . ?'

The man straightened his tie. He shook off the red dust that was covering his trousers. He took a handkerchief out of his pocket, and with it carefully cleaned the blood off his wrists.

'My real name is Ezequiel. Ezequiel Ombembua.'

'And the fake passport?'

'I bought it from a Congolese man.' Jamal, aka Ezequiel, paused slightly, as though assessing the density of the air in front of him. He sighed. 'I came here to kill you, brigadier.'

'Now?'

'No, not now. The first time I came, I wanted to kill you. Now I've come to explain myself and to try and understand. You can search me. I'm not armed . . .'

'Understand what?'

'You really don't remember?'

'Remember . . . ?'

'You really don't remember me?!'

'No!'

'That's why I didn't kill you last time. If you don't remember, then you're no longer Brigadier Kaley. The person I came to kill is buried away somewhere inside your head. I don't know how to kill him. I can't.'

'Why would you want to kill that person?'

'Because that person killed the best there was in me.'

'When was this?'

'It was in 1995. I was a primary school teacher. I taught classes in Luanda. That year my mother died and I had to travel to Bailundo, for the funeral. UNITA were in Bailundo.'

'Yes, I know – that I do still remember.'

'One day some soldiers showed up at my house and took me away. They said I'd stolen a stash of diamonds.'

'And I was the person who interrogated you, of course.'

'Yes. You remember that?'

'I don't. But it's what I did – my job was to extract information.'

'You tortured me, senhor, for a whole night.'

'You had nothing to do with the robbery?'

'You beat me with a hammer . . .'

'Did you or didn't you?'

'I was a believer. I believed in God. I believed in people . . .'

'What did you do with the diamonds?'

In a quick movement, Ezequiel's hand was on the gun. The next instant he was on his feet, the barrel of the weapon pressed into Hossi's neck. Adriano leaped towards the two of them, and he could have brought his right fist, thick and heavy as an iron ball, against Ezequiel's delicate head, had Hossi not prevented him.

'Take it easy! Nobody move!'

Ezequiel spluttered like a choking dog. He was sweating heavily. The red dust was running down his face and dripping onto his shirt.

'Fuck! Fuck!'

'Make a decision,' said Hossi, very calmly. 'If you want to kill me, now's your chance.'

'You don't remember?'

'I don't remember anything.'

'You beat me badly. You crushed my knee with a hammer.'

'And the diamonds?'

Again Ezequiel pressed the barrel of the gun into Hossi's neck. I thought he was going to fire. I struggled to my feet, leaning on the table, my knees trembling:

'Don't do it. Please, don't shoot!'

The man turned his frightened dog-eyes towards me.

'Who are you?'

'I'm a journalist.'

'You're a friend of the brigadier's?'

'Yes, I'm a friend of his.'

Ezequiel let his arm fall. He sat down. Hossi moved towards him and took the gun from his hand. He put it back down on the table. I took a few hesitant steps, almost at random, then I started to make my way down the cliff.

'Where are you going?' – Hossi's voice.

I didn't answer. I didn't even look back. I made my way down the trail. The further I went, the firmer my steps became. When I reached the blue bungalow, my legs were trembling again, but it wasn't fear now, it was rage. I threw my clothes into my bag, packed away my laptop, and left without closing the door. I put the suitcase in the trunk, got into the car, sat back and turned on the engine. And I fled.

18.

Domingos Perpétuo Nascimento has green, very light eyes. In a city like Luanda, a mulatto with green eyes grows up surrounded by all kinds of privileges. That's how it was in colonial times, and it's still that way today. In high school, he must have dated all the prettiest girls. Everybody invited him to their parties. That, perhaps, explains the confidence with which he looks at the world and at other people. The firmness of his convictions. There he was, sitting opposite me, at the editorial office of *O Pensamento Angolano*, in Quinaxixe, legs crossed, cigarette in the corner of his lips, with the discreet serenity of a champion sharpshooter.

'I liked the article you wrote about me,' he said. 'You seem an honest man. Somebody told me you wrote another article about a plane, a Boeing 727 that disappeared from Luanda airport in 2003.'

'Yes, they never found the plane . . .'

'Do you remember the pilot's name?'

'I do.'

'Charles Padilla.'

'Yes, Charles Padilla, an American. Why are you asking me this?'

'He disappeared along with a mechanic. Do you remember the mechanic's name?'

'No, I just remember he was Angolan.'

'No, he wasn't Angolan. He was Congolese. His name was, or rather, is, Jean Mpuanga. Good mechanic. I was with him the other day.'

'You were with him? Where?!'

Domingos Perpétuo Nascimento stubbed out his cigarette in the ashtray. He was clearly pleased at my surprise. Like all good storytellers, he allowed himself to remain silent for a long moment, smiling sweetly, savouring his triumph. Finally he spoke.

'In Recife.'

'In Brazil?'

'Yes. You see, I joined TAAG in 2000. I met Mpuanga, I thought he was a good guy. Pretty special. He liked reading. He read a lot. Books in French with long titles. We played football a few times. I ended up going round to his place to eat a *mufete*. It was a very good *mufete*, incidentally. His wife was from Dondo. She knew how to grill the fish. She used *cacusso*. Proper freshly caught *cacusso*. Oh, those black beans with the palm oil ... Just remembering it makes my mouth water. But to continue – two weeks ago, I went into a little bar, in Recife, to have a beer, and there the guy was, sitting in a corner, about fifteen years older but with the same smile. He had a kind of crooked smile, as if he'd suffered a stroke.'

'So they stole the plane?

'I don't know.'

'You don't know?'

'I have no idea.'

'You didn't ask him?'

'No. I'm not a cop. I'm not a journalist. I just asked him what he was doing there and he said he was Charles's partner. They've got an air taxi company.'

'An air taxi company?!'

'Yeah, they're rich, though Mpuanga still keeps a modest lifestyle. Every evening, around six, he goes to that same bar to drink a caipirinha and read the papers.'

I sat there without speaking, looking into the limpid green eyes of Domingos Perpétuo Nascimento. Outside it was raining, the way it'll rain at the end of days. Heavy water was punishing the asphalt, beating the cars and windowpanes. The noise of the rain falling was superimposed over the snoring of the generators, the furious honking of the *candongueiros*, the shouts of the *zungueira* women hawking their wares, sheltering in the large entrances of the buildings.

'Burburinho,' said Domingos.

'What?'

'That's the name of the bar – Burburinho.'

I made a note. I said goodbye to him with a hug. I watched him dive into the storm and he disappeared within seconds, dragged off by the dark torrent. When I left it was no longer raining. In the entrance hall of the building a girl offered to carry my shoes, while another said she'd follow after us with a bucket full of clean water and a towel. When we reached the car they would wash my feet. I refused. An even more enterprising lad was renting out wading boots. I congratulated him on his initiative, but told him it wasn't worth it. My shoes were already old. So were my feet.

The increasingly frequent floods were creating new lines of employment. There are people who offer to carry others on their backs, which appals me because it reminds me of some engravings I saw, from the late nineteenth century, early twentieth century, with black men carrying whites piggyback. There are also some who sell plastic bags, into which people stick their feet, and which you then stick to your knees with sellotape. When the water dries up, the streets are covered with thousands of black plastic bags, as well as shoes and food leftovers. The unpleasant smell sticks to your skin.

I walked across the flooded pavements. I couldn't find my car. The square where I'd left it was now a muddy lake. It looked like you'd stand a better chance of finding hippos and crocodiles there than cars. I gave up and looked for a *candongueiro* to take me to Talatona. It took me nearly two hours to find one. As usual, it had its name written in black ink on the back window: *Informal Parliament*. I sat down between two thin, sweating young men, who despite their tiredness still managed to find the strength to make light of their own misfortune.

'We're so screwed,' one of them said to me. 'They're trying to kill us from rain now.'

'With rain,' I corrected him.

'You're a grammar teacher, are you, old man?'

'No, I'm a journalist.'

'What do you reckon's going to happen to the revos?'

'I don't know.'

'That girl – Karinguiri – she got that name from a little bird they have down in Benguela. It's a teeny little bird, but very brave. It helps the others. It faces up to their enemies, making an almighty racket, to save its companions. If we had more like her the country wouldn't be in this state.'

His friend agreed:

'Oh, man, yeah! Here in Angola the honest people are in prison, and the crooks are in charge.'

My soaking wet shoes were bothering me. They'd shrunk in the water. Or maybe my feet had swollen. I considered taking the shoes off. I thought that if I took them off, I'd never manage to get them back on again. I kept them on. A lady sitting behind us joined in the conversation, saying that by having kids arrested the President is only showing himself to be scared and weak.

'It was the rain that wet him, but he punishes the dew,' she added, with a loud tut.

Everyone laughed. Everyone but me. The other passengers noticed my silence.

'And what does the journalist think about the whole business?' asked the driver.

'I think there are other ways of fighting for democracy,' I answered. My feet were hurting me. 'There's no need to disrespect the President.'

The young man sitting to my right couldn't hold back:

'It's the President who's disrespecting us every day! It's disrespect stealing from the people, the way he does it, and then sharing out what he's stolen among his children.'

The other got nervous.

'Take it easy, pal. The old man's allowed his opinion.'

Nobody said any more. When I got out of the *candongueiro*, close to the Belas shopping mall in Talatona, it was raining again. I arrived home drenched. Baltazar ran away from me. I took a hot shower, put on an old pair of jeans and a freshly washed white shirt, and turned on my laptop. I found a message from Moira. In the first few paragraphs she talked about the light in Lisbon. She'd been in the Portuguese capital a few days earlier to take part in a joint exhibition bringing together new African artists. She had woken up very early to lean out of the veranda, naked, while the sun rose over the homestead. She was taking photos of clouds. She thought that morning's sky might be useful for her when constructing dreams. After this long preamble, she told me she'd exchanged messages with Hélio, and that she'd decided to visit him in Natal a week later.

'Are you coming?'

The question just floated there on the computer screen. I imagined Moira on some beach in Natal, walking along with Hélio, hand in hand, and I felt a stab of jealousy. It occurred to me that I could stop in Recife, before going on to Natal, and find out what had happened to the Boeing 727. Now that really would be a great report. I phoned Alexandre Pitta-Gróz, director of *O Pensamento Angolano*, and asked him if the paper could pay for a flight for me to Recife. I let him laugh for a few minutes. He laughed and coughed. Then he laughed again. Alexandre is always coughing. He picked up that cough nearly forty years ago, when he was imprisoned, shortly after independence, accused of links to the Angolan Communist Organisation. I insisted:

'Please, Alexandre. This might be one of the most important reports of my life.'

'Might it?' (Cough.)

'It might.'

'Wrong answer. If you'd said it *would* be the most important report of your life, I'd have been ready to pay out of my own pocket. Things are looking bad, you know that. The paper doesn't have a budget for international travel.'

'Fine. I'll pay for the trip. The trip and my expenses out there. I just need you to let me stay in Pernambuco for a week.'

'OK, now I'm getting interested. I'll give you a week. I'll even give you two weeks and I won't care if you come back fat and suntanned, so long as you bring me back a good story.'

19.

Lucrécia's bitterness towards me accumulates in her soul, each year, like muddy water gathering at an abandoned dam. One day the weight of the mud is going to destroy the barrier. There's not a lot I can do about it. I realised, some time ago, that any action of mine will displease her, whether it's a gesture of approach or of confrontation. When I left home, a good few years before the divorce, Karinguiri was very small. For the first fifteen months, Lucrécia wouldn't let me see the girl. She moved them both to her parents' house, refused to answer my phone calls and gave instructions to the guards to keep me at a distance. One of them even went so far as to threaten me with his gun. Alexandre Pitta-Gróz, a lawyer by training, though he has never practised, made me understand the pointlessness of going ahead with a court case to demand my paternal rights.

'This country is divided into those people who can insist on their rights, and those who don't have rights at all. Your wife is in the first group. You used to be in her group once, when you were married, then you came back to ours. Get used to it.'

I got used to it. Fifteen months after I'd left the house, Lucrécia called me. She said I could go to the apartment of an aunt of hers that afternoon, to see the girl. I went. Karinguiri had just turned four. I held her on my lap. I asked her:

'Do you know who I am?'

The girl gave a happy smile:

'You are my papá.'

I returned home devastated. From that day on I started visiting the girl, two or three times a month. I started writing stories which we'd read together. We'd play with dolls. We'd do drawings, lying on the floor, while she told me about her best friend, a very blonde girl, the daughter of a French businessman who was a friend of Homero Dias da Cruz. I would arrive home on those nights with my knees aching, my skeleton all out of joint, as if I'd spent two hours working out at the gym.

The following year, Lucrécia let me have Karinguiri for a week, during the Easter holidays. In those days, I still lived in Armando Carlos's apartment. I remember the shock on the girl's face when she came in.

'Where are the servants?'

'We don't have any servants.'

'Who's going to look after me?'

'I'm going to look after you. I'm your father. It's my job to look after you.'

It wasn't always easy. The hardest part was combing her hair. For years Karinguiri had a thick mane of hair, which shone in the sun like a cool copper flame. You could have stuffed cushions with her curls.

A friend of my father's, Pedro da Mata, an administrator of

the Railroad, lived on the Lobito breakwater with his wife and nine children. In the colonial days, we used to spend the March holidays at their house. After independence, the Mata family moved to Portugal. The youngest son, Mauro da Mata, stayed behind in Lobito. I ended up visiting him often, after my father moved back to Benguela. We became good friends.

Mauro had six children by two wives, one Mozambican and the other from Benguela. Both of them lived with him, with no weirdness or conflict, taking care of the children and sharing the domestic chores. I'm not sure whose the children are. I suspect even they no longer know for certain which belly they came out of.

When Karinguiri was seven or eight years old she and I went to spend a few days' holiday in Lobito. We were put up in Mauro's big mansion, the same room where I used to sleep with my brothers. That mansion brought back happy memories. I remember an enormous casuarina tree, in the yard, which leaned out over the sea. One of Mauro's brothers had attached a swing to one of the uppermost branches. We would sit on the swing, swinging, gaining altitude, a great altitude, eight metres, ten metres, and then we'd dive head first into the warm water. At the end of the afternoon we'd get hosed down to clear our sun-punished skin of sand and salt. I lay in bed, eyes open, watching while on the ceiling, through the mosquito net, geckos were chasing after insects. The bed was still the same. Perhaps the mosquito net, quite hole-ridden now, was the same, too. On the ceiling, the great-grandchildren of the geckos of my childhood still chased insects.

I thought it cruel to subject the girl, every night, after a

prolonged period swimming in the sea, to the painful cere-
mony of reordering her hair. After three days, Karinguiri was
already sporting some solid dreadlocks, the kind that were
enough to make any Rastafarian die of envy. Seven days later,
when we returned to Luanda, she was carrying an extravagant,
impenetrable forest on her head. The first hairdressers I asked
for help refused to take on the challenge. When I asked a friend
for advice, she recommended the salon of a Russian, one Igor,
that operated in a five-star hotel. So that was where we went.
Igor got up out of an armchair printed with the flag of the
defunct Soviet Union. He took two horrified steps towards my
daughter. I held out my hand, while explaining my crisis:

'I need to return this girl to her mother, tomorrow morning, and I'd like her hair to be in a decent state.'

'I presume you aren't together, you and the child's mother?'

'No!' said Karinguiri. 'They're speculated.'

'Separated,' I corrected her. 'She means separated.'

'Naturally,' said the Russian, icily. 'I hope your ex-wife has
you killed. If I were her I'd kill you myself with my bare hands.'

I didn't laugh. The man wasn't joking. When I returned
three hours later, I found Karinguiri sitting in one of the
chairs, very upright, very serious, while four pretty young
assistants were finishing untangling her hair. The operation
went on for another hour.

'This girl is a heroine,' murmured Igor, when he finally
returned her to my hands. He looked at me with contempt.
'Let's see if you might learn to deal with her hair yourself.'

I did learn. A friend explained to me that, after washing
her hair, I should always comb it from the ends, moving up

firmly towards the roots. The best combs are wood. Brushes also work well. Other friends recommended softening creams. In the days after a wash, it's enough to use a good hydrating oil. You spread the oil with your fingers. You can use a comb just to give it a bit of body.

In the kitchen, though, rather than learning, I was forced to regress. There were to be no more of the sophisticated dishes with which, at first, I'd tried to win her over. Karinguiri preferred sausages and fries. Pancakes. Eggs over easy – though she refused to eat the yolks. She also wouldn't eat, for ethical reasons, things-with-eyes; green-things; slimy-things, like okra; things-with-many-legs, like octopus or centipedes; and things-that-maybe-pray, like cats or praying mantises. (I swear I never forced her to eat cats or praying mantises – and not even centipedes.) As a result of these complex and, occasionally, somewhat mysterious dietary restrictions, trips to restaurants could turn into moments of great drama. I wasn't too surprised when, at the age of sixteen, my daughter announced she was a vegetarian.

The second time I went to visit Karinguiri, I found her more determined than ever. I hugged her. She was hot and incredibly thin. She was just skin and bone and between the two of them the pure fire of idealism. She told me she'd started giving English lessons to the other inmates and asked me next time I visited to bring her some exercise books and pens. I explained I wouldn't be able to visit her for the next two weeks.

'Where are you going?'

'Brazil, for work.'

'What work?'

'Dreams. I'm going to look for dreams and dreamers.'

'You don't need to go that far, Papá. I have so many dreams. The other prisoners, the policewomen, we all dream a lot. You wouldn't believe the dreams that fit inside this prison.'

I went back to my apartment, and even though I was alone I locked myself in the bathroom. Though I wasn't totally alone, in truth. Baltazar was stretched out in the sun, in the living room, next to the window that overlooks the gardens of the condo. But a cat doesn't count as company. You can't have a cat's company. Sharing a house with a cat is just an elegant kind of solitude.

I closed the bathroom door, turned the key, sat down on the edge of the bath and cried.

20.

It was gone midnight when I disembarked in Recife. The border police officer received me with a tired smile.

'On holiday?'

'I've come to Recife to look for an aeroplane, a Boeing 727, that's been missing since 2003. I'm also looking for a machine that can film dreams.'

'Seriously?! And what do you do?'

'I'm a journalist.'

The man shook his head, in silent criticism of my folly, stamped my passport and handed it back to me. I waited twenty minutes for my luggage. I came out into a warm, humid night, almost identical to the ones we get in Luanda, but without the torture of the noise. A sleepy taxi driver, as wordless and sad as a ghost, drove me to a hotel I'd chosen from home in Luanda, by searching on the internet, just for its location in the historic centre of Recife, very close to the bar Domingos Perpétuo Nascimento had told me about: the Hotel Nassau. There was a lad dozing barefoot on the other side of the reception desk. He woke up, startled, when he saw me arrive. He put on a pair of flip-flops and only then did he stand up.

'Are you Senhor Daniel?'

I handed him my passport and watched as he filled in my registration card. He couldn't have been more than eighteen. The low-cut sleeveless T-shirt revealed his thin chest and feeble shoulders, one of which bore a tribal tattoo. On the other it was possible to read, in Gothic letters, *My Name is Solitude*. The lad climbed two flights of stairs, carrying my suitcase. He went along a small corridor painted in a pale red, before stopping at door number 13.

'This is your room. I hope you don't mind.'

'Mind what?'

'The number.'

'I have nothing against any numbers. There are no bad numbers.'

'Are you sure?'

'Totally.'

He opened the door. He put the suitcase down in the entrance hall.

'My name's Cain.'

'I don't believe you. I'd find it easier to believe if you said your name was Solitude. Nobody in the world is called Cain.'

'No need to worry, senhor. I'm an only child.'

I smiled. I gave him a ten-*real* note.

'Thanks, Cain.'

'Do you need anything else, senhor? You don't want me to send up some company?'

'Company?!'

'A girl to keep you warm?'

'Thank you very much, that won't be necessary. It's a hot night. If anything, I'd rather have a girl to cool me down.'

'They don't exist. At least, not in Brazil.'

I took off my shoes, lay down on the bed and thought about Moira. A line of poetry formed of its own accord. I sat down at a small table beside the window, opened my laptop, and wrote all the rest. I sent the poem to the person who had inspired it. I went back to bed and fell asleep. I awoke with the sun burning my face. I checked the time on my phone. Nearly seven. I got up, took off my crumpled clothes, cleaned my teeth, had a quick shower. When I went down to the foyer I was a new man. Cain was still there, sitting on his chair, barefoot, his head thrown back. He was snoring unevenly. He didn't wake up. I left without making any noise. Thousands of people were hurrying along the pavements. On one corner, there was a small snack-bar called Peace & Quiet. I sat down and ordered a papaya juice with orange and a cassava crêpe with ham and cheese. I wouldn't mind living in this city. I'd get a job with one of the local papers. I'd rent a room. I'd marry a dark-skinned woman with small breasts and wide hips, called Janaína, or Inaê, or Yara, and at breakfast time she'd cook for me. I'd eat cassava crêpes, drink Surinam cherry juice, or acerola cherry juice, or cashew juice. I'd read the *Diário de Pernambuco* and the local poets. Perhaps, just very occasionally, memories of Angola would come to me, and I'd quickly dismiss them with a careless shrug. I thought about this, I thought about Karinguiri and tears came to my eyes. I got up, leaving the crêpe half-eaten. I paid and left. For several hours

I walked, aimlessly, around the noisy streets of Recife. I was in many places and in none, as if passing through dreams that light up for a moment and then are plunged back into darkness. Evening was already drawing in by the time I was myself again. I found myself in a large square, beside the sea. A huge penis-lighthouse, with a florid glans, like some exotic illness, rose up from a stone promontory a couple of hundred metres ahead. People were pointing at this enormity and laughing. A young couple asked me to take their photo. I took the picture, following the instructions from the young man who asked that I include the penis-lighthouse within the frame. I asked him if he knew where the Hotel Nassau was and he directed me. On my way, to my surprise, I stumbled across the Bar Burburinho. I went in. There weren't many people. At a remote table, in the darkest corner, a man in his fifties was reading a thick book. It was a novel in French with a discreet plain Gallimard jacket. I knew at once this was the man I was looking for. I walked over.

'Jean Mpuanga?!'

The man dropped the book with a start. He took off his glasses and looked at me.

'Who are you?'

I held out my hand.

'Daniel Benchimol – journalist.'

Mpuanga ignored my outstretched hand.

'What do you want?'

I sat down opposite him.

'What happened to the plane?'

'Are you a cop?'

'No, I told you, I'm a journalist.'

'You could be a journalist and a cop. A lot of people have to combine several jobs in these tough times.'

'Well, I don't. I'm just a journalist.'

'My name's Paulo Costa Pinto, Brazilian, born in Bahia, businessman. I don't know what plane you're talking about.'

I got up.

'I'm sorry, I got the wrong person. Have a good night.'

The man gripped my wrist, firmly. He had a slightly wonky smile, unusual but not unpleasant.

'Sit down. Sit down.'

I sat back down.

'But say we just pretend I'm that fellow. The one you were talking about. Mpuanga's the fella's name, right?'

'It could have been an Angolan name, but yes, he's Congolese.'

'Or was. You don't think a person can change nationality?'

'You can change passport. You can't change identity.'

'Why not?'

'Because a chameleon is always a chameleon, even when it changes colour.'

'Oh no, man, a chameleon becomes several different chameleons. We're several different people over the course of our lives. A person can be Ukrainian up to a certain point and Brazilian from then on. That's what happened with Clarice Lispector.'

'Clarice never actually got to be Ukrainian. She was two months old when she arrived in Brazil.'

'Right. What about Coetzee?'

'What about Coetzee?'

'He's Australian now, isn't he?'

'No, he's a South African Boer who has an Australian passport.'

The man shook his head and smiled.

'Nabokov?'

'Never stopped being Russian. He went on being Russian, even when he was writing in English, even when American.'

'I can tell our journalist doesn't believe a person can remake his life, completely, with a different identity and a genuine feeling of belonging to the country that took him in. And I'm not going to be able to convince you.'

'No, you aren't. A person is his past. The past doesn't change.'

Jean Mpuanga, or Paulo Costa Pinto, whoever he was, burst out laughing.

'Oh, I'm sorry for you, Mr Journalist. You have no imagination at all! To anybody with any imagination, the past is constantly changing. You think the present is born out of the past, but it's the other way around. The present creates the past. Somebody with imagination isn't bound to the past, let alone to borders. I'm Paulo Costa Pinto, Brazilian, native of Cachoeira, in Bahia. I've lived in France and Portugal for a long time, hence my accent.'

Now it was my turn to laugh.

'I'm sorry, I really can't imagine you as Brazilian . . .'

'That's because you – and I'm sorry to have to insist – don't have an iota of imagination.'

'That's just as well. I'm a journalist. For a journalist,

imagination is a failing. Curiously, not long ago, when I was arriving in this country, I was accused of showing too much imagination for a journalist. I might have replied, but I didn't, that it's the reality I work with that tends to exhibit an excess of creativity. I'm not to blame. I'd prefer a reality which was – how should I put it – less creative.'

'I can believe that. However, I'm going to ask you to make an effort. Imagine I am, or I was, this Jean Mpuanga you're looking for. Can you imagine that?'

'That's easier for me than imagining you're a Brazilian called Paulo Costa Pinto.'

'Very well. Now imagine yourself into the skin of that man. You're a mechanic. One night, you decide not to go back home after work. You're tired and you know that back home you have five children waiting for you and a wife who never shuts up . . .'

'I've heard she's a good cook.'

'Yes, she was a great cook, that she was.'

'But you were tired.'

'Jean was tired. He couldn't take any more. The idea of returning home was unbearable. He started drinking. There was a Boeing 727, belonging to an American company, abandoned on the tarmac, and sometimes, after it got dark, Jean would board the plane, sit in one of the business-class seats, and sleep. Which is what happened on that Friday in May. That night he overdid it on beer and *caporroto* spirits. He climbed the steps and made his way, tripping over his own feet, up the aisle. He dreamed that he was waking up and seeing the lights of Luanda, through the small window, sinking away into the darkness. He saw a great moon floating over the black water. The next morning, he opened the door and didn't find the stairs. He also didn't find the airport. He didn't find Luanda. The plane was sitting on a long beaten-earth road. There were no buildings around, no vehicles, no ploughed land or plantations, nothing to suggest any human presence. The savannah stretched out to the horizon. Acacias breaking up the pastureland. You know what I mean, you must have seen a lot of landscapes like that. I remember hearing a vague buzzing, but I couldn't see any insects.'

'Where was this?'

'Don't interrupt me. I was very scared. I sat back down. I shut my eyes, counted to a hundred, and then got up and looked out the door again. The savannah was still there.'

He fell silent. The bar had filled up. Two Portuguese men were arguing at the tops of their voices. One was accusing the other of having robbed him. I never found out what he had stolen. Paulo Costa Pinto / Jean Mpuanga stood up. He took some money out of his pocket and put it on the table, next to his empty glass.

'I've got to go. My wife's expecting me for dinner.'

'You married again?'

'I was never married before.'

He held out his hand.

'I've enjoyed talking to you very much, Mr Journalist. Have a good night.'

I looked at him, scandalised.

'You can't leave me here without telling me what happened to the plane.'

'I don't know.'

'What do you mean, you don't know?'

'I never wanted to know. When Padilla found me, when he realised I'd travelled as a stowaway, albeit an involuntary one, he reacted badly. He shouted at me, that is, he shouted at Jean. He nearly killed me. But then he decided to help me. I mean, to help that guy, Jean.'

'And did he?'

'I owe him everything. I owe this new life to him.'

'Can I talk to your friend?'

'Padilla is travelling.'

'When's he back?'

'Forget it. He won't want to talk to you.'

'Why not?'

'You know very well why not.'

'I promise not to publish anything. I give you my word of honour. I just want to know what happened.'

'What's your email address?'

I took a card out of my trouser pocket. I always carry a dozen of them around with me. I chose one that looked less worn than the rest, smoothed it out, and handed it to the mechanic.

'You promise you'll talk to Padilla?'

'I will.'

'I'm relying on you.'

Jean hugged me, holding me tight against his strong chest, as if I were an old friend. Then he turned his back on me and left. I sat at the counter and ordered a Coke. The night was swirling, beyond the door of the bar, and now it was as noisy and dirty as nights in Luanda.

No, I wouldn't like living here.

21.

Dear Daniel,

The ancient Greeks, like the Chinese and the Hebrews, had no word for the colour blue. To all of those people the sea was green, brownish or wine-coloured. Sometimes black. In Western painting the sea only started to be portrayed as blue in the fifteenth century. The sky wasn't blue, either. Poets described it as pink, at dawn; aflame, at twilight; milky, on melancholy winter mornings.

Maybe it's names that give things their existence. Isn't that what the Bible says? 'In the beginning was the word and the word was with God and the word was God.'

I'm imagining a secret society of powerful demiurges. I can see them over the centuries blending in with the crowds, on their fantastical mission, going from village to village, spreading names in the most varied languages – and, as these languages are enriched, so the universe gains colour and complexity.

Contradicting the above theory, I feel that what happens often in my soul is a tumult of feelings that have never been named. Perhaps they'll become common, many years from now, when somebody names them. For now, though, I'm like a painter who, at the heart of the Middle Ages, chooses a particular shade of blue to colour the sea. This before the word blue existed. As they stare at this painter's canvas, looking at those waves in that impossible colour, the people are unable to hide their surprise and their horror. I imagine if you knew what was going on in my soul you'd feel a similar revulsion. You and everybody else.

I'm somebody who's arrived too early. Imagine another woman wandering about among the dinosaurs. I'm that woman. A monster – or so the dinosaurs would say.

This morning I awoke with that certainty and I wanted to share it with you before you arrived. I received your poems. I'm not the person you're inventing in them (we always invent the people we love). It's more complicated than that: I'm a person you could not invent. I'm beyond your imagination. I did, however, like the poems. I liked feeling, just for a few moments, that I was that other woman who inspired you.

Kisses,

　　　Moira

22.

The driver who took me to Natal, Arzílio Takimoto, killed a man. Two lads got into the taxi one rainy Sunday. One of them sat on the passenger seat to his right. The other behind him. They asked for some vague address in one of the most run-down neighbourhoods on the outskirts of Greater Recife. When they arrived, the lad sitting in the back seat held a knife to Arzílio's neck:

'You lose, old timer! Don't move a muscle . . .'

Arzílio took hold of the blade with his right hand, pulling it away from his neck, and with his left he shot a violent punch at the nose of the guy sitting beside him. The poor wretch brought his hands to his face, which was covered in blood, opened the door and ran off. The other boy pulled the knife free and stabbed it five times into the driver's thick back, before the man managed to undo his seat belt, turn around, and elbow him so hard that he broke his two upper canines. The attacker dropped the knife and escaped out of the right-hand window. Arzílio followed him in the car across a huge patch of open ground covered in trash and creeping vegetation until he hit him. He got out of the car and approached the body lying on the ground.

'My leg!' whimpered the young man. 'You broke my leg!'

Arzílio kicked him in the chin. He held down his neck with his left boot and with the right he started to stamp on his head, once, twice, three times, till the kid had stopped moving.

'When I left him, he no longer had a face.'

The streets of Natal followed on from one another, deserted and identical. The night enclosed them, totally still, as though it had always been there and never intended to leave. Once we reached the hotel, Arzílio helped me get the suitcases out of the trunk and then took off his shirt to show me the scars. He also had marks on the palm of his right hand and on his fingers. He told me he'd lost more than fifty kilos since that violent Sunday. Even so, he was still vast and solid as a baobab tree. I said goodbye to him and went inside. A clock hanging from the wall, over the reception desk, said 02.17. The hotel was called the Alma, a name whose meaning – 'soul' – was totally unsuited to the building, a glass tower without any personality or the vaguest trace of sentiment. I opened the door of my room and sat down on the bed, anguished. I noticed a screen print on the wall, of a dragon breathing fire. It reminded me of something. I took the card Arzílio had given me out of my pocket, looked at it a few seconds, thought about throwing it in the trash but didn't do it. I was ashamed of myself. Karinguiri wouldn't have listened to Arzílio's story in silence. She'd have objected. She'd have demanded that the driver stop the car. She'd have got out, dragging her suitcase with her, into the vast darkness, and she'd be left there laughing to herself – and her laughter would move the stars.

I suddenly missed my daughter, and with that feeling came a sharp pang of remorse. I'd failed as a father. I hadn't been able to protect her.

I undressed and lay down. On the other side of the wall I heard a woman moaning. To begin with it was a prolonged lament, but it quickly gained in intensity to become a hoarse howl, then convulsed crying, and finally a triumphant laugh. I heard a man's voice in a pointless entreaty:

'Quiet! Quiet! You're going to wake everybody up!'

Then came silence.

The next morning, I woke with a slight headache. I went down to reception. Breakfast was being served in an adjacent room. I chose a table by the window. I ordered a crêpe with ham, cheese and tomato. I was finishing the dish when Moira came in. She had covered her tall hairdo in a huge turban in effusive shades of blue and red, and she was wearing a very short dress in the same colours. She approached me with a smile. I got up and hugged her.

'So here you are,' she said. 'I didn't really believe you'd come.'

'What number room are you?'

Moira sat down. She crossed her long legs in a practised movement. She smiled, her eyes meeting mine.

'You like it?'

'Very much.'

'I'm not staying in this hotel any more. I've moved to Hélio's house.'

I got up. I poured myself some coffee. My hands were trembling. I sat back down.

'And the machine? That machine for filming dreams?'

'Amazing! You've got to see it for yourself. I'm working with them, with Hélio's team. For me, it's an artistic project. It's going to keep me busy for many months. Maybe years.'

She told me, her eyes shining, waving the metal blue of her nails before my own dazzled eyes, that she had spent the previous days painting watercolours. She'd painted animals, plants, all kinds of objects, atmospheric phenomena, rivers, waves, geographic accidents. The watercolours were then digitised, and collected up in a huge image bank. First, Hélio studies the brain activity of sleeping volunteers. The volunteers are woken at very short intervals. Each time, they recount what they have been dreaming. The neuroscientist and his assistants look for patterns that might be associated with different images. The data is inputted into a computer. Finally, reversing this process, it is possible to produce short films from the cerebral activity of somebody dreaming.

'I still don't believe it!'

Moira laughed. My disbelief seemed to please her.

'Up till now, they have been using photos taken from the internet. What came out of this weren't exactly films, but successions of disconnected images. With watercolours and a decent computer, it's possible to achieve a certain fluidity. Some kind of movement. They're still very imperfect films, but they're films.'

'I'll believe it when I see it.'

'You will. But for that, you can't sleep tonight. You'll have to arrive at the lab tomorrow in a sleep-deprived state. They'll hook you up to a machine, you fall asleep, and they'll record your dreams.'

'I don't know if I want to do this.'

'That's the only way you're going to know if it works.'

I had to agree. I finished my coffee.

'Right. I'm in!'

Moira smiled.

'Can I ask how you plan to stay awake for the next twenty-four hours?'

'Reading. Writing. Drinking coffee.'

'Reading?! You wouldn't prefer to have me help you, to get through that whole cruel eternity?'

I held her gaze, trying to work out whether or not she was joking. Moira held mine, her smile still in place. That morning she took me to Lagoa de Pitangui, a lagoon some thirty kilometres from Natal. We had lunch around there, sitting at a table partly submerged in the water. That afternoon we went to see the Cajueiro de Pirangi. The state of Rio Grande do Norte takes an inordinate pride in this particular tree. This specimen, which is really two, or maybe even more, is claimed to be the biggest in the world. Moira curled herself around me while we walked beneath the green noise of the vast and multiple tree.

She kissed me on the lips.

'Do you still dream about me?'

I said no, I'd never dreamed about her again. It did seem to me, however, that wherever she was, reality was shadowed and distorted, just like in dreams.

'It's as if there can be no reality, where you are. Just like the way nature abhors a vacuum, reality can't abide you. You're a kind of orchid in human form.'

She looked at me, surprised.

'Should I take that as a compliment or an insult?'

I shrugged.

'I don't know.'

We had dinner at a small Japanese restaurant. It was midnight when we got to the hotel. Moira came up with me. She accompanied me into the room.

'What about Hélio?' I asked as her fingers moved inside my shirt and pinched my nipples.

Moira raised her eyebrows.

'What about him?'

I didn't answer. I lowered the straps of her dress, kissed her breasts, and once again I was overcome with a feeling of having experienced this exact moment before. Some piece seemed to have been broken or become corrupted in the meticulous gears of time. It was as though it was jumping, going back, stopping, then leaping forwards a few minutes. There I was in the bed, with Moira laughing, eyes closed, at a gallop, on top of me. Her whispering obscene words in my ear. And before this – or after this – me holding her hips, marvelling at the glow that was coming off her. Behind us, the dragon breathing fire. Laughter, again. There was a point at which I fell asleep, or thought I was falling asleep, but Moira immediately shook me, shook me, impatiently.

'Don't sleep! You mustn't sleep!'

I got up to open the windows, because it had become impossible to breathe inside the room. A breeze came in. A bewildered little light came in. I saw Moira kneeling on the bed, smiling, stroking her sex.

'Come!'

In the taxi, on the way to the sleep lab, Moira kissed me lightly on the forehead. She made an effort to tidy my hair a bit, which was growing in all directions, as if trying to flee from my head.

'Give us a smile. You don't look like someone who hasn't slept – you look like someone who hasn't even woken up yet.'

Hélio met us at the door of the sleep lab, a small white building flanked by a pair of tall palm trees. Inside floated a colourless, merciless light, like the one which no doubt illuminates the souls in Purgatory. I lay down on a small folding bed. A freckly red-headed woman attached a web of wires to my head.

'Relax,' said Hélio.

I was nodding with sleepiness. I looked at the woman's face. Her freckles were spinning, on her very white skin, like minuscule crabs dancing on the sand of a beach. A shadow passed across the brightness and I realised it was a great hound. I woke up. Hélio was looking at me.

'What were you dreaming about?'

'A dog, a wild dog . . .'

'Cool. Go back to sleep.'

A train. A train making its way through a dark forest. I'm there, but apart from everything. Trees passed us, whose names I didn't know, and all of them ignored me. There were people sitting in front of me, but they were faceless.

'And now? What were you dreaming about?'

'I can't describe it. I was on my way to Berlin, on a train.

I remember two men, in front of me, they didn't have faces . . .'

'Right. And relax . . .'

'One of us will destroy the other –' I heard the voice and turned around. I saw the old man standing against the sunset. He was incredibly tall, dressed all in black, and even though I couldn't see his legs, because the man was in long trousers, I knew they were made of glass.

'Did you dream?'

'Yes. A really tall man. A man with glass legs. I shot him in the legs.'

Round about the tenth time Hélio woke me up, I started to get annoyed. I said it might be best to suspend the experiment. He smiled. He made me drink a slightly sweet infusion that tasted of mint and of honey. This time it took me longer to fall asleep. I dreamed that I was waking up with a terrible itching in my shoulder blades, and that soon I was growing wings. My mother thought I was being transformed into an angel. My father disagreed with her, shouting:

'He's an ostrich! Can't you see he's an ostrich?!'

Then I dreamed that I was having an affair with a pair of Jamaican contortionist twins. I was travelling with them. I folded the twins up carefully to pack them in my suitcase. Halfway through the trip I took the twins out of the suitcase and had sex with both of them.

'I dreamed of a pair of twins,' I tried to explain when Hélio woke me up. 'They were contortionist twins. They came out of a suitcase.'

Finally, I awoke of my own accord. I checked my watch: 12.32.

I realised that once they had exploited me to the maximum, stealing all my dreams, they'd decided to allow me to sleep. I struggled to my feet, in a daze, and went off to look for Hélio and Moira. I found them in the building's small bar. They were sitting at one of the tables. They didn't see me come in. Hélio was leaning forwards, holding on to the Mozambican artist's narrow wrists. He looked shocked, as though he'd just learned, from her, some dreadful news.

They saw me. Moira pulled her hands free. Hélio jumped to his feet.

'Ah! You woke up!'

'I'm not sure.'

'I'm grateful for your patience. One guy tried to thump me when I woke him up for the thirty-sixth time.'

'I can understand that. What you people do is torture. Somebody trying to hit you is the strangest thing that's happened?'

'Oh, no, we've had some really weird situations.'

'How do you know people aren't lying when they say they've been dreaming about this or that?'

'In some cases, it's possible to check. For example, you said you dreamed about a dog, a wild dog, and that tallies with the data we had already, because other people have also dreamed about dogs before now. Sometimes, the dreamers do lie. They get embarrassed—'

'Erotic dreams,' Moira interrupted him, smiling.

'Yes, erotic dreams do happen, but not only that. Imagine you dream you're committing some horrendous crime. You probably wouldn't want to tell us that dream.'

'But you can find out by watching the movies.'

'Yes, you're right, sometimes we find out.'

'Don't you feel like a kind of voyeur?'

Hélio laughed.

'Oh, definitely, but I'd rather call myself a dream watcher.'

I remembered what Moira had said in Cape Town:

'You mean like a birdwatcher?'

The woman got up.

'You must be exhausted, my Angolan friend. Let's get some lunch and then I'll take you to your hotel.'

Hélio proffered his hand.

'Thank you again.' Then he took an envelope out of his jacket pocket. 'Before I forget. This arrived for you.'

I recognised the writing. Hossi Apolónio Kaley had tracked me down. I thanked Hélio, folded the envelope and put it in my trouser pocket. I had lunch with Moira in a small by-the-kilo restaurant and then we called a taxi. Minutes later, in bed, she said:

'It's hard to tell a lie when we're naked.'

Since both of us were naked, her words sounded genuine to me.

Moira went on:

'You know that's how it is. All lovers know that. Torturers, too.'

'Which is why torturers strip their victims?'

'Exactly. It reminds me of this Israeli researcher, Edith Spencer Cohen. She says men lie much more in the cold months, when they're covered up with clothes – coats, scarves, hats. Women lie only slightly less during hot months. In general, we women lie a lot. Really so much more than men. We also talk more. We use on average twenty thousand words per day. For you it's something like seven thousand. A thousand of those are curse words . . .'

I burst out laughing.

'Seriously?'

'We lie because we're complex beings. A lie is a work of art that those who are simple-minded can never really master.'

'I agree. Telling a lie, doing it well, with imagination and elegance, that's a manifestation of intelligence and sophistication. Otherwise, I've always thought the truth very overrated. In democracy there isn't one truth, there are versions. In a dictatorship, well, yes, then there's only one truth – the official version!'

'I don't believe it! Are you saying you're in favour of lying?'

'You started it . . .'

'I didn't. I started saying that I wouldn't lie to you because we're naked, and it's hard to lie when we're naked. And I hope you won't lie to me. If you do, I'll know.'

'Deal.'

She sat down on top of my chest.

'Was it true, what you said the other day, that you'd dreamed you were in bed with me, in this bed, in this actual hotel?'

'It's true. Back in Cape Town. I dreamed about us. I dreamed about that dragon on the wall . . .'

'And all the other dreams?'

'True. I swear on my daughter's good health.'

'You know what Hélio thinks about your foreshadowing dreams?'

'You haven't told him about my dreams about you, I hope?'

'I've told him about the others.'

'Just as well. Either way, I'm not interested in Hélio's theories . . .'

'Well, you ought to hear them.'

Time is a dimension, just like length or breadth or height. And so it makes no sense to say that time passes. It doesn't pass. It is. We are only able to travel along it in one direction – the direction of entropy, of destruction – but that doesn't mean it runs out. It just means that we're moving forwards. A road doesn't disappear as we get further along it. That big baobab tree on the side of this road existed before we passed it and will continue to exist after we've left it behind. In this way, according to Hélio, it might be possible for us to remember future events, if they're very important or very traumatic. It might be that we experience, just occasionally, brief memories of people we haven't met yet, but who are going to mark our lives profoundly.

'Hélio believes that certain people, like you, have developed a special aptitude for remembering the future,' concluded Moira. 'He thinks you remember me because I'm going to be – because I am! – someone who's very important in your life.'

'And you believe this?'

'I do like the idea.'

'Of being an important person in my life?'

'I like the idea that you can remember somebody I haven't yet become. I look at myself in your eyes, like looking in a magic mirror, and I see who I'm going to be.'

It was only when the sun was already high in the sky, after Moira had left the room, that I remembered the letter Hélio had given me.

23.

Luanda, 24 October 2016

My dear fellow countryman,

You must be wondering why I'm writing you a letter, a real letter, on good paper, when we live in the age of email and immaterial communication. First, because I'm a man of another century, the same age as you but so very much older, so old that I'd rather write by hand than type on a computer. I like the smell of paper and permanent ink. And then, because I don't want the thought police to read what I'm writing now. You should believe it, my friend, they're watching us both. They rummage through all our email. And so I've written this letter and handed it to a friend travelling today to São Paulo. I asked him once he's disembarked to mail it.

I didn't understand why you left, running, as if you were fleeing from the Devil, on that damn afternoon. Did you really think I was going to kill the man?

There were no bullets in the gun.

I didn't tell you because I needed your shock – I needed your shock to be authentic to create the mise en scène. It worked. Our Mr Jamal, or Ezequiel, whatever his name is, hasn't bothered me again.

What scares me is these holes in my memory. Somebody comes towards me and I don't know if they're an old friend coming to hug me or a somebody with a grudge and a gun in their hand. So as a matter of survival I treat everybody as my enemies.

I wanted to apologise, in case I upset you.

However, the apology wasn't the reason I decided to write you these lines. I'm doing it because I learned, visiting my nephew, that a few days from now he and his companions are planning to start a hunger strike. They're demanding to be released, with no conditions. They'll only eat again the moment they get out of prison. I left the place really troubled. The President won't give way. I don't believe the kids will, either. It's going to be a tragedy. Somebody has got to persuade them to give it up. Unfortunately, the only person they listen to is your daughter. I'm hoping that your daughter listens to you. Meanwhile, I've started thinking about some kind of operation to free them. An operation more closely connected to my military experience and the glorious tradition of 4th February than to your ideals (yours and those of the kids). Pacifism, my dear brother, is like mermaids: it can only breathe in the sea of fantasy, reality doesn't suit it. Let alone this reality of ours today, which is so very cruel. Angola is no place for the faint of heart.

Please, my friend, come back as soon as you can. The struggle continues.

Sending you a hug –

Hossi Apolónio Kaley

24.

Arzílio Takimoto was waiting for me at the hotel reception, at six-thirty in the morning. He put my suitcase into the trunk of his taxi and then opened the door for me, smiling:

'So did you like Natal, senhor?'

'I don't know yet.'

On the drive back, I reread Hossi's letter. Everything about it terrified me: the conspiratorial tone; the warning about the cops; the revos' declared intention to begin a hunger strike; the grim, and probably correct, prediction that the President would ignore the situation; the determination to organise another 4th February, that is, an attack on the prisons like the one that tried to release a group of nationalists in Luanda back in '61. Not only were no nationalists released, but forty guerrilla fighters were killed. The date is commemorated in Angola as the start of the armed liberation struggle against Portuguese colonialism.

The telephone beeped, announcing the arrival of a new message into my mailbox. It was a telephone number in Pernambuco: *Padilla is prepared to talk to you.*

Jean Mpuanga!

I called him.

'Hello? I'm in a cab, on my way back to Recife. I'm flying late this afternoon to Rio, and from there I'm going back to Luanda.'

'Man, that's a shame – Padilla arrived yesterday, but he's leaving again after lunch. It would have to be before two p.m.'

I sighed, on edge.

'Got it. OK, I'll try and see if I can change my flight.'

I called a travel agent in Recife, with whom I'd spoken just hours earlier begging her to bring the flight forward by three days. She didn't bother to hide her irritation.

'Really, senhor, would you please make up your mind!'

Half an hour later I had managed to change the flight again, to the following day. Arzílio left me at the door of the Hotel Nassau. I gave him a good tip. Cain greeted me with a broad smile.

'You came back, senhor?'

'Just for one night, Cain.'

'You aren't going to want a girl?'

'No. Just a room.'

I left my suitcase with him and walked over to the Bar Burburinho. I found Jean at the table where I'd seen him for the first time. He was with a short, stocky man, with very smooth black hair, a square face, big gentle eyes. Both men stood up as I arrived. Jean shook my hand, warmly, while he introduced me to his companion:

'Charles Padilla, the greatest aeroplane thief in the world . . . Daniel Benchimol, the greatest investigative journalist in Angola . . .'

Padilla smiled, uncomfortably.

'It wasn't a theft . . .'

The three of us sat down.

'It wasn't a theft!' Padilla insisted, more firmly now.

I took advantage of the cue:

'So what was it?'

'You might call it a recovery.'

'Excuse me?'

'The plane's original owner, a small company in Miami, Cheyenne Airlines, hired me to recover it. Do you know an Angolan general by the name of Amável Guerreiro?'

I knew the story. Amável Guerreiro had become a businessman after the end of the war. Many other generals did the same. First, he invested in a fleet of lorries. Then he decided to create an airline. It seemed like a good business to be in at the time. The general went to the United States, evaluated various options, and finally opted to buy a Boeing 727, in good condition even though it had many flying hours behind it, from Cheyenne Airlines. He paid the first agreed instalment and Cheyenne Airlines commissioned Charles Padilla, an American of Cuban heritage, to pilot the plane to Luanda. However, in one of those cruel ironies at which life always surpasses fiction, the general died in a helicopter crash in Huambo just days after the deal was completed. His children argued with each other and the plane ended up being left forgotten on the runway, in Angola, accumulating fines and parking charges.

I listened attentively to Padilla. The information tallied with what I had discovered for myself, all those years ago.

'It was a short flight,' Padilla went on. 'I took the plane to a runway somewhere in the interior of the Congo, where there was another general waiting for me, also a businessman – but not Angolan, this one was Congolese – who handed me a small box. I checked the contents of the box, and then I hitched a ride to Kinshasa.'

'We hitched a ride,' said Jean.

'Right, we did. By the time I realised I was carrying a stowaway, it was too late. I told the Congolese that Jean was my business partner. If I'd told the truth . . .'

Jean Mpuanga laughed.

'If you'd told the truth, I wouldn't be here. They'd have hacked my body into pieces with katanas. Those people don't mess around when they're on duty.'

'Jean helped me a lot in Kinshasa,' Padilla continued. 'If it hadn't been for him, I suspect I never would have made it out. I still wake up in the middle of the night with terrible nightmares. Well, it's the same nightmare, really. I'm there, in Kinshasa airport, trying to board a flight for the U.S., I go up the stairs to the plane, but then a soldier comes and drags me away.'

I wanted to know what was in the box.

'What box?'

'You said that the Congolese general gave you a small box.'

'Diamonds, what else could it have been? Finally, we managed to get a flight to Paris. I returned to Miami, handed over the diamonds, received my share, and used that money to invest in a small air-taxi firm here in Brazil. We've only got two small planes. I fly one of them myself. It isn't a big business, but it's enough to pay the bills. I called Jean to help me with the aeroplane maintenance. He's an excellent mechanic.'

'Can I publish what you've told me?'

'You can. I've done nothing wrong. I'm not a criminal.'

I stood up. I'd managed to get my story. To tell the truth, it wasn't as interesting as most of the fictions that had been woven around the plane's disappearance. A young Pakistani businessman, in a Chinese-run underground casino in Luanda, had assured me the Boeing had been stolen by Islamic fundamentalists.

'They're going to fly the plane into an American warship. Boom! It's going to be a huge success, my friend, big world news.'

Years later, at a wedding in Benguela, at the house of the groom's parents, I spent hours talking to an old-time nationalist, who had been imprisoned by the Portuguese and almost lost an eye during a series of brutal interrogations. He was a scrawny man with completely white hair, but his skin was still smooth and shiny, stretched over his cheekbones like a leather drum-skin. The old man dragged me by the arm over to a corner of the yard and there, the two of us hidden behind five or six healthy banana trees, he burst into a violent speech against the President and his entourage, accusing him of having betrayed the ideals of Mário Pinto de Andrade and Viriato da Cruz and looting the country like common criminals. At one point, he brought his mouth close to my ear. The powerful stench of alcohol nearly knocked me over.

'Remember that plane that disappeared, the jumbo?'

'It wasn't a jumbo, senhor, it was a 727. The jumbo, the Boeing 747, is much bigger.'

'Listen, kid, it was a jumbo. It was a jumbo. I know very well it was a jumbo. But even if it was a 727, or a 747, or even 007 himself – the point is, it disappeared, and I hear you're interested in finding out how . . .'

'Yes, yes, of course.'

'Well, I'll tell you. Do you know Pascal Adibe . . . ?'

'Naturally. He's that former arms dealer, French or Colombian, I'm not sure, now naturalised Angolan, and our ambassador to the Vatican . . .'

'He's one of the President's henchmen . . .'

'He's just a front.'

'Front, back, whatever – a total bastard. Anyway, the plane went to Darfur, loaded up with weapons, on Comrade Adibe's orders.'

Alexandre Pitta-Gróz would be happy if I gave him one of those versions. No matter, I thought, he was just going to have to be satisfied with the truth.

'I talked to General Amável Guerreiro two or three times.' Padilla said this while holding out his hand to me, to say goodbye. 'He was a very odd man.'

'Insane!' Jean interrupted him. 'He was insane – confirmed, signed and sealed. He spent some time interned in Cuba, in a mental asylum. He was hearing voices.'

'Yeah, he'd been hearing voices. He told me that when he was locked up in Cuba, all the lunatics dreamed about an angel with purple wings and that the angel would give them advice. The angel had advised him to buy an aeroplane . . .'

'The general told you that?'

'Yes, that's how he explained the purchase of the plane.'

'And the guy all the lunatics dreamed about, what was his name?'

The two men exchanged a look. Then they looked at me as though seeing me for the first time, and as if I had an impressive rhino horn bursting out of my forehead.

'What was whose name, the angel's?'

'The man in purple.'

Padilla shook his head:

'You're joking, right?'

I got up again. I forced a smile.

'Sorry . . .'

As I walked into the hotel, just minutes later, I found Cain talking to a somewhat cross-eyed young woman, with crooked teeth, who smiled at me as though I were a prince.

'Valquíria really likes you, senhor.'

'Valquíria doesn't know me.'

The girl straightened up. She put her hands on her waist and pushed her chest forwards. She had breasts in full bloom, round and hard, which her very low-cut T-shirt revealed quite unambiguously.

'I don't, but I'd really like to get to know you.'

My response was brusque.

'That won't be happening today.'

I leaped up the stairs, two at a time, opened the door and dropped onto my bed. Lying on my back, I could see a piece of sky through the window. Hours earlier, when I'd woken with my arms around Moira, my right hand holding her left breast, I had been dreaming about an identical cloud. In my dream, a young Mucubal, called General Popular Resurrection, was crossing the Namib desert carrying a long stepladder. He was walking adrift, alone, across the vastness. From time to time he would unfold the ladder, plant it firmly in the sand, climb up to the top step, and weave small white clouds out of his own saliva.

I got up and walked over to the window.

I closed the window.

25.

I went to visit Sabino. I arrived at the prison disgusted, and left even worse. I was so stressed I managed to get lost on my way home. I stopped the car and went into some cheap joint and ordered a beer. I didn't want to talk to anybody. I needed to breathe.

Just breathe.

I asked Sabino how he was. He didn't talk about himself. He started to unfold an account of other people's sufferings. One of the guys is doing real badly, he said – malaria. 'Please, uncle, I need you to get me some medicine.' Another was suffering from diarrhoea. A third had his glasses broken by the guards, out of pure malice, and without his glasses he could see very little, he couldn't read. Then he went on to enumerate the problems of those imprisoned for common crimes, with whom the revos had formed a friendship.

'And you?' I interrupted him. 'I want to know how you're doing.'

The boy raised an eyebrow, surprised.

'I'm fine, uncle. I'm strong.'

I put my hand on his forehead. I lowered my voice. I told him not to worry.

'I'm going to get you all out of here.'

'How's that going to happen?'

'I've talked to a few of the guys, from the days of the struggle . . .'

'No, uncle! Please, not that!'

'You don't want to get out?'

'Not through violence. Please, promise me you won't try anything crazy.'

They're going to start a hunger strike, he told me. They're sure a hunger strike will wake people up, even a lot of the people who're still supporting the regime, showing that it's possible to resist without firing a gun. I tried to talk him out of it:

'You're a kid. You don't know what you're talking about. The men who are in power have no heart. If you open up their chests all you'll find will be hundred-dollar bills. Wads and wads of banknotes.'

'Everybody's got a heart, uncle.'

I got annoyed. I raised my voice.

'You think you're going to save the country?'

He looked at me very seriously. He looked just like my father.

'If we're going to save Angola, no one must be left out. It's a challenge we need to face together. All of us together.'

I was there in that cheap joint, with Sabino's words still echoing in my head, when I sensed somebody sitting down beside me. I looked up from my beer. It was 20Kill. I noticed his small hands, with their polished nails, his hair, close-cropped, so precisely it looked like it had been drawn with ruler and compass.

'Something the matter, brigadier?'

'What are you doing here?'

'I was out for a stroll. It's part of my job – going out for a stroll. So I was out for a stroll when I saw you, and I decided to give you a piece of advice. Since the war ended you've led a good life. We've treated you well, haven't we? We've been very generous towards the defeated. Nothing like it has ever before been seen in the painful history of the world. Even in Cuba, where you were living at our great nation's expense, recovering from your dangerous emotional mess, eating and drinking the best that money could buy. Then you came back to your birthplace and opened that tiny hotel of yours out in Cabo Ledo. And I ask you – where did all that filthy cash come from?'

'I got a loan from a bank.'

'And who do they belong to, the banks in this fine country of ours? Who does everything belong to? Listen to me, pal, we've been patient. We've closed our eyes to certain irregular situations . . .'

'What situations?'

'The hotel is built practically on the beach. That's not allow, man, the beach is pubic land.'

'Public, for fuck's sake. Can't you pronounce any of our national languages properly?'

The guy looked at me, confused.

'Portuguese is the only language I speak.'

'Then you've got to pronounce it properly. Your Portuguese is a total wreck.'

The guy took a deep breath.

'Like I said before, Senhor Hossi, with all due respect, I've just come to give you a piece of advice – don't get yourself mix up in the politics. Right now, you shouldn't be seen with that journalist, the one who's always in a bad mode. The crazy girl's father. He's real bad company. *And talk to your nephew. Talk to him proper. You got to convince him not to get into more trouble. This hunger strike business, for example, if that goes ahead it'll be real demoralising for the country. It's not worth it . . .'*

'Sabino doesn't listen to me.'

'Well, make him.'

He said this, gave a quick nod of his tiny head with its so delicately combed hair, and disappeared. I finished my drink, paid and left. It was deep night outside. The darkness was roaring down the streets. I ran to my car. I felt my skull splitting, as if there was another night, an even more ancient one, expanding in my brain, struggling to get out. I thought, terrified, that maybe all that dense blackness was coming out from inside me, coming out my ears, my nose, my lips, as I breathed. I was exhaling the night, without meaning to, just like all those poor prisoners once did, in my hands, pissing, secreting blood, sweat and fear.

I drove down hostile roads almost blindly, until finally the weak light of a gas lamp illuminated a bend in the road that I recognised.

It's two in the morning now. I just arrived home a few minutes ago. I had a hot bath. I took two Xanax. I loaded the Glock. It's under the bed, at arm's reach.

Friday, 4 November 2016

I've written to Daniel Benchimol, telling him about my visit to the prison. If he can't persuade Karinguiri to cancel the hunger strike, I'm scared a tragedy might happen.

This morning a miracle happened. I was at the beach, pretending to fish, focusing on the luminous movement of the waters and the beautiful sound that the small waves make as they break against the sand. So much light. So many eternities following one another beneath the sun. Then I heard footsteps behind me and I turned around. A woman was standing there, about thirty metres away. When I looked at her, she dropped to her knees, covering her lips with her hands, as if trying to contain a scream. I let go of the fishing rod and jumped to my feet. It took me eighteen years to run those thirty metres. I knelt down beside her, and there we stayed, the two of us, in that position, crying in each other's arms.

26.

The TAAG flight leaves Rio de Janeiro for Luanda at 9.45 p.m.
I arrived at Galeão airport in Rio, coming in from Recife, at
around 5 p.m., I checked in, passed through border control,
and sat down to wait for my departure. I closed my eyes. Once
again I saw General Popular Resurrection wandering, winged,
across the infinite sands. I saw the big scarlet vulvas of the wel-
witschia plants, and their tentacles calcined but still alive. The
plants watched General Popular Resurrection without surprise,
without curiosity. They'd been there for four hundred years,
six hundred years, some of them a thousand years, holding the
sky onto the ground with their incredibly deep, nail-straight
roots. These plants' ancestors had breathed the same air as
the dinosaurs. Being so ancient, nothing surprises them. The
phone woke me. Lucrécia! I closed my eyes again. I didn't want
to answer. I couldn't bear hearing that damn voice, so bitter
and imperious. And yet I did answer. As soon as I'd said hello,
she started to cry. It was as if she were holding me, her head buried in my chest, so I could feel the scent of her hair, her hot hands
stuck to my back, the dampness of her tears on my shirt.

'Our girl's going to die,' she moaned.

I got up. I ran over into a corner, to hide. I didn't want the other passengers to see me crying.

'Nonsense, Lucrécia. That's not going to happen.'

'She's not eating. She doesn't want to eat anything. They're on hunger strike!'

'Already? I didn't think that was happening for a few more days . . . !'

'So you knew? You knew about it and didn't tell me anything?!'

'I'm in the airport, in Rio. As soon as I get off the plane, first thing I'll do is go to the prison to talk to her.'

Which I did. Armando Carlos was waiting for me. I went home, took a shower, we had lunch in an open-air restaurant, a place my friend liked to go, and then he accompanied me to the prison. At the entrance, seeing my ID, the guard frowned. He picked up the phone and made a call.

'You're going to have to wait, gentlemen. You can sit outside.'

We sat down on a stone bench, on a narrow patio hemmed in by high walls, in the lace-patterned shade of an old cashew. The top of the tree, its crooked branches in disarray, seemed to be playing tag with the sun. Chickens pecked about distractedly on the dusty ground. A huge lady, wrapped in colourful cloths, came over and hugged me. She introduced herself.

'I'm Dona Filó, Lila's mother. Karinguiri looks like you, she's got your nose, though if I'm honest I think she's much more beautiful. No offence – she's taken after her mother, even the colour of her skin. But the boys tell me she's got your heart. You must be very proud of her.'

'Yes. I am.'

'Be strong! We need to learn to summon up our courage from our children,' she said, then left.

I didn't know who Lila was. As soon as Dona Filó had gone inside, I asked Armando. My friend got annoyed:

'Seriously, you don't know who Lila is?'

'Sorry, no. Should I?'

'Of course you should. You should know the names of all the revos who were arrested with your daughter. Lila Monteiro is a singer. She's Bogeyman's girlfriend.'

'One of them is called Bogeyman?!'

'It's one of his names. Good kid. He's worked with me.'

'He was an actor?'

'Yeah, he was an actor. Then at a certain point, he got into rap. He became a very famous rapper. Hated by the regime. The problem is that you, and a lot of people like you, may *be* here in Luanda, but you don't live here, with us. You don't suffer with us.'

'This is me you're talking to, Armando. It's not like I'm Lucrécia!'

'You're not Lucrécia, I know that. But you also don't live here. You stay shut up in your house reading your books. You go out less and less. In the old days, you used to immerse yourself in the real Angola from time to time, at least to interview some poor bastard or other. You don't even do that now.'

'That's not true.'

'It is. In the last few years, the only things you've done as a journalist have been interviewing writers and artists, almost all of them foreigners, or living abroad. Do you have friends in the neighbourhood?'

'No.'

'No. Right.'

'You know I don't have many friends.'

Armando put his hand on my shoulder:

'I'm your friend.'

Then Armando told me about the revos. The magnificent seven, as some of the papers were calling them. Five lads and two girls. One of them was my daughter. The other, Lila Monteiro, aged twenty-five, is a singer in a rock band. She was born in Benguela and lives there most of the year. She became relatively well known not just as a singer, but also as the organiser of a heavy metal festival which, every September for the last five years, has brought together thousands of young people from several cities all around the country. I'd never heard of the festival. Lila's boyfriend is the oldest guy in the group, Ivan Teixeira, known as Ivan the Terrible or Bogeyman. Bogeyman is thirty years old, and besides being an actor and musician, is also a butcher.

Napoleão Pacavira, aged twenty-two, is a photographer. He started out working for a gossip mag belonging to one of the President's sons, before being sacked. He isn't proud of his past. He prefers to photograph demonstrations, strikes, protests, and everything that makes up what the revos call mass movements. For the last three years, he's been documenting the drama of people who've been turfed out of their homes by force as a result of property speculation. While Armando was talking about him, I recalled a Portuguese magazine where I saw a series of portraits, in black and white, of victims of forced demolitions. Yes, my friend was able to confirm, those were Napoleão's pictures. He won a prize for that piece of work.

The intellectual of the group is called Rubem Monteiro. He studied African literatures in Lisbon. He's published two books of poetry. He's produced Portuguese translations of a range of works on the techniques of peaceful resistance. He was at Tahrir Square in Cairo, in January 2011, at the start of the Arab Spring.

Semba Lopes is a stonemason. Two years ago, during one of the many demonstrations against the dictatorship, a giant nicknamed Exterminator split his forehead open with an iron bar. The thug in question was head of a militia, which called itself the Spontaneous Movement for Democracy, set up and supported by the Political Police. Semba kept on demonstrating, now with a scar dividing his forehead in two, a vertical line running down to his nose. He manufactures and sells his own T-shirts with slogans against the President.

Sabino Kaley, Hossi's oldest nephew, is twenty-five, and an electrician. He works for a firm that installs and repairs generators. It was originally his idea to storm the conference, interrupting the President's speech and flinging bloodstained thousand-dollar notes in the old dictator's frightened face. The notes were fake, the blood wasn't. It was Ivan the Terrible who had sourced the blood. Chicken's blood, it would seem.

'It was either that or make a nice risotto,' concluded Armando, and we both laughed.

A policeman interrupted us.

'Daniel Benchimol? The director would like to speak to you.'

They led us along a dark corridor to a small, austere room, where we were awaited by a man with broad shoulders and timid eyes. He got up to greet us. He held his hand out to me:

'I've read some of your articles. It's a pleasure to meet you, senhor.'

He asked us to sit down. He praised my daughter's fighting spirit, regretted the situation she found herself in. Then he gave a sigh, placed his hands on the desk and looked at his fingers as though expecting them to answer for me.

'Your daughter, senhor, as you know, insists on harming the image of this country. For the last three days, she's refused to eat any solid food. This regrettable eating disorder—'

'It's not an eating disorder,' Armando Carlos interrupted him. 'It's called a hunger strike, and it's a means of non-violent protest.'

'An eating disorder,' continued the director, ignoring my friend. 'A regrettable eating disorder, through which she has infected the other political dissidents – or perhaps I should say, the other dissident politicians. Your daughter, though she's very young, is the one who's leading this association of wrong-doers who made an attempt on the President's life.'

'They're political prisoners!' protested Armando.

The director glanced at him briefly. There was more irritation in his expression than fury. Then he went back to focusing on his own hands. When he continued speaking, his tone was slightly tense.

'I'd like you to talk to your daughter. Show her that this course of action could do her a great deal of harm. To her and all the others, too. Please, allow justice to take its usual course.

Justice mustn't be subject to pressure. Angola is a democratic country and follows the rule of law.'

'Is my daughter all right?'

'She's only drunk water for three days. She's been seen by a doctor. Yes, I think she's all right. The Angolan government is concerned for all its citizens, even the rebels, the arguers, the troublemakers.' He looked up at Armando Carlos. 'It is concerned even for the most ungrateful of its children. We are going to transfer the young people to the São Paulo prison-hospital, where they will be able to receive adequate medical assistance.'

Armando Carlos stood up.

'I know the São Paulo prison well. I spent three years there.'

The director didn't seem surprised.

'Well, Senhor Armando – whose work I have also been following – I hope you learned some lessons from that experience.'

'I certainly did. What doesn't kill us, makes us stronger.'

We went straight from there to the visitors' room, where Karinguiri was already waiting. She smiled when she saw us.

'So my father's brought the great actor with him. Such an honour.'

Armando Carlos gave a theatrical bow:

'The honour is all mine.'

We spent a good fifteen minutes chatting, as if we were sitting round the kitchen table, laughing together, remembering old jokes and anecdotes. When the laughter died down I put my sweating hands onto Karinguiri's nervous fingers.

'I'm worried about you, girl. Your mother is, too. I think

you've already achieved what you wanted to with this hunger strike, you've got the attention of the press, inside the country and outside. You can stop now, start eating again . . .'

'No. Getting the press's attention is good. But that's not the aim of our action.'

'What do you want?'

'We want to be free while we wait for our sentencing. Which, incidentally, we have a right to be. That's all.'

'What you've done, what you're doing now, requires huge courage,' said Armando with his radio announcer's voice. 'You know I was in prison, too, many years ago, with some of the other guys, other dreamers, and we also went on hunger strike. It didn't come to anything because in those days there were no social networks and we were completely cut off from the world. Nobody wanted anything to do with us. It's different today, there aren't those islands any more, information circulates now. The overwhelming majority of people, both in the country and abroad, are on your side. The regime will have to give way—'

'I'm not sure they're going to,' I interrupted him.

'They will. However, you must drink a lot of water, you have to stay well hydrated.'

'Armando, please . . .'

'Take it easy, my friend – let me speak. They want to send you all to the São Paulo prison, where I was, right after independence, and which has now been transformed into a prison-hospital. It's a good idea. You'll be all together there, and you'll get medical help. Accept it.'

'I understand, Uncle Armando,' said Karinguiri. 'We'll accept that.'

'A hunger strike is a means of struggle that requires discipline. For it to work, you have to stay healthy and lucid. The first few days demand immense willpower. You have that willpower, I don't know if the others are going to. You'll feel a lot of pain, because your organism will start to devour itself, first your muscles, then even your bones. You might suffer cardiac arrhythmia. You'll get very weak, any small infection might be dangerous. That's why it's important you're in a hospital bed, in a clean environment. And don't forget, you've got to drink a lot of water.'

'I will, Uncle Armando. And you please keep an eye on my dad.'

'I will.'

'And you, Dad – try and support Mum. Be patient with her.'

A police officer approached shyly. She bent down and murmured something in Karinguiri's ear.

'I'm really sorry, Dad. You guys are going to have to leave.'

She handed me a sheet of paper folded in four, which I tried to hide in my trouser pocket.

'Read this when you have the time.'

We walked out into the sun. I sat down, anguished, on the stone bench, in the shade of the cashew tree. Armando Carlos sat down to my right. He hugged me. A short while later we saw Dona Filó coming out. She sat on my other side (it took her a little while to settle there) and she hugged me, too.

27.

I travelled to Cabo Ledo two days after landing in Luanda. It was a Saturday. When I arrived, the sky was bleeding over the sea, not in its usual way but with a funereal halo around it, like an ill omen. I was surprised to find Hossi in the company of a well-fed woman, wide-hipped, round-faced, with a clear, frank smile. Hossi took her hand and led her towards me:

'I want to introduce you to Ava. I've told you a lot about her.'

It took me a few seconds to remember.

'Ava?! That's not possible . . .'

She greeted me with two kisses.

'*Encantada.*'

That night, as the three of us sat at a table with a sea view illuminated by a giant moon, Ava told me how after her husband's death, six months earlier, she had decided to leave Cuba and find Hossi.

'Nicolás died aged ninety-one. But no, he didn't die of old age, he was tough. He was healthy. He died of stupidity.'

The Spanish she spoke was very beautiful. She seemed younger when she spoke, too.

'Stupidity?' I asked. 'How so?'

'Nicolás liked playing cards with a group of other old men. One night on his way home he was surprised by a kid, a boy of fifteen, sixteen, who showed him a blade. Instead of handing over his watch, the only thing of value he had with him, Nicolás gave him a punch in the nose. Old fool.'

'Did he die right away?'

'Not immediately, no. They called me. He died in my arms, asking my forgiveness for the trouble, because he was getting blood on my new dress.'

Some days later, while sorting through her husband's things, Ava found a letter addressed to her. Nicolás, anticipating his death, not by stabbing, of course, but owing to his advanced age, was saying goodbye to her. He explained that he had a bit of money stashed away in a Spanish bank. Ava bought a ticket to Madrid. She spent a month in Spain, withdrew the money, and flew from there to Luanda.

'All those years, there wasn't one day I didn't think about my Angolan man. After Hossi disappeared I received a visit from a State Security agent.'

'Captain Pablo Pinto?' asked Hossi.

'Pablo Pinto?! No, his name was Juan Ernesto.'

'A short man, with John Lennon glasses?'

'That's right. Juan Ernesto. I knew him. He was married to a cousin of mine. He was put in prison two years later. For paedophilia. He died in prison. Another one of the prisoners killed him. But that's not relevant now. He showed up at my door. I was scared, because I could tell it was something to do with you. I didn't invite him in. He took off his hat – he was wearing a panama on his head, as if he was any old tourist – he took it off and told me you'd gone back to Angola.' Ava was silent a moment. She wiped away a tear with a paper napkin. 'He told me he was very sorry. That you'd told him you would love me for ever and you'd wait for me in Angola. That was why I came. I owe my happiness to that bad man.'

Ava didn't know a single person in Angola and she hadn't the faintest idea how to find Hossi.

'What about Facebook?' I asked.

She laughed.

'I've never used Facebook. We didn't have a computer at home. And the internet on the island, you know . . .'

On the plane, en route to Luanda, Ava met a young Angolan businesswoman called Rosa Prata, who despite not being rich had been managing a company buying and selling craftwork with some success. Ava told her she was going to Angola in search of a man she'd fallen in love with, eighteen years earlier. She had lost him, thanks to the treacheries of life, but she had never forgotten him. Rosa hugged her warmly:

'We're going to find this man of yours, girl. I promise.'

The woman insisted on having Ava stay with her. She lives in Quinaxixe in a nice apartment she shares with a niece. It wasn't hard to find Hossi. An ex-guerrilla with whom Rosa does business remembered him well. Two or three more phone calls and somebody mentioned the Rainbow Hotel. Two days after that, a Saturday, Rosa drove Ava to Cabo Ledo.

'I was so afraid Hossi would be married, happily married,

with a wife and kids. I didn't want to disrupt his life,' said Ava. 'My second biggest fear was that when he saw me like this, all old and fat, my *preto* wouldn't like me any more.'

Hossi shifted in his chair, and took the woman's hand.

'You haven't got old, my love. You're even more beautiful.'

I got up.

'I don't want to get in the way . . .'

The old guerrilla smiled, nervous. He hesitated:

'No, no. Stay! Don't you like seeing me in love?'

'On the contrary. I just think I'm in the way. I'll leave you both with this huge stunning moon . . .'

'I ordered it specially for Ava,' said Hossi, taking my arm. 'Stay. Drink with us. You can toast your friend's happiness.'

We toasted. We drank. Hossi ordered more beer. Ava kept pace with us, with that fabled Cuban courage. Around eleven at night she excused herself and stood. She was tired. She needed to sleep to recover from those last highly emotional days. As soon as she'd gone, Hossi's voice hardened.

'We've got a lot to talk about.'

He told me what had happened on his visit to the prison. I told him about my conversation with my daughter. He was furious with his nephew. I tried to calm him down. Sabino was right, I said. The hunger strike was an extreme measure, but undoubtedly more sensible than attacking the prison, all guns blazing. Hossi banged the table, knocking over the glasses. I pushed my chair back, as the beer trickled and dripped onto the floor. The other guests stopped their conversations. Adriano, the mute waiter in dark glasses, rushed over with a damp cloth and cleaned the table. He looked askance at me, mistrustful, as he picked up the bottles and withdrew again. Hossi didn't even notice him.

'For fuck's sake, Daniel! Whose side are you on?'

'Take it easy! I'm on your side, but I've got to agree with Sabino . . .'

'Who said we had to fire guns?'

'What do you mean – what did you have in mind?'

'I've talked to some of the boys. Totally trustworthy guys . . .'

'I'll bet one of them's Adriano!'

'You win your bet. We went through hell together. He'd give his life for me.'

'I hope that won't be necessary.'

'It won't. My plan's very simple. The simplest plans are always the best. We arrive at the girls' prison at four in the morning with two ambulances. Then we go to fetch the boys. You're in a captain's uniform, with two soldiers, I'm in a nurse's. We're carrying documentation that authorises the transfer of the revos to São Paulo prison-hospital. Nobody will be surprised because it's already been announced that they're going to be transferred there.'

'And where are you going to get hold of the ambulances?'

'One of the guys I mentioned, he works at the military hospital . . .'

'Jesus, you people are everywhere.'

'We really are.'

'Don't expect me to be a part of it.'

'Why not?'

'I'm not doing anything illegal.'

'Illegal?!'

'What you're suggesting is definitely illegal.'

'So you'd rather wait for your daughter, my nephew and the other kids to starve to death?'

'No! Of course not. We need to start organising a solidarity movement.'

'A solidarity movement?! You? You, who've never organised anything, who've lived your whole life on your knees . . .'

'I haven't lived my whole life on my knees!'

'You haven't?'

'No!'

'Looks like it to me. And not just me,' he said, getting up. He held out his hand. 'I wish you luck! All the luck in the world – you're going to need it.'

That was the last time I talked to him. In a conventional way at least, face to face, rather than in dreams.

28.

My darling,

I'm attaching a video file with one of your dreams. A film of your dream. I hope you don't get too scared, but just a little, since, as I told you once (I think it was in the yard behind my house, as the sky was darkening and your eyes were filling with light), art ought to unsettle, it ought to frighten, and – at least to me – these videos are also part of a great artistic intervention.

I've been thinking about you.

I'm sorry you spent so little time with me, but I understand your reasons. I pray for the situation with your daughter to be resolved soon.

To tell the truth, I miss you.

Sending you a kiss –

Moira

29.

Hossi turned his back and walked away. I sat down again, controlling my urge to run after him and knock him over with a punch on the chin. I'd never do that, obviously. I haven't hit anybody since primary school. I don't know how to fight. I abhor all kinds of violence. I've got fragile fists and a heart of sponge.

I noticed a guy watching me, sitting at a faraway table. It was the agent the hotel owner seemed afraid of. That 20Kill guy. I raised my glass in a mocking toast. The man smiled, copying my action. He gave me a wink. Then he got up and disappeared. I ordered another beer. It seemed a good night to get myself drunk, something that hadn't happened in many long years. Then my phone beeped, announcing the arrival of a new message – Moira! – and my mood changed. She missed me. I opened one of the video files. I watched it three times, one after another, first with surprise, then with shock, and then, finally, with a mix of horror and shame.

I paid and went to my room. I sat down on the bed. I watched the video again. It was an animated movie. It was easy to recognise Moira's features. A naked woman, with a coloured turban on her head, was unspooling, like a ball of yarn, while another identical figure jumped out from inside her. Everything about both figures looked like the artist: the angular faces, with small wrinkles at the edges of their lips, the slender bodies, the coloured turbans. Moira had done it on purpose. She had drawn the twins like this, identical to her, as a way of mocking me. I imagined her watching the video with Hélio, the two of them laughing loudly together, exchanging winks and vile comments.

The truth was, I was angry because I really had dreamed this. I told them I'd dreamed about a pair of Jamaican contortionist twins. Neither of them asked me how I knew the women were Jamaican. Neither of them asked me anything about the shapes of their faces, if they were beautiful or ugly, or who they looked like. I dreamed about twin women and in my dream I knew they were Jamaican, but I couldn't explain why. I didn't tell them – I never would have told them – that it was Moira, split in two, with her prodigious hair covered in a colourful turban.

I answered Moira's message with a simple question: *How did you know?*

I waited fifteen minutes and an answer came: *I didn't know, my love. I couldn't know. I found out through the machine. The machine works.*

I stretched out on the bed, exhausted, and fell asleep fully clothed, with my shoes on. I woke up suddenly, in the deepest darkness, with the harsh bang of a gunshot. Then immediately afterwards another gunshot, which vibrated in the eternal silence, very quick, and then a woman started screaming. I heard men's voices yelling orders, a quick stamping of boots. I turned on my bedside lamp and got up. My head ached. I grabbed my phone, and went out of the bungalow. The moon was climbing vertically upward, huge and round, illuminating the sands all the way down to the vast blackness of the sea. It took me a few seconds to realise that the screams were coming from Hossi's bungalow, and I ran over. There were two bodies lying on the ground. One of them was Adriano, the mute waiter. He'd fallen onto his back, a solid mass, abandoned, his face turned towards the moon, eyes wide open and yet closed to any light. On his white shirt, a thick dark stain was spreading. The other was Hossi. Ava was holding his head. She was kissing him, desperately, shouting curse words in Spanish. A lean, elegant man, forty or thereabouts, was kneeling on the sand, trying to calm her. I don't know what he said, but the woman went quiet. By this time, there were already five or six people standing around the scene. The man turned to us.

'I'm a doctor. We've got to get him to Luanda. Anyone have a car and can drive?'

I took a step forwards:

'Let's go!'

The doctor gave instructions to two of Hossi's employees concerning what had happened, and while I went to fetch the car he disinfected the wound and tried to staunch the haemorrhaging. We put Hossi on the back seat. A tall, very beautiful woman, wearing a white T-shirt, jeans and flip-flops went up to the doctor and hugged him. She tried to persuade him it would be best if he went with us. She finally pushed her husband into the car, turned around and sat in the passenger seat:

'Get in!' she commanded. 'Drive!'

I obeyed. We were out on the road in just a few minutes, headed for Luanda. The tarmac shone in the moonlight. Here and there the black silhouette of a baobab tree stood out against the starry sky, like an ad for some African beer. I thought about turning on the radio, but decided against it. If I turned on the radio and Anselmo Ralph was singing, then, yes, I really would feel like I was in a commercial. Now wasn't the time.

'My name's Melquesideque,' said the man. 'I'm a doctor at the Muxima clinic. You know where that is?'

'I do. Can he hold out till there?'

'I think the bullet's perforated his right lung. He's lost a lot of blood. Go as fast as you can.'

While the car made its way across the night, the woman introduced herself. She said her name was Tukaiana and she had a furniture store in Talatona. She and her husband spent weekends in Cabo Ledo, at the Rainbow.

'It's a simple place, unpretentious, and we like simple places,' said Melquesideque.

Tukaiana turned to me.

'So what happened then?'

'I don't know.'

'Robbers?'

'In Cabo Ledo? Doubt it . . .'

'Who could have wanted to kill Hossi?'

'He's got a lot of enemies . . .'

'Hossi?!' said Melquesideque, amazed. 'Old Hossi has enemies?'

'I don't believe it,' said Tukaiana. 'The old man can be a bit rude – sometimes he shouts or goes off on a bit of a rant – but he helps everyone. The staff like him. The fishermen even more. You know that school for the fishermen's kids? Hossi paid for that building to be built with what little profit he made from the hotel . . .'

'Hossi belonged to the UNITA Secret Services,' I explained. 'He did terrible things during the war.'

'My father was an agent, too,' said the woman, 'not on the UNITA side, but on our side. I mean, the government's side. He also committed a lot of crimes . . .'

'For example, he killed my parents,' Melquesideque interrupted her, without any apparent sign of hurt or bitterness in his voice. 'I've already forgiven him.'

'He was always a good father,' Tukaiana went on. 'I don't like what he did. I hate what he did. And yet I can't help myself loving him. We didn't speak to him for years. I didn't want to see him. I was very unhappy. Then my husband showed me the way. The only way is forgiveness.'

'And what about him, your dad? How does he manage to live with his past?'

'For years he drank. We thought he was going to die of cirrhosis. But then from one day to the next he gave up alcohol. He's like a different person now.'

'What happened?'

'I don't know.'

'My father-in-law was a believer, he had great ideals. He

believed sincerely in the socialist revolution, and that to save the revolution somebody had to get his hands dirty. He used that euphemism a lot – get his hands dirty . . .'

'Your father-in-law is a thug!'

I glanced in the rear-view mirror. Hossi had opened his eyes. He was coughing. Each time he coughed, he spat out some blood. I thought about the job I was going to have, the following day, to wash out all that blood. I was ashamed at having thought it. Melquesideque started to fret:

'Take it easy, old man. Don't speak. Try not to move.'

Hossi gave a long moan, then went quiet.

'Who did this to you?' I asked. 'Did you see the gunman's face?'

'Now's not the time for an interrogation,' said Melquesid-eque. 'I need him to calm down.'

Hossi coughed.

'Serious thug, your father-in-law. Even worse thug than me. I hope the crocodiles get him. Oh, those crocodiles! There were so many of them! The river was full of them.'

'He's delirious,' murmured Tukaiana. 'That doesn't look good at all.'

Hossi fell silent. I suppose he must have blacked out again. For a good half an hour, none of us spoke either. Finally, Tukaiana said, with a sad sigh:

'He's right. Yes. He's a thug. He's a thug and a good father. I don't like the thug, but I love the father he is to me.'

30.

As the days went on, the hunger strike of the seven activists took on dimensions that the regime hadn't anticipated. Newspapers from all over the world tried to keep track of the prisoners' health. In Lisbon, a group of Portuguese and Angolans came together outside the Angolan consulate in a peaceful vigil that began at eight in the evening and didn't end until the small hours. The demonstrators were carrying candles. Some of them wore masks of the prisoners' faces. In Praia, in Rio de Janeiro, Maputo, London, Paris and Berlin, similar initiatives took place. The international repercussions gave the democratic movement a new lease of life. Twenty-five high-profile names, including writers, musicians, artists, actors and cultural agitators, posted a video on social media demanding the freedom of the magnificent seven. All around this initial nucleus, a wave of solidarity was growing. There were young people from the outskirts, and others from powerful bourgeois families, linked to the ruling party. Some were taxi drivers, electricians, trades unionists, small businessmen, others were human rights activists, journalists, university professors.

Armando Carlos was unusual among the original group for being one of the oldest. One afternoon he showed up unannounced at my house. It was a Saturday. He dragged me to a ruined villa in the lower town, which for decades has housed a variety of theatre companies and capoeira groups, artists' studios and a lively bar, with a stunning terrace, called Nomenklatura.

Armando's company, the Mukishi, occupies one of its rooms. I wondered whether we were going to see a new play by the group. The place was full. I noticed most people were wearing white. Many had T-shirts with the faces of one of the seven young imprisoned activists and the slogan 'Freedom for Angola!'

Strangers came up to hug me.

'Be strong, old man! We're going to get your daughter out of jail!'

'Karinguiri's an inspiration to all of us.'

'You must be suffering so much, senhor. Please know we're suffering with you.'

Dona Filó, Lila Monteiro's mother, was also there in a big group. She was wearing a T-shirt with her daughter's face on it. She moved away from her friends to greet me. She held me firmly against her huge chest.

'Just as well you came! It's so important having you here. How is your friend?'

'Hossi?'

'Yes, Sabino's uncle.'

'Still in a coma.'

'Do you know anything new?'

'No.'

'You're never going to know,' said Armando Carlos. 'It was an operation carried out by State Security.'

I got annoyed.

'What are you saying?'

'You told me yourself – that night, just a few hours before the attack, you saw an agent who'd been watching Hossi.'

I grabbed him by the arm and dragged him to the bathroom.

'Seriously, man, are you crazy?'

'What do you mean?'

'You're telling people I know who it was that shot Hossi?!'

'Yeah, I'm telling everyone. I tell them you saw a skinny black man with close-cropped hair, that 20Kill guy . . .'

'Are you trying to get me murdered?'

'They won't kill you, not you.'

The bathroom door opened, and – bright as an apparition – in walked 20Kill. He was wearing a silk shirt printed with orchids in very bright colours, which made him look like a tourist strolling down Copacabana beach. He didn't seem surprised to see me. He smiled:

'I've been looking for you.'

I turned to Armando:

'Talk of the Devil . . .'

My friend looked 20Kill up and down, with a cruel smile.

'This is it? This multicoloured thing is a murderer?!'

The agent took a step back. He opened the door, as if he was going to leave, but he didn't. He stood there, one foot out, one foot in, his anxious eyes flitting between me and Armando:

'And who are you?'

'Come on, comrade. You know perfectly well who I am. You must have studied my file. I've got to admit, you've got some guts showing up in this lion's den.' He laughed darkly. 'But guess who the lion is today?'

20Kill sighed.

'It wasn't me who attacked Senhor Kaley.'

'It wasn't?'

'No. It wasn't us. Why would we do something so stupid, at this exact moment, right when we've got every journalist focusing on Angola?'

'Because you are stupid!'

'Careful, Senhor Armando! I don't know you. I've never shown you any disrespect . . .'

Armando leaped across the room, grabbed 20Kill by the collar and threw him against the urinals. The man brought his delicate hands to his shirt, which had been torn from top to bottom, while at the same time giving us a look of genuine distress.

'Such an expensive shirt, Senhor Armando. Such an expensive shirt . . .'

I positioned myself in front of Armando:

'Calm down! Calm down!'

My friend pushed me away. He hit 20Kill in the chest with his open palm. The little man was left sitting in one of the urinals. At that moment, three young men walked in. I recognised one of them: Flávio da Cunha, a former pro basketball player, one of the partners in Nomenklatura.

'What's going on in here?' asked Flávio.

'This is the guy who shot Hossi,' said Armando.

'Seriously? . . .'

'Yeah, it's him.'

They shoved him out to the bar. On the stage, a young Rastafarian stood tall and thin in front of a microphone, even taller and thinner than the microphone itself, while with large gestures and loud yells, in a deep booming voice, he declaimed lines by Pablo Neruda:

'If each day falls, / into each night, / there is a well / where clarity is trapped. / We must sit on the edge / of the well, of the shadow / and fish for the fallen light / patiently.'

Flávio said something in the Rastafarian's ear. The lad bowed slightly and moved off, surrendering his place by the microphone. The ex-basketball player adjusted the mic to his height.

'Good evening, friends, comrades. I've got a surprise for you.'

Armando and the other young men forced 20Kill onto the stage. The murderer looked more embarrassed than terrified, like a shy bridegroom at his wedding forced to give a speech.

'What's your name?'

'Rui. Rui Mestre.'

'Very well, Comrade Rui. What do you do for a living?'

'I'm a civil servant . . .'

'Speak louder!'

'I'm a civil servant at the Ministry of Information and Security . . .'

The whole room exploded into violent booing. Flávio raised both his hands, asking for silence. The audience took a while to settle down.

'And tell me now, Comrade Rui, what did you do to Senhor Kaley?'

More boos, kicking. Shouts of 'Murderer! Murderer!' 20Kill straightened up. With a worried look, he scanned the room, as though hoping to find some help. Then he coughed, clearing his throat, a solemn expression on his thin face. He tried to rearrange his torn shirt. He straightened himself up, puffed out his chest, like a head of state addressing the nation:

'I solemnly declare, as Africa and the world are my witness, my complete and utter innocence. I swear by the holy blood of Christ that I did not shoot Senhor Kaley. I don't kill people. I never have, I don't, and I never will.'

Five policemen, two of them holding nightsticks, the others light machine guns, opened a path through the crowd. They climbed onto the stage, struggling to ignore the hostile clamour around them. They came back down, almost at a run, protecting the fragile body of 20Kill between their own. The man passed me and smiled. He said something that was lost, stifled beneath the shouts of the mob. One lady standing beside me was laughing heartily, pointing at the agent's wet trousers:

'Hey, look! The little fag totally pissed himself!'

The rest of the night went by without any further upsets. My brothers, Samuel and Júlio, showed up accompanied by their respective wives. Júlio also brought his two eldest daughters, one of whom, Ginga, is Karinguiri's age. They've always been very close. We hugged. We hadn't hugged in years. I also saw, or thought I saw, Melquesideque and his wife. A lot of people made speeches, recalling the young people in prison, praising their courage and determination. The Rastafarian with the deep voice and big gestures recited some more Neruda, and then Fernando Pessoa, Viriato da Cruz and Agostinho Neto. Three very well-known singers, who had never performed together before, got up on stage to do some old Angolan songs from the fifties and sixties. The sun was already rising when Armando took the microphone to announce the end of the vigil, to read messages of support that had come in from several countries and share the next actions to be taken. I remembered the piece of paper Karinguiri had handed me during my visit to the prison, I got up, and took a couple of steps towards the stage.

'Can I read a message from my daughter?'

Armando looked at me, surprised. The people applauded while I climbed onto the podium. I unfolded the piece of paper and read.

31.

Dear Dad,

It pains me so much to know that you and Mamã are suffering because of me. I wish there were some other way of doing what I thought was right without upsetting those I love. Since I haven't been able to think of any alternatives, I do at least hope I might help you understand how we got here. I'm sure you'll support me if you understand. Supporting me doesn't mean trying to get me to give up on this hunger strike, or trying to get me to keep my mouth shut from now on, or saying yes to all the things my heart renounces. You'll be supporting me when you manage to give me your hand even when you disagree; you'll be supporting me whenever you show that you're proud of me, because I'm doing what I understand to be right.

When you and Mamã separated, it tore me right down the middle. I grew up divided between you and her. Suffering at every argument between you. Hiding from one of you the love I felt for the other.

I grew up divided between different worlds, too. Worse than that, I grew up a stranger to my own country. At first, I thought Angola was the name for the network of condos that are home to Mamã, my aunts and uncles, my grandparents and all their friends. I thought

Angola was this big network of condos separated from one another by pieces of waste ground: Africa. I believed our employees lived in condos, too, with names like Rocha Pinto, Cazenga, Golfe or Catambor. One day I asked Teresa (my nanny – I hope you remember her) if the swimming pool in the condo where she lived was bigger than ours. Teresa told me that where she lived, they call the swimming pools rain puddles and each person has their own. At the time, I didn't get the irony.

Later, I thought Angola was mostly made up of bohemian artists who on Saturdays would gather at each other's homes, to drink beer, to smoke dope, to discuss plans they would never carry out. Almost all of them expressed contempt for money and mocked the luxury condos where my mother and her family live. Today I know they despise money only because they have enough so they don't have to think about it. Poor people don't despise money.

I only got to know the Angola of the poor – I won't say the real Angola, but the one that represents the overwhelming majority of Angolans – a few years ago. Strange as it may seem, I recognised myself in it. I've ended up in this prison because I decided to be Angolan. I'm fighting for my citizenship.

Fear destroys people. It corrupts more than money. I've seen that happen in Mamã's Angola Condo. I've seen that happen in your Artists' Republic. I see it happen, too, in the Angola where almost all Angolans live.

Fear isn't a choice. There's no way to avoid feeling fear. And yet we can choose not to give in to it. My companions and I have chosen to fight against fear.

They call us revolutionaries – revos! – as if that were an insult. Despite what they're accusing us of, it was never our intention to bring down the President. I'm not saying we wouldn't like to bring down the President. Yes, we'd like the President to go. We'd like Angola to be a free, just, democratic country. But the thing is, we're just half a dozen young people – half a dozen and one, to be precise – and we're in no position to bring down the President. We don't even have the power to bring down the president of the Coqueiros football club.

We've discovered, however, that it is possible to combat fear. If we, who aren't representing anybody, who have no strength, are able to confront the President and his whole apparatus of repression – then anyone can do it.

By demanding our imprisonment, by accusing us of an attempted coup, the regime has shown that it is afraid of us. It's afraid of seven young people who don't even have the power to bring down the president of the Coqueiros football club.

How can you be scared of a regime that trembles when seven young people with absolutely no power raise their voices?

Think about that, Papá.

With a big kiss, from your girl,

Karinguiri

32.

On Sunday, the morning after the vigil, I woke up tired and with aching joints. But all the same, I felt strong, animated by an energy I hadn't experienced in years. It was past eleven. I fed Baltazar, and then I prepared a toasted sandwich with cheese and tuna. I turned on the TV and sat on the sofa, to eat. A picture of a man with a very swollen eye appeared on the screen. The unharmed eye spun around anxiously, side to side, while a policeman standing in front of him was speaking into the camera.

'This person was arrested at his home, after an intensive police investigation lasting several days. It didn't take him long to confess to the crime. Say what you did, Ezequiel . . .'

It was only at that moment that I recognised Ezequiel Ombembua, or Jamal Adónis Purofilim. I felt sorry for him. The man stammered:

'It was me. I shot and injured Hossi Kaley and then I killed his bodyguard, Mr . . .'

'Adriano Patrício,' whispered the policeman.

'Exactly. I killed that Adriano man with a shot . . .'

'With a shot to the chest,' the other man completed the phrase for him.

I turned off the TV and went to have a shower.

It was midday when I received a call from Dona Filó. She told me that this morning her daughter had suffered a cardiac and respiratory arrest. They were able to attend to her at once and, according to one of the prison doctors, she was very weak but stable.

'I'm heading over to the prison. Will you come with me?'

I said yes. Ten minutes later an old Citroën DS, a model I hadn't seen in many long years, pulled up outside my building. I went downstairs. Dona Filó had her enormous bosom resting against the steering wheel. She didn't look very comfortable. She was sweating, wedged against the leather of the seat. Despite the discomfort, the heat and her daughter's condition, she received me with a big smile.

'Come in! Don't be scared.'

I got in and off we went. Dona Filó raced over the tarmac, dribbling around the other vehicles, the pedestrians, holes in the road, with movements of great precision and complete confidence. The distress with which she spoke to me, repeating what the doctor had said to her and telling me about episodes in her daughter's life, were not reflected in the way she held that steering wheel. The woman who was talking to me, I knew already; the one holding the wheel, calmly euphoric, she was a surprise.

'You're like Fittipaldi.'

She laughed.

'I learned to drive from my godfather. My godfather was a

motor car racing legend around here. You're from Huambo, you must remember the *6 Hours in Nova Lisboa* . . .'

I did remember. People came from all over the country, even from Mozambique and South Africa, to watch the races. They'd put up bleachers along the city's main roads. The roar of the engines used to drive the birds and dogs crazy. The air smelled of burned fuel. I liked the smell.

'My godfather took third place once, in the *6 Hours in Nova Lisboa*. And he won other important trials, in Moçâmedes and also here in Luanda,' Dona Filó went on. 'This used to be his car. I take very good care of it.'

She told me her godfather's name. She seemed surprised I didn't recognise it. I've never taken the least interest in any sports at all, least of all car racing. We reached the São Paulo prison faster than I'd expected. A guard blocked our entry.

'It's not visiting hours.'

Dona Filó phoned the doctor who had notified her about her daughter's condition. The man came out to speak to us. He leaned on the high wall, hunched over, looking at the ground. He took a cigarette from his shirt pocket, lit it and put it between his lips. For an interminable minute, he smoked in silence. He couldn't do anything, he said regretfully, never looking up. He asked us please not to call his cellphone again. He'd call as soon as he could. Lila was fine. In his opinion, however, she could not continue with her hunger strike. They were thinking about force-feeding her in the coming hours.

'That's not possible,' Dona Filó protested. 'My daughter left a signed document stating that she refuses any force-feeding, even if she loses consciousness.'

225

'If she insists, senhora, she's going to die. Is that what you want?'

'Don't be stupid! And it's up to my daughter to decide if she wants to go back to feeding herself or not. Let me in. Let me speak to her.'

'I'm sorry. That won't be possible.'

'Very well. We're going to protest.'

She turned to me.

'Come. I've got the stuff in the car.'

She opened the trunk of the DS and took out two large sheets of paper. She put one on the hood of the car and wrote in black marker, in thick letters: *Freedom for the political prisoners!*

She handed the paper to me.

'Hold this. I'm going to make another one for me.'

The other said: *Free our children!*

'And now?' I asked, nervous. 'What do you want to do with this?'

'Now we're going to go out to the road so everyone can see us.'

'They're going to arrest us.'

'So let them.'

I followed her. As soon as I held up the poster I again felt that same energy and joy as I'd felt on waking up. The car drivers slowed down to read the posters, then sped up again. One of them gave us a thumbs-up, smiling at us. There was a good breeze. To the east, the sky was darkening. The sunlight was beating directly against a black wall of clouds. It wasn't long, just ten or fifteen minutes, before five police officers approached. One of them, the tallest, moved ahead of the others. He made a beeline for me, giving me a solemn nod.

'If you will excuse me, senhor, the boss has told me to ask what you're both doing . . .'

Dona Filó laughed. In the distance, a lightning bolt shot across the sky. It was as if the distant rumbling was echoing her laughter.

'Tell your boss we're protesting. We'll be here, on permanent protest, until they let us see our girls.'

'The boss isn't going to like that, Mamã.'

'We're free citizens, and we know our rights. Our children were arrested on a ridiculous charge. The period of pre-trial detention has expired and they still haven't released them. They're being illegally detained, which is why they've decided to go on hunger strike. My daughter nearly died this morning . . .'

'I'm very sorry. I don't know anything about politics.'

'It's not about politics, it's about human rights. You're a police officer. Your duty is to protect our rights. We have the right to protest.'

'I'm just following orders . . .'

Another of the policemen stepped forward:

'Please, if you stay here, we're all going to have problems.'

'We're staying,' I said. 'We're staying till they let us in to talk to our daughters.'

'Don't make things more complicated, old man,' begged the first officer. 'You can come back during visiting hours. Until then, go for a walk, have a soda, and then come in with the other visitors. It would be better for everybody.'

'My daughter nearly died,' insisted Dona Filó. 'She's suffered a cardiac and respiratory arrest. I want to see her now. I want to talk to her.'

The policeman shook his head.

'You're real stubborn, senhora. OK, we'll pass that on to the boss.'

We stayed there, holding our pieces of paper. We saw the rain advancing, in a rapid tumult, even as the light receded. Then the water fell on us, like a vertical river, ripping our words of protest from our hands. We remained unmoving, soaked, clothes stuck to our bodies, hair streaming down our faces, while the cars drove past, indifferent, and the storm disappeared into the distance as quickly as it had come.

33.

I found Ava sleeping, sitting in a chair, next to the bed where Hossi was fighting against death, or was allowing himself to be lulled by it, I'm not really sure which. The hotel owner arrived at the Muxima clinic in a coma, and had been hooked up to equipment ever since. Melquesideque, who met me when I arrived, made no attempt to hide the seriousness of the situation.

'Pray,' he said. 'Even if you're not a believer, pray for our friend.'

I promised I would pray, even though I didn't know how, lacking the practice and the conviction. I asked him if I could contribute towards the expenses of the clinic. The doctor smiled. He said not to worry, as Mr Tolentino de Castro had insisted on bearing all the costs. He escorted me to the room and left me there. I sat opposite Ava. The woman was sleeping, sitting up very straight, supported on the ample architecture of her own torso. She woke up suddenly, with a start, as if a ghostly hand had shaken her. She looked at me with no surprise.

'Hossi would like to talk to you.'

'What? He's woken up? He spoke?'

'I dreamed about him. I dreamed about him, just like I used to, back in Havana.'

'That's not possible.'

'Lots of things are not possible. All the same, I dreamed about Hossi. He told me you have to find his journal.'

I knew Hossi kept a journal. One evening we'd talked about it. I found it strange that we both kept journals. It's not very common. The hotel owner disagreed: he said maybe it wasn't a common habit in Luanda, perhaps just because Luandans are bone idle and disorganised, but that in those guerrilla days a lot of people wrote them. Savimbi himself had kept a journal. And the head of the guerrillas encouraged his commanders to do the same. Keeping a journal – according to Savimbi – was a good exercise in discipline. Hossi told me that when he was killed, in the forests of Lucusse, in Moxico, Savimbi had several volumes of his private diaries with him, along with notes towards an autobiography. Many of the UNITA leaders have published autobiographies. So when Ava mentioned the journal, I shivered.

'Hossi's journal?'

'Yes. Hossi is scared the police will find his notebooks.'

'He didn't say who the shooter was?'

'No. He didn't say.'

'Did you sleep here last night?'

'No. At six in the evening they made me leave. Rosa came to fetch me. My friend Rosa, the one I met on the plane. I've been spending the nights at her house. I'm not sleeping. I can't sleep. I arrive here after lunch, and I fall asleep. I dream about him. I'm back with him again.'

I went to find Melquesideque.

'I need to sleep in the clinic, in Hossi's room, or in one nearby.'

The doctor laughed – a joyless laugh.

'Are you ill?'

'I could be ill, yes, it could happen at any moment. What kind of illness could I have that would justify my being kept in overnight?'

Melquesideque sighed.

'I'm not going to ask you any questions. I'm going to trust you, even though it means risking my job. I'm going to trust you, because you're Karinguiri's father. I was there, at the vigil, senhor, and I was very moved by the letter you read.'

That night I slept at the Muxima clinic in a room next to the one where Hossi lay. It cost me more than a night in a five-star hotel in London, Paris or New York, though it still wasn't as expensive as a night in a four-star hotel in Luanda. A nurse appeared, just as I'd switched off the light, to take my temperature. She consulted her thermometer, took a look at my clinical file and left the room, laughing mildly:

'That Dr Melquesideque . . . !'

Melquesideque woke me at eight in the morning. He opened the curtains and the sun gushed in, burning my eyes.

'Did you manage to get what you wanted?' he asked.

I sat up in bed, struggling to reorder my thoughts.

'I did.'

'Then you're cured. Can I discharge you?'

'Yes. I'm very grateful.'

I got dressed and left. I climbed into my car, checked the

fuel gauge (the tank was almost full) and drove to Cabo Ledo. I couldn't think of anything but the dream, which seemed to have stretched out to fill the whole night, repeating with small variations, like a landscape seen through the lens of a kaleidoscope.

The Rainbow was closed. There was no one to be seen. I went down to the beach, came back, and sat at the restaurant to look at the ocean. Finally, when I was sure there was nobody watching me, I got up again and headed for the yellow bungalow. At the door, to the right, there was an ironwood sculpture, representing a life-size mermaid sitting on a rock. The rock was genuine, a dark stone, which the sea had worked over, latticing it, softening its edges, for thousands and thousands of years. I crouched down and reached behind it, feeling around between the rock and the bungalow wall. There it was: a key.

I got up and opened the door. There were several folders scattered around the floor. Others were open on the bed, in total chaos. I walked across to the small bathroom. In the cupboard beneath the washbasin I found a shoebox. I didn't need to open it to know that Hossi's journals were still there. I took the box, left the bungalow, closed the door again, put the key in my pocket and walked quickly to the car.

A man emerged from the shade of the mango tree, blocking my path. I dropped the box, amazed. Hossi!

34.

Dear Moira,

I've been going through some difficult, intense days. My daughter is still on hunger strike. Another girl, in prison with her, nearly died three days ago, from a cardiac arrest. She has in the meantime started eating again. The good news is that the solidarity movement for the political prisoners has been growing substantially, both outside and inside the country. Every day I receive dozens of phone calls and emails, whether from people I know or complete strangers, telling me they see themselves in those young people's attitudes. They give me courage – like giving me their hearts.

I talked to you, once, about a friend of mine, Hossi Apolónio Kaley, the owner of a small hotel, who invaded other people's dreams. Hossi was attacked. They shot him twice. He's in a clinic, in Luanda, hovering between life and death. One of the hotel's employees was killed in the same attack. The police arrested the alleged criminal. Poor bastard. I don't believe he's the real killer. I suspect – but I have no way of proving this – that our Political Police are mixed up in the crime. One of the young people in prison is Hossi's nephew.

My friend had made up his mind to get him out of prison, at any cost, and he might have said something he shouldn't have.

Since Hossi's been in the clinic, a number of the patients have started dreaming about him. One of the dreamers is his girlfriend, Ava, a woman Hossi met in Cuba many years ago. She showed up in Luanda, all of a sudden – she just dropped out of the sky, shortly before Hossi was attacked. She lost him once, and refuses to accept she might lose him again. She goes to the clinic, she sits in a chair and falls asleep. That way, she can dream about him.

I spent a night in the room next to the one where they're keeping Hossi. I dreamed I was on a plane, flying over a vast ocean, and that Hossi was still there beside me, wearing a purple coat, covered in badges and medals, like the porter of some grand hotel. The stewardesses were on skates, whizzing from place to place. I was surprised to see them with so much to do, given that the plane was almost empty.

'Just as well you came,' said Hossi. 'I've been waiting for you.'

One of the flight attendants leaned over us. It was you, in a dark blue blouse, a matching skirt in the same colour. On your head, a huge turban, with little yellow aeroplanes on it. You held out a tray covered in starfish:

'Try one . . .'

Hossi grabbed my arm:

'Pay attention to what I'm telling you.'

It wasn't easy, because while Hossi talked, you were starting to undress.

'Come with me, you two,' you whispered, opening your blouse and removing your bra. 'We've got a beach in first class.'

'Pay attention,' Hossi insisted. 'Focus on my voice. You've got to go to the hotel. Make sure nobody's watching you. There's a key

234

hidden behind the mermaid. Open the door, go in and walk over to the bathroom. My journals are hidden in the cupboard, in a shoebox. Keep them for me.'

The next morning, I went to Cabo Ledo, to Hossi's hotel, I found the key, opened the door, took the shoebox from the cupboard and brought it with me to Luanda. The journals are amazing. I'll have to tell you about them some other time. What I'm planning now is to have you come here to me. I hope you can convince Hélio to come, too. I'd like him to film my dreams, in the clinic. My dreams and Ava's.

One of Hossi's closest friends, a Portuguese lawyer who is covering the cost of his treatment, is prepared to pay for your trip.

There's no shortage of reasons for me to ask you this, but the first is the need to find out who shot my friend. For Hélio, this might be a unique experience. Maybe it'll even confirm some people's ability to get themselves dreamed about by others.

Of course, there's a chance I've made up everything I've just written because I need you beside me. I need you, because I've decided to face my fear, and whenever you embrace me I grow a little and become stronger. I need you, to be a better person.

Sending you a kiss –

Daniel

35.

My love,

I don't know how to help you right now except by answering yes, I'll come visit you, as soon as I can, and you don't need to invent miracles to convince me. I'm convinced.

It'll be harder to persuade Hélio. They want to speak to the doctor who's taking care of Hossi, by phone or Skype. Do you think that might be possible?

We've made a lot of progress in recent weeks. We're using a new programme. We've managed to create short films, and they're almost perfect.

Till soon –

Moira

36.

I experience moments of happiness whenever I'm with Ava, and I'm with her all the time; and moments of distress whenever I think about Sabino and the other revos, and I think about them a lot.

If it wasn't for Ava, my Ava, I might be dead. I can see now that Daniel was right to reject my plan. As soon as I saw him, the first day he showed up at the hotel, I knew he was a coward. A coward who, from time to time, suffers from outbreaks of bravery. Cowardly people are, as a general rule, smarter than brave ones. Most heroes, the guys who stride bare-chested into enemy fire, are not distinguished by their clarity of thought. I've never met a hero who was a good chess player.

Ava also went crazy when I told her about my plan. She said if I went ahead with it, she'd go back to Cuba. I dropped it.

Today is the anniversary of my first death. In previous years, I've got up early in the morning and gone out for a walk on the beach, trying not to think about anything. Not thinking about anything, when your heart is heavy with pain, is very difficult. I used to just walk. The sun on my head, growing stronger every minute, until a certain moment when I would drop to my knees. I wanted the light to wash me. Light can wash you, it can clean away the bitterness, but it doesn't help you to forget. I've never told anybody what happened that day. I've never been able to. This morning I sat down on the sand, my feet in the sea, Ava's head in my lap, and I told her everything. I talked for a long time. When I'd finished, I was finally at peace.

Adriano was the only person in my life who knew what happened. Now Ava also knows. But he was there. He witnessed it all. He saw, as I saw, my wife dragged by the hair, screaming. He saw when they pushed her face into the red dust. He saw when they brought the katana to her neck. He saw them kill my boys, too. Paizinho was three years old. Dudu, five months.

I think Ava has come back to save me.

Yesterday, when we woke up, Ava kissed me on the lips, and said:

'I dreamed about you.'

'Yes, I know,' I replied. 'We were both in a huge garden filled with butterflies.'

She pulled back, looked at me a little frightened:

'How did you know?'

I told her the truth. I'd dreamed the same dream. But . . . I was lucid the whole time I was dreaming, if that makes any sense. It was the way Pablo Pinto, or Captain Juan Ernesto, whatever his name was, had wanted it to happen, back in Havana, all those years ago. The dream progressing and me wandering through it, talking to Ava as if she was awake.

Tonight it happened again. So I dreamed again. And I was dreamed again.

37.

The man emerged from the shadow of the mango tree and looked at me head on. His expression disturbed me more than the impossibility of this meeting. Hossi was staring at me without the least trace of recognition, as though seeing me for the first time. I dropped the shoebox. The box opened and the journals scattered across the ground, six thick notebooks, five of them tied with red ribbons.

'Hossi, what are you doing here?!'

The man hesitated:

'What's happened?' He was exactly like Hossi except without the hurt that seemed always to cover him, like a shell. 'Who are you?'

And then I understood.

'You're Jamba, aren't you?'

'Yes, who are you?'

'I thought you'd died. Hossi told me you'd died in the war.'

'I didn't die – on the contrary, I came back to life. I woke up.'

We sat at one of the restaurant tables. I introduced myself.

I told him that Hossi had been shot and injured, very seriously, and that he'd asked me to come here, to Cabo Ledo, to recover some texts and documents. I didn't mention that his brother had asked me this in his dreams. Jamba told me his story. In July 2001 he'd gone to Lisbon, to attend a telecommunications course, and never came back. He worked for a few months in a friend's bar, in Nazaré, waiting tables. Two years in Paris followed, washing dishes in the restaurant of another one-time Angolan deserter, and from there he went on to London. He'd also been in Barcelona, in Amsterdam, in Berlin, always irregular arrangements, changing jobs and cities to escape the police. In 2010 he met a Namibian woman, of German origin. They married and went to live in Swakopmund, a small coastal city with German colonial architecture, not too far from the Angolan border.

'And this whole time you never managed to speak to your brother? You really couldn't track him down?'

Jamba shrugged.

'Finding him was easy. But Hossi always refused to speak to me. He tells everyone I died in the war.'

'But why?'

'It's a sad story.'

Jamba had been a major for the government forces, a telecommunications expert, when in October 1999 these forces retook Bailundo. Jamba and Hossi's father, Graciliano, had fled Huambo and set himself up in the village working as a mechanic. Hossi had dinner with his father, just a few days before the re-conquest, said goodbye to him and went off with the guerrillas. A few days later, by which time the government forces had entered the city, Jamba showed up for dinner. The old man hugged him with the same warmth he'd hugged his other son, he sat him down at the table, gave him what food there was, which wasn't much, only manioc meal and fresh mushrooms. They talked about trips on the *comboio-mala*, the old steam trains, subjects that made Graciliano smile.

Before they had finished their dinner, a group of soldiers came into the house and took the old man away, accusing him of collaborating with the guerrillas. Jamba shouted, protested, but it did no good. Several witnesses, over the days that followed, identified Graciliano not only as a sympathiser with the so-called 'Black Rooster', but as a militant occupying a lofty political position. Maybe it wasn't true. What's for sure is that the old man died in prison, days later, in obscure circumstances, and Hossi never forgave his brother.

'I did everything in my power,' said Jamba. He was sincere, I think. 'They ended up arresting me, too, for a few weeks. I lost my faith in the army. As soon as I had the chance, I deserted. Hossi never spoke to me again.'

Jamba returned to Angola because of his nephew's imprisonment. He entered the country, at the wheel of his car, over the Santa Clara border. In Lubango he gave a ride to a young Brazilian agronomist, a keen surfer, called Caio César, who'd travelled from Porto Amboim on his own, after hearing about the amazing waves in southern Angola. 'Down in Namibe, they've got this left tubular wave that's three kilometres long!' he said, excitedly. 'Oh, man, such an awesome wave, so perfect, you can drop in anyplace you want.'

Jamba thought about stopping in Huambo to sleep and see

relatives, but Caio offered to share the driving with him, in four-hour shifts. The Brazilian was in a hurry to arrive, too. And that was what they did. In Porto Amboim they said good-bye like old friends. The old soldier had no trouble finding the Rainbow Hotel. He pulled his car up alongside mine, in the shade of the mango tree, a little curious at the lack of any visible activity, and got out. That was when I appeared.

'And now?' I asked, once Jamba had finished his story. 'What do you plan to do?'

'I'll go to Luanda now. I'll go see Hossi.'

I was silent for a bit, looking at the sea.

'Does anyone know you're here?'

'No, I didn't want to announce my presence. I was afraid of being detained on entry for desertion.'

'That's probably best. Don't tell anyone. I'll take you to my place till things calm down. I suspect Hossi was waiting for you, and that there's a role for you to play – I just don't know what it is.'

38.

A bougainvillea exploding in a ruddy and silent din. The ruined wall. At the back, a frieze of palm trees, like lacework edging.

It was my dream!

The crow, which wasn't actually a crow, but Hossi Apolónio Kaley, in the shape of a crow; and then the same crow again, resting on my friend's shoulder. Hossi & Hossi. The Hossi in human shape dressed in that ridiculous porter's coat. The other, anchored to his shoulder, sharpening his beak on the brass medals.

'Yes!' I said. 'That's exactly how it was.'

Silent cinema.

I had tears in my eyes.

'It's just, that's exactly what it was like.'

We were in my apartment. Apart from me, sitting on the sofa in the living room and in three other chairs, were Moira, Hélio, Armando Carlos, Jamba and Melquesideque. Hélio had hooked his laptop up to the TV. This was the fifth time we were watching the film the Brazilian scientist had made while I slept.

Moira and Hélio had arrived three days earlier. She was staying with me. Hélio was installed in Armando Carlos's apartment. The two of them got on at once. They shared an identical horror of consumer society, the same contempt for social conventions and very similar tastes in literature and music.

Despite what I'd feared, Melquesideque raised no objection to our trying to communicate with Hossi through dreams. On the contrary, the experiment excited him. He notified the clinic director that a Brazilian neuroscientist was going to try a new technique to get Hossi out of his coma. The director, an obese, narcoleptic man, a former deputy from the ruling party and brother-in-law to one of the President's sons, showed little interest. He wanted to know who would be paying for the Brazilian's visit and all the treatment. Then, after a long pause and a huge yawn, he asked whether Dr Tolentino might not be inclined to make a donation to the clinic. Melquesideque reminded him that Dr Tolentino, a much-loved and well-respected man, with influential friends, already spent a lot of money supporting a home for abandoned children.

'Right,' said the director. 'But I still don't understand your devotion to this one old guerrilla, some old Bailundo guy, who to top it all is the uncle of a terrorist.'

'I think it's called friendship,' retorted Melquesideque. 'Hossi is our friend.'

Melquesideque had another bed put in Hossi's room. We agreed that I'd be the first to try out the machine. Hélio put a kind of cap on my head, covered in wires, insisting that I should forget all about it and relax. I stretched out on the bed and waited for sleep to come.

'And what did Hossi say to you?' asked Moira, while we were watching the film. 'It's such a shame we can't record sound.'

I told them we'd exchanged memories from our childhoods. Nothing relevant. After the death of my grandmother, when I was thirteen, I used to climb up the avocado tree to one of the highest branches. There was a hole in the trunk. I would talk into the hole, convinced the avocado tree would be able to establish some kind of magical connection between me and my grandmother, wherever she might be. I recalled this episode and Hossi, the crow, laughed, a soft laugh with no cruelty in it, while the other Hossi, the hotel porter, remained unmoved, looking at the fringe of palm trees in the distance with half-closed eyes. Then Hossi, speaking through the crow, told me that, at the same age, he and his brother used to go every Saturday to the cemetery, unbeknownst to their parents, to talk to their older sister. The girl had died, at eighteen, on Christmas Eve, on her way out of Midnight Mass, run over by a sergeant from the colonial army.

'There's no difference between talking to a cross in a cemetery and talking to a hole in a tree,' said Hossi. 'It's nonsense either way. But I think it's more beautiful nonsense talking to the hole in a tree than to a stone cross.'

'That never happened,' said Jamba, as soon as I had stopped talking. 'We've only got one sister, Judite, and thank God she's alive. Alive and well. She's Sabino's mother.'

The silence that followed was almost an accusation. I shook my head, annoyed.

'So my dream is a lie?'

'It's just a dream,' said Hélio. 'Why does it have to be any more than a dream?'

'Yeah, a dream, but not just any dream. I dreamed about Hossi, in that purple coat. Ava's dreamed of him, too, like she did in Havana. At least we've been able to prove there's some truth ...'

Hélio interrupted me.

'It proves nothing. You dreamed about Hossi, you dreamed about him wearing that coat, because you're still obsessed with that whole story.'

'Hélio's right,' said Armando Carlos. 'Of the two possible hypotheses, common sense says we should choose the simpler one.'

Moira hugged me.

'I'm sorry, my love. I wish I could believe it ...'

'Oh, really?' I stood up. 'So what about the dream where Hossi told me where to find his journals, out in Cabo Ledo? How could I have known where he hid the key to the bungalow? Where he kept the journals?'

'I'm not sure,' said Hélio, shrugging. 'What do you think?'

'I don't know what to think any more.'

'There are several possibilities. Hossi could have mentioned the journals, he could have told you where he usually kept the bungalow keys. Time passed and you forgot. Or thought you'd forgotten. A lot of memories we think we've forgotten come back to us in our dreams.'

I sat down again, defeated.

'Maybe.'

Later, that night, Moira wound herself around me. I remained distant, motionless. She found my alienation strange.

'What's up?'

I didn't answer. Jamba was snoring, stretched out on the living-room sofa. Might he be dreaming? What would he dream about?

39.

They had cut off her braids. Her hair had grown back on the side she'd shaved, covering over the tattoo of the word 'Freedom'. Lying on the bed, very thin, her skin pale and dull, my daughter reminded me of one of those old engravings of saints that the priests used to hand out at catechism. She also reminded me of a report I'd seen, some years ago, about an earthquake in a Middle Eastern country. The firemen were making their way across the debris, carrying a stretcher with the body of a girl who'd spent several days buried and had survived. Her face was covered with a fine layer of white powder. The body looked dead already. Yet her eyes, wide open, were filled with light. That's what my daughter's eyes were like.

I sat down beside her and took her hand. Karinguiri turned all that limpid light towards me, with a sad smile:

'Oh, Daddy, you're so skinny!'

It had been twenty-one days since Karinguiri, Sabino and Bogeyman last ingested any solid food. The other revos had given up their hunger strike, some of them owing to serious health issues, like Lila, others under family pressure. The

President hadn't broken his silence. The government hadn't made a statement. João Aquilino, my old boss at the *Jornal de Angola*, had published a vicious op-ed, railing against the 'international press, in the service of neo-colonialism' and the 'journalists betraying the fatherland, supporting and giving a voice to dangerous political delinquents, with the aim of bringing down a legitimate government, which is loved and supported by all the Angolan people.'

I left the São Paulo prison, as I always did, my heart heavy with distress. A Portuguese journalist, who had been sent to Luanda by a cable channel with a huge audience both in Portugal and in Angola, was waiting for me at the gate in front of a small group of young demonstrators. There were more policemen – all of them armed, some holding dogs – than demonstrators.

'Good afternoon!' the journalist greeted me. 'How is your daughter?'

'Bad, very bad. How would you expect her to be?'

'Do you still hope the President might be moved, that he's going to make a gesture of compassion and free these young people?'

The interview is available to watch in various places online. It's possible to witness the exact moment when Devil Benchimol took me over. My body stiffens and I raise my voice. Some people say I even shouted, but I don't know, I've never watched it.

'Compassion?! That would be like cracking a snake's egg in the hope that an angel might burst out of it. You can't expect anything from an evil, corrupt man except corruption and evil.' A brief pause for breath. 'That man you call the President is no better than a cowardly tyrant, who keeps himself shut up day and night behind the walls of a colonial palace, because he hasn't got the guts to come out into the street and face the people. He's a son of a bitch!'

I said two or three more things, some of them more intelligent than this, but it was these first words that made me famous. Well, almost famous. Until that day, very few people in Angola knew my face. Abroad, naturally, no one had ever heard of me. In two hours, that all changed. I was in the Muxima clinic when my phone started ringing. It rang all afternoon. Journalists called from Portugal, Brazil, Mozambique, Cape Verde, France, Germany, all wanting me to confirm what I'd said. A lot of friends called, too, some of them to show their support, others to reprimand me. I was unsurprised to receive a call from Lucrécia, incredibly annoyed, saying that with my rude, stupid, irresponsible interview I had thrown two weeks of 'diplomatic efforts involving a lot of respectable people' (her words) into jeopardy, given that the President had already committed to releasing Karinguiri. The only demand was that our daughter agree to return to Lisbon to complete her course. The government was prepared to forget the whole business, and even offer her a generous scholarship for her studies. I asked her if she'd consulted the girl in question about this plan. She didn't answer. She shouted that I'd always been a terrible father, that I would never stop being a disaster as a father, and hung up.

I went back home. There was an encampment stretched in

front of the building, which over recent months had been filling up with tents. As I got out of the car I saw an old man, sitting on a rock, in front of one of those tents. I recognised him. I saw him there often, in rain or shine, looking at me as if holding me responsible for the misfortune in which he found himself. This time the thing that caught my attention was his coat. The old man was wearing a coat in such an unusual colour, a reddish blue, almost purple, onto which were pinned a series of bottle-tops and small aluminium discs, cut out of drinks cans, standing in for military medals. I walked over to him.

'Where'd you get that coat?'

The old man threw me a mocking look.

'It's my general's coat. I made it myself. I used to be a tailor.'

'I like it a lot. How much will you sell it for?'

He laughed, happy as a bridegroom, exposing his bare gums.

'Two thousand kwanzas.'

It was ludicrously cheap. I shook my head, half astonished and half amused, and gave him four thousand. The old man counted the notes, and put them away in a very worn leather purse. Then he took off the coat and handed it to me. Bare-chested, and very thin, he reminded me of a Buddhist monk in an advanced state of self-mummification. I took off my shirt, which he accepted without a word of thanks, and put on his coat. Dressed like this, I went into my apartment. Jamba, who was sitting on the living-room sofa, watching television, burst out laughing.

'Is it Carnival now, or have you just decided to dress up as a lunatic to evade the police?'

He'd seen the interview, minutes earlier, on Portuguese TV. He thought I'd gone too far. In his opinion, the best thing to do would be to seek political asylum at the Swedish or Brazilian or Cape Verdean embassy. Not the Portuguese one, he insisted, never the Portuguese embassy, since in all likelihood the Portuguese would hand me back, handcuffed, together with an apology to the Angolan government.

I admitted that he was right. I insisted he should remain in hiding, to watch out for journalists, and not open the door to anyone. I put away the strange purple coat, or the nearly-purple coat, and went back out. I parked the car close to the Muxima clinic. Hélio and Moira were in Hossi's room, trying to convince Ava to connect herself to the dream-filming machine. The Cuban woman refused.

'No! It'd be like having someone spying on us through the window. I can't do that.'

I switched off my phone to focus on what was happening in this conversation. I admitted Ava was right. I suggested we try to find other people to do it. Moira offered to spend the night in Hossi's room herself. I looked at her, surprised.

'You? You didn't even know him.'

'All the more reason. I'm not as suggestible as you are.'

I replied that in that case, I'd stay there, too. I didn't fancy the idea of going back home anyway. Jamba had called me ten minutes after I'd arrived at the clinic to tell me that there was a pack of reporters lying in wait like highwaymen at the entrance to the building. One of them had even managed to get inside. He'd gone up in the elevator and rung the apartment doorbell.

Ava said goodbye at around six o'clock, and left, in floods of tears. Melquesideque appeared soon afterwards. He looked sadly through a file that one of the nurses brought him. He leaned over Hossi's parched face. He looked like he was whispering something in his ear. Finally he turned to me.

'Our friend's getting worse and worse. I think he's given up on living.'

He invited me to join him for a coffee at a bar just next to the clinic. We sat down at one of the tables. I noticed that the other customers were murmuring to each other, looking at me furtively (some of them with respect, others with open hostility).

'They're talking about you,' said Melquesideque, smiling. 'You're the topic of the day.'

He gave me another amused smile:

'Congratulations on the insanity.'

'I'm glad you chose that word,' I admitted. 'Most people, of the ones who're on my side, are congratulating me on my courage. I think you chose the right word – it wasn't courage, it was insanity. A moment of madness. But that being the case, I don't deserve anybody's admiration.'

'You do. On the whole, there's no beauty in madness. In those cases where there is, it's worthy of admiration. That outburst of yours, let me tell you, that outburst of yours was a wonderful moment.'

He showed me a message that had been going around phones and social media, calling the population of Luanda to a great demonstration, that night, in Independence Square. 'You can't expect anything from an evil, corrupt man except corruption and evil. Come out into the streets to demand the immediate release of all political prisoners. Down with the dictatorship! Long live freedom!'

I said goodbye and went back to Hossi's room. I was sitting in a corner, reading the many messages that were still coming in, when Armando Carlos called me. He was in Independence Square.

'There are dozens of people here, bro. So much excitement. So much happiness. There are kids with drums, dancing and singing. You should join us. After all, a lot of these young people are here because of you.'

'I'm at the Muxima clinic.'

'Want me to come fetch you?'

I hesitated. I told him Hossi was doing really badly. He might not make it through the night. Armando Carlos understood. He knows me well.

'Are you scared to come?'

'Of course I'm scared.'

'After that interview, I think there's no turning back for you. You have to keep moving ahead. I don't see many cops here yet, just half a dozen embarrassed-looking officers. They don't even know what to do. I imagine the ninjas – the real repression pros – won't be long. The more people there are in the square before they get here, the harder it'll be for them to assault us. Come!'

I said yes, I'd go.

I got up. I even said goodbye to Hélio and Moira, who were

otherwise paying me no attention. I didn't go. I sat back down. I watched as the Brazilian scientist helped Moira to put the cap on her head and whispered instructions. She lay on the bed. He turned off the light, settled himself comfortably in the other chair, and disappeared into the images that followed one another like coloured lightning flashes across the screen of his small laptop. I turned off my phone, shut my eyes, and surrendered to my tiredness.

I woke suddenly. Two nurses were trying to resuscitate Hossi, one of them, the older one, shouting instructions to the other. I leaped out of the chair. A young doctor, a friend of Melquesideque's, ran into the room.

'What's going on?' I asked him.

The man moved me aside with a brusque gesture, as if I were an impertinent child, and joined the nurses. The sun was coming in through the open windows. Hélio and Moira were not there. There was no sign of them. I turned on my phone and the messages started coming in. The first ones were from Armando Carlos.

11.17 p.m.: *The ninjas have arrived. Going to try and talk to them.*
11.28 p.m.: *Total chaos. They've let the dogs loose. They're coming towards us with nightsticks. Lots of kids injured.*
11.58 p.m.: *I've also been bitten on the arm. They're taking us to the police station. Hope they don't take our phones.*
00.18 a.m.: *I'm at the 29th precinct. They're starting to search everybody. There are 15 of us here. Tell your journalist friends abroad. Tell everybody.*
7.38 a.m.: *Where are you? They released us after a whole night of*

questioning. Total madness. Only just given back my phone. Going to a clinic to sort out my arm.

8.00 a.m.: *What's going on? Something very strange. Do you know what's happening? Call me!*

The doctor interrupted me:

'I'm so sorry,' he said. 'Your friend's died.'

I looked at him, uncomprehending.

'Hossi died?! Now?'

'He was doing really badly. He didn't have a hope . . .'

It was only at that moment that the dream occurred to me. It didn't happen the way it usually does. Normally I only remember a dream the moment I wake up and it almost always breaks apart and I lose it. Sometimes I wake up, get out of bed, go wash my face, and then some particular smell, some small occurrence, illuminates a vague image amid the darkness, a few words, an idea. If I'm lucky, I can grab on to that hand that's reaching out to me and save the dream, almost in its entirety, with long dialogues and complex scenes. This time it was different. The dream emerged out of the blue of my mind, bright and complete, like a huge silver fish shattering the smooth mirror of the waters. I ran out the room. I didn't wait for the elevator. I raced down the stairs and got into the car. I called Armando Carlos:

'Where are you?'

'Home. I'm with Hélio and Moira. You got to get over here.'

'I'm on my way now.'

I turned on the engine and pulled away. There were a lot of people out on the streets. Some were holding placards:

Freedom now!

We won't have peace without democracy.

Let's crush the tyrant!

I accelerated. I arrived at Largo da Maianga in fifteen minutes. I parked on the pavement, in front of Armando Carlos's building, and ran up the ruined steps. The door was open. I found my friend in the living room, sitting on a beer crate, in front of Hélio's laptop. His right arm was bandaged. Moira and the scientist were standing behind him.

'You've got to see this!' said Armando Carlos.

I went over and looked, incredulous, at the moving pictures.

'It's my dream! You guys recorded my dream?'

'It's not your dream,' said Moira. 'It's my dream.'

'It's not yours or his,' said Armando Carlos, very calm. 'Seems that tonight, in Luanda, everybody's had the same dream.'

'What do you mean?'

'That's just what happened,' said Moira. 'Go out into the street and talk to people. You'll be amazed. All those people, out there, they all dreamed about Hossi. The same dream I had.'

'Not me, unfortunately – I didn't dream,' said Armando Carlos, regretfully. 'I was being questioned. But still, I think I can still say it's ours! It's our dream!'

40.

The door to the palace was closed, but there were no soldiers defending it. Then Hossi passed through the wall. He went through it with complete confidence, in a firm elastic leap, as if the destiny of walls was to be passed through. The President was waiting for him, standing in an enormous office, in front of a desk strewn with papers. He was still a well-groomed man, with a dancer's poise, despite being past seventy and suffering from a serious bone disease.

Hossi and the President faced up to each other like a pair of birds in a cock-fight, seconds before they're launched onto each other.

'What do you want?' asked the President.

'Everything!' replied Hossi.

He said this while, in a simple movement, splitting the President down the middle. From inside the President another smaller President popped out, even more upright than its predecessor.

'Why?' asked the Little President.

'You stole our country.'

'Nobody can steal what already belongs to him,' answered the Little President. 'We are all Angolan.'

'We are, yes – but what was agreed was that the nation's riches would be used for the general good. You have destroyed our children's future. You destroyed our dream. Tell the truth.'

'What truth?'

'Why did you lock up the revos?'

'They're terrorists.'

With the same simple movement, Hossi split the Little President down the middle. Then another little man – tiny – who barely came up to the old guerrilla's knees, emerged from inside the Little President.

'Why did you lock up the revos?' Hossi asked again.

'They're dangerous,' said the Tiny President. His voice wavered. 'You've lived through the war. These kids haven't. They don't know the horror of war. They're starting fires. Dividing society. I had them locked up because I don't want a new war.'

Hossi split the Tiny President down the middle. What appeared to take its place was a minuscule, frightened thing, with a tiny, squeaky little voice.

'Stop,' begged the Minuscule President. 'What do you want?'

'Tell the truth. Why did you lock up the revos?'

The Minuscule President gave up.

'They aren't scared! Those kids aren't scared! Have you ever seen such a thing?! They're crazy, they show no fear, and that's a contagious illness.'

'You're talking about courage?'

'They're crazy. Can't you see they're crazy? If I let them go, they'll infect everybody else. They'll destroy me – me and my family. They'll destroy everything we've built. I can't let them go.'

Hossi stamped on the Minuscule President, crushing him.

People were starting to come through the walls: young people with drums; old people carrying hoes and katanas; mechanics, their dungarees stained with oil; Mucubal lads, with zebra manes on their heads. Barefoot boys, *quimbandeiros*, soldiers, students, fishermen. And also teenage prostitutes, women pedlars, fisherwomen, hawkers, money changers, the most ancient *bessangana* women, bent double with the weight of their age; pregnant mamãs, with one child on their back and holding hands with another; cooks, washerwomen and nannies.

All those people were there, in the vast presidential office, going round and round like fish in an aquarium; looking wide-eyed with amazement at the pictures on the walls and the open cupboards, in which they could see thousands of busts of the President, in gold and silver; the stuffed heads of former fractionists and enemies of the people who had disappeared long years ago; glass jars filled with anxious little hearts, still alive and palpitating, and next to them, crystal globes in which there floated, in a sky as blue as on my happiest childhood days, the games to be used first by the teenage prostitutes and the barefoot boys.

'It's all here,' said one of the *bessanganas*, pointing all around her. 'All the days they stole from us.'

She started crying.

Crying and laughing.

That old *bessangana* woman was all of us.

41.

As soon as my eyes met Jamba's I could tell he already knew. To this day, I don't know how. Maybe some radio station had broadcast the news. He was standing by the window. He turned, and I remembered a filthy goat I'd seen, tied to the rusty shell of a military tank, in one of those difficult years we went through. I hugged him. At first, he tensed up, as if he wasn't willing to accept my hug. Finally, he yielded. We also didn't exchange a word about the dream. It wasn't necessary. I made some tea for us both. We drank in silence. I went to the wardrobe to fetch the purple coat. I gave the coat to him.

'Put this on.'

Jamba didn't seem to find this strange. He put the coat on over a white shirt.

'We're going to the Palace, right?'

'Right.'

Armando Carlos was waiting for us in the car. I sat in the driver's seat and turned on the engine. As we moved closer to the upper town, the number of people on the streets increased, in a crescendo of outcry and commotion. The atmosphere was festive, as if it were Carnival, with men and women singing, dancing, improvising slogans. Some police officers were joining in with the party. We saw just one agent, surprised, shouting, leaping about, hemmed all around by the laughter and mockery of the people.

'That one must have been up working all night,' commented Armando Carlos, smirking. 'Probably one of the ones questioning us.'

In Coqueiros, the crowd was so dense we decided to ditch the car and continue on foot. As soon as Jamba stepped out onto the tarmac, with his extraordinary purple coat, there was a confused uproar that spread in concentric waves, followed by an awesome silence – and all those people moved aside to let us pass.

We went on, like a kind of miracle, with people reaching out their nervous fingers to touch Jamba, but never hindering our progress. We didn't make it right up to the Palace because we found it surrounded by a powerful military force.

'Those guys are from the Commander-in-Chief's Special Protection Forces,' said Armando Carlos. 'They're dangerous.'

'And what about the dream?' asked Jamba.

'Who knows? Maybe they're trained not to dream,' joked my friend.

The people all around us had gone back to shouting their slogans: 'Why'd you lock up the revos? Why, Mr President? Why'd you lock them up?'

The soldiers looked at Jamba in terror. I was sure none of them would dare to fire at him. Maybe at the people, yes, maybe at me and Armando Carlos, but not at him.

'So what now?' asked Jamba. 'What do we do?'

'Tell them you want to speak to the officer in charge,' suggested Armando Carlos.

'We want to speak to your commanding officer!' shouted Jamba. 'Let us pass!'

Jamba's shout made the soldiers tremble. The crowd fell silent. Here and there, somebody coughed. A child was crying. In the distance, the sound of car horns. Finally, an officer appeared, holding a megaphone. He moved the soldiers aside, gesturing with his free hand that we should come forward.

'Come! Quickly! The President is willing to talk to you . . .'

We walked past the soldiers. Some of the demonstrators tried to follow us, but were kept at bay with rifle-butts. Then a terrible shouting rose up. The people, far from retreating, were throwing themselves against the barriers. The officer handed me the megaphone.

'Say something to calm them down. This is going to end in bloodshed.'

I took the megaphone with both hands.

'Calm down!' I shouted. The words came out of my mouth without my thinking about them. 'Calm down! We're going inside to talk to the Old Man. Be patient, wait here till we come back.'

Jamba took the megaphone from me.

'We'll be back! Freedom for the revos!'

The crowd shouted, in a vast chorus: 'Freedom for the revos!'

'This isn't a rally!' The officer got annoyed. 'Give me the megaphone and let's go!'

He took the megaphone and led us into the Palace. We

walked through rooms about which I don't remember a single detail except for the dusky half-light, and even that only because it seemed to be pulsing, gaining in confidence each time the mob out there cried: 'Freedom! Freedom!' and then corridors and more corridors, all of them deserted, until we reached a spacious hall, lit up on one of its walls by three enormous oils on canvas. The triptych seemed to me to represent a mermaid, floating in an emerald sea. Armando Carlos almost got angry. No, no! He could see at once that it was a spaceship, a spaceship soaring through the infinite blue! Jamba disagreed with him and disagreed with me, as it seemed obvious to him that the painter was merely attempting to depict, with great fidelity, an ancestral figure dancing on the rain-damp savannah. That was what we were doing, arguing about the meaning of the triptych, when the same officer who had first brought us in reappeared, stood to attention, and announced:

'His Excellency, the President of the Republic!'

The President came in. I noticed how short he seemed, weak, almost an old man, compared to the figure with the smooth voice and upright bearing we were used to seeing on TV giving lethargic speeches, and whom we'd got used to hating without any great commitment, because he also didn't seem someone capable of very arduous feelings, and if he did order the murder of a journalist here, a dissident there, he wasn't doing it out of any true hatred, but just with the effort of somebody carrying out a duty, and it actually wasn't hard to believe that he might have remained in power for so many decades rather out of forgetfulness or ignorance than for any real, ferocious desire to command.

He held out his hand:

'Have a seat,' he said, nodding towards a huge yellow sofa. When he spoke, he went back to being the man we saw on TV, just a bit weaker and a bit more hunched over. 'I've been expecting you.'

We sat down. None of us knew what to say. So then I leaned towards him and explained that we had come in peace and that our only objective was to negotiate the young people's release. The President ignored me. He turned to Jamba with a placid smile.

'I don't know how you did it. That trick with the dream . . .'

'It wasn't a trick,' murmured Jamba.

'A trick, a miracle, whatever it was, please, don't do it again. In fact, they tell me you've died, Senhor Hossi. They told me that just moments ago. They called me, assuring me you are dead. That you're in a coffin in the Muxima clinic.'

Jamba smiled. His voice was firmer now.

'And yet here I am, as you can see.'

'Naturally. Oh, if you weren't aware, it was us who killed you. I'm very sorry about that, you gave us no choice.'

'I imagined it was your men. In fact, along with my nephew, and the other young people, I'd also like you to free Senhor Ombembua . . .'

'He's already been released. He was released two days ago. As far as I'm aware he's currently in a hotel room in Brazzaville, recovering from the shock. You can rest easy, the man received fair compensation. But as for you . . .'

'As for me?!'

'As for you, since I find it hard to believe that you are dead, in the Muxima clinic, and at the same time alive, here, talking to me, I deduce that your name is not Hossi, but Jamba. My intelligence services are not up to much, I know, but it wasn't at all hard to discover the deception.'

'Of course not. I have friends in the forces.'

'Some enemies, too. I'm very sorry to disappoint you, but soon, on TV, we're going to be denouncing your fraud. We're going to show pictures of your brother's body, and photos of you with him, a long time ago. People will see that they've been deceived. This farce of yours ends here.'

Armando Carlos gave an angry laugh. It sounded like a god laughing.

'It ends here?! Can you really not hear the people outside? Listen . . . !'

He made a big sweeping gesture, as if he were knocking down the walls, and then the turbulent cries of the people could be heard clearly: 'Freedom! Freedom!' and for a fraction of a second I thought I spotted a spark of terror in the President's eyes, but then he raised his own right hand, with its very thin, well-tended fingers, and at once the shouts were subdued, or seemed to be.

'Don't be under any illusions, my dear Armando. These people who are protesting against me now will be cheering me before long. The people are fickle and stupid, and they have no memories.'

'It is you, senhor, who are under an illusion,' I replied, fighting the urge to shout. 'Tell me, where is everybody?'

Only then did the man look at me.

'Everybody who?'

'Your people. Your generals. Your ministers. Your secretaries and assistants. All those people who only yesterday were jostling to get into this Palace.'

'They'll come when I call them.'

'No. You've called them already and they didn't come.'

'Have you seen the soldiers out there . . . ?'

Jamba stood up.

'I've been a soldier, Mr President. Not one of those men would risk his life to save yours. If we don't leave here in the next ten minutes, the people will advance on this place and nobody will try to hold them back. Free the kids.'

Armando Carlos also stood up. I did the same.

'Free those young people, now. Call the prison. We want to hear you give the order.'

The President remained seated.

'Very well,' he agreed at last. 'I'll give the order to free them. But before that, Senhor Jamba, tell the crowd to return to their homes.'

'No! You give the orders first!'

The President took a silver telephone from his jacket pocket, made a series of calls, and I noticed that he spoke no longer with a voice of command but of entreaty. He put the phone away and looked at us, with the stunned eyes of a man who is clinging, hopelessly, to his final moments of glory.

'You can go fetch your children. It's over.'

We made our way through the deserted Palace, without

exchanging a word, and emerged from the perpetual dusk of its halls into the harsh light of this afternoon of wonders. The crowd received us with a single cry: 'Freedom! Freedom!' as it surged forwards, in an inexorable movement of rejoicing, to meet the vast helplessness of the soldiers.

EPILOGUE

I look up and see Moira floating, as if levitating, on the translucid crystal of the sea. Karinguiri is sitting beside me, reading. She's taken advantage of the Easter holidays to come visit us. She arrived ten days ago and already she knows the island better than I do. The young university students – the Fort is home to a university – welcome her like a prophetess. Here, too, there are people who believe in utopias.

Not me. I just watch. I'm an indolent and dispassionate observer: a Bantu *flâneur*.

I've read in the papers that the President is at risk of being deported, not to Luanda, but to one of the many countries where he's stashed his money. Now that he's lost power, there are a lot of his former partners, his former confreres, his former best friends, who're demanding his imprisonment. Ever since he fled to Russia, on a luxury jet with his wife and all his children, the news has been coming in about the collapse of his huge financial empire. The generals who came to power as his successors, promising free and fair elections, which get postponed every six months, do not want him back. A public trial would upset a lot of people.

Just yesterday I received an email from Armando Carlos: *We're waiting for you. We need to finish what we started. The struggle continues.*

I didn't reply.

I feel good here. I lead a peaceful life. I teach at the university. I read a lot, swim in the sea. Moira has left Cape Town for good. She re-established her studio in an old ruin, right in front of the ancient family mansion, with its walls as thick as ramparts, where we live – and where I am concluding these memoirs. She still dreams, she still creates depictions of her own dreams, and her work has lost none of its unsettling power. But she's found a new calm since getting pregnant.

Island of Mozambique, 2 March 2017